PRIMITIVE
DEPARTURE

LW MONTGOMERY

Copyright © 2012 LW Montgomery

All rights reserved. Except as permitted under U.S. Copyright Act of 1976, no part of this publication may be reproduced, distributed, or transmitted in any form or by any means, or stored in a database or retrieval system, without the prior written permission of the publisher.

The characters and events in this book are fictitious. Any perceptible similarity to real persons, living, dead, comatose, or simply insecure is entirely coincidental and not intended by the author.

The author herewith acknowledges the following for their inspiration, support, and/or patience: etiennefish, Max Friz, Kevin Moore, WLH, MJM, EEM, Tom Cochrane, Davidoff & Cie, Justin Vernon, The Edrington Group, Justin Furstenfeld, Gregory Alan Isakov, James Vincent McMorrow, DFW, CM, RMP, Lerxst, Dirk, Bubba, Carberry Distillers, Brandi Carlile, Harm Lagaay, C&B, Bill & Margie, Helmsman Walt Grace, SPI Group, Joy & John Paul, Sanjay Gupta, DWP, Sam Mettler, Jean-Max Bellerive, Richard W. Hotes, Elizabeth J. Kucinich, Bryan Lourd, William M. Pohlad, Paul G. Vallas, SP + everyone at J/P HRO

LIBRARY OF CONGRESS CATALOGING-IN-PUBLICATION DATA
Montgomery, LW
  Promise of Departure / LW Montgomery. = 1st ed.
    p.   cm.
  ISBN 978-0-9851197-9-9
  LCCN 2012905665
  2012

25% of your purchase today is donated to J/P HRO to support their dedicated relief and rebuilding efforts in Haiti. Please visit their website to learn how you can help even more: www.jphro.org

Pou tout moun nan Ayiti, ak tout kè m '.

1

Printed in the United States of America

Promise of Departure

Janet,

I can't do this. I won't survive divorce. I know I've said this a hundred times, but it's the truth. I want what's right for you and Maggie, and please believe that I held on as long as possible, but I just can't do this. I can't watch the garage door close behind you for the last time.

Running away like this is selfish. I know. I can't ask you to understand or forgive me or anything like that, but every last fiber of my spirit is telling me to run...just GO. Be anywhere but here.

I've transferred everything to you (minus a little cash until I end up somewhere) - the IRA and money-market funds are yours. The house, should you decide to move back home (I suspect you will), the titles to the cars and bikes (not Gerty, obviously), savings...everything I think.

I know most people manage to handle this like adults. They find a way through. I wish I could, too, but I just won't be able to. I wish I was the boy you once loved, the man you trusted and understood. It's not there now, and I know it's taken me a long ~~thing~~ time to see (or accept) it, but maybe I finally do. I fully realize that leaving a letter on the kitchen counter like this is heroically cliché, but you know this isn't what I want. I want you. I want Maggie, but I can't have you so I can't have her. That's just an ugly fact of American fatherhood I suppose, but I'm not going to convert her to currency.

I don't know where I'm going (somehow having a 'where' implies a return). Tell your attorney that he's won. I lied about mine (I never had one).

I love you. I always have. I love Maggie. I always will. I'm sorry. I'm sorry. No garage door.

Greg

ring like crazy, ring like hell
turn me back into that wild haired gale
ring like silver, ring like gold
turn these diamonds straight back into coal
— *Gregory Alan Isakov*

I've dropped the bike.

It's a mantra before the big BMW even introduces rattle-can grey to diamond-waffle steel.

I've dropped it.

I've dropped the motorcycle.

I've been in Haiti eight seconds, and I've dropped the goddamned bike.

The pretty hipsters I'm blocking farther up the ramp freeze and stare at me with a sort of meerkat uncertainty. They don't offer to help or ask if I'm alright, and while this strikes me as peculiar, it's *how* they're staring that has me worried.

Am I saying this out loud? Did I say that out loud?

"Did I?"

Oops.

"Uh, dude?"

He's the nearest of five, closer to twenty than I am forty, and impossibly laid back with a casual I-straight-rolled-outta-bed-and-wore-this-shit-again swagger I know is anything but unintentional. My rattled brain hammers fast to fix the slip.

"Did I seriously just do that?"

Their staring stops, mercifully replaced with snickering and lock flopping head lolls. I tell myself I really don't care what they think (though I sadly do), and that it's simply too bad they'll have to wait a minute. But other passengers are starting to line up behind them now. Older, boring, *normal* passengers. And this, on the other hand, does bother me as I feel a sense of obligation to them as one of their own. They're confused, just now starting to peer around the cool kids and the expensive camera gear they're rapidly stuffing into expensive camera gear bags made from materials that likely didn't even exist a few years ago.

I need to get the bike up, but I'm facing a Real Problem and while the 'what' is simple, the 'how' is simply not. This steel ramp, slapped between the cargo freighter behind me and a temporary floating pier farther down, is a narrow five footer. The bike fell to the right and onto a sidecase that has luckily struck just one inch shy of a retaining lip welded to either edge of the gangplank. Had I been walking her down a little more to the right, that composite case would've surely struck the lip. But the lip would've been less a lip (or any sort of retaining barrier, for that matter) and more a what-are-the-goddamn-odds fulcrum rendering the big BMW truly precarious.

I sincerely dislike dropping bikes. It's embarrassing and it's stressing and it always plays out in slow-motion. Slow enough that there's this microsecond just before the point of no return where you actually think you'll snooker gravity. You won't, of course, and the parabolic arc of the falling machine mirrors your own crashing self-esteem. Somewhere between that microsecond and the rest of your life, you realize it's done. Time to let go. Let it crash.

Still, I am pretty lucky. Teetering on that fulcrum/lip wouldn't have been likely, but entirely expected. A skittering/teetering against the salt-crusted steel at such a precarious angle she might've tipped right over the edge, pulled bay-water bound by a rather top-heavy load. I loaded her this way just over one month ago. My decision. And now, mere seconds into this harebrained trip, I've literally let her down. It's rookie shit. I know better. I'm nervous this morning. I feel weak and I'm shaking and everything feels totally wrong now that I'm really here. Had Sissy (the name my little girl settled on) fallen overboard I can't even...

Christ. What then?

No, not had fallen. *Would've.* I'm pretty sure I would've keeled over as well, tumbling all gave-up some forty feet down to the drink. Mercifully, poor ol' Sissy just waits on her side instead.

Lucky.

Unfortunately, the old tried and true dead-lift method isn't going to work here. I've dropped a few bikes in my life, often enough that I've developed a little MTBD*allowance, so I know full well that method simply won't work here. Which means I have to find a way to *pull* her up. But even that's not the Real Problem. It's just the task, the thing that needs doing before the cool kids and the normal people and the other types of people I can't yet see (but are assuredly backing up behind everyone else) all lose their collective shit. This is a disembarkment, after all, and as all travelers inherently understand in a very primal and largely unspoken fashion, it is vitally important to put immediate distance between yourself and whatever run-down conveyance you've stumbled from. I get it. I'm sensitive to this. I'm not a complete asshole.

The Real Problem is that this fully loaded BMW R 1200 GS Adventure weighs just shy of a thousand (stupid) pounds I need to somehow leverage my buck seventy against. I am not happy about this. In fact, I'm certain I'm far less thrilled about the next few minutes than all the sighing and pissed-off people behind me on the ramp could ever possibly be.

I know it won't work, but I yank on her anyhow. Stuffed sidecases still attached, topped-up top case on, and full of fuel. And Scotch. Really good Scotch, too (not that lesser quality single malt would likely alter the weight). Thankfully, there are perfect spots on the bike to grab for this exercise, and as expected, she doesn't budge an inch.

I retrieve the little key ring from the ignition, unlock and

*Mean Time Between Drops

remove the left pannier, pop the latch on the top case (which I heave to the ramp below), and slip the jingly keys back between the grips.

"She weighs less now!"

Damnit!

But the cool kids don't say a word. They don't even notice the second filter failure. They just stand there, staring at expensive cell phones held an inch beneath overlarge sunglasses that must be polarized (judging from their furrowed brows), likely texting one another in fractured language no better spoken aloud in the three square feet separating them.

Fine. Usually not a complete asshole...

Sissy does move a little. Not quite enough to fully right her, but through sheer determination (commonly known in these situations as garden variety embarrassment) I'm able to rock her back to me just enough to realize she's still in neutral. Which means she suddenly rolls half a foot farther down the ramp. Which means I drop her again.

"On purpose!" I want to object, but it's only obvious to me why I've allowed such a thing to happen as everyone, not just the cool kids now, but every last one of them stares skyward to say increasingly exasperated things to clouds.

"Thanks a ton for helping out. Really. Never mind that we'd have her up and halfway down the ramp by now if any of you cared about anything other than yourselves. Really, I got it. Thanks."

This I manage not to say aloud. I bite my tongue and slam the shifter down into first with my palm (which hurts far more than I'm prepared to publicly acknowledge), grab Sissy by those previously tested scruffs, and struggle her back up to me once more. I'm her surrogate gravity and she reacts accordingly, rolling up slowly on cambered tires designed to work this way. The overextended tendons in my quads argue that this is far past foolish, but I ignore them, just as I'm ignoring my pounding palm I've just glanced at which is already bright red and surely the same shade of everything north of my shoulders.

Once upright and safely on the side stand, I reassemble her and verify that the key is still there in the ignition. This last bit's a paranoid habit as I tend to misplace motorcycle keys for one reason or another. My mesh riding pants (part of an armored outfit I never ride without, and to be fair, are also likely made of materials that didn't even exist a few years ago) simply aren't equipped with front pockets. No pockets at all, in fact, other than those sewn in for the removable armored pads. It's taken years, but I've finally realized if I just keep the damn key in the ignition I tend not to lose it as often. I'd guess that in over ten years and a tick over 4.015 times around the planet, I've lost the key for every bike I own a number of times I've just now chosen to forget.

The drop is my fault. The fellow in front of me came to what most people would politely refer to as an abrupt halt. He made it halfway down the ramp with a mountain of boxes stacked in his arms before one of them started to shimmy loose.

What if he'd—

Nah. It's not his fault. I was too close. *I* dropped the bike. I can shed blame left and right, but it's my fault and I should slap those two truths together to form a little song about stuff I'd rather not be dealing with already. I don't even know if he dropped that box. I was too busy dropping Sissy.

Christ! Have I tried walking her before? Loaded like this?

I rode her up a very different ramp back in Portland, so...nope. First time. I should have done the safe thing and rode her down in neutral, but I had to go for the showy version of a thing better left to larger lads.

I hear tinks and thuds on the steel ramp (and watery reports in the harbor water far below) before realizing the theatrics of getting the bike upright have jostled things free from jacket pockets I've clearly forgotten to zip shut. Maybe it's just useless stuff. Coins. Three-year old gum. Maybe the cell phone, if I'm really lucky. Heavy lint?

Please be heavy lint!

But the tinks imply metal/composite (important/expensive). It really seemed like a good idea, donning my riding gear back on the boat. Mesh pants, mesh jacket, new riding boots (which squeak with every step and will do so for several weeks). I had it all lashed to the rear seat for transit in the cargo crate, but it felt a bit dicey leaving it bungeed down while walking her. Plus, I didn't know if it was windy out. Not to mention the simple fact that I didn't have to try cramming it all into already overstuffed cases this way. In other words, I thought I did a pretty smart thing just ten minutes ago.

A wiry man in tattered clothes two sizes too large waits for me at the bottom of the ramp, grinning and handing out pale green sheets of paper. It's impossible not to notice just how precious few teeth he's got left in that happy mouth of his.

"You did that? You drop?" he asks, thrusting a copy at me that I struggle to grab with my left hand while my right temporarily balances the whole of the big bike between us.

"I— yes. I guess I did."

"Why? Why you do that?"

His expression doesn't change. There isn't a trace of contempt in his voice. It doesn't even sound slightly sarcastic (though I'm not certain I'd recognize it through the heavy accent). I think he's just sincerely asking, as a child might, and I'm far too dumbfounded by the frankness of it to be offended because I know I'll be asking myself the very same thing for the rest of the day.

"Just getting it out of the way early, I guess."

I want whatever I say to make the most sense to him, something that satisfies him and his reasons for asking (my reasons will be quite different). I tend to do this with people I don't know. I can't really tell if he even understands me.

Maybe he thinks I'm being sarcastic! Did I sneer?

But his expression hasn't changed a bit. He just grins at me.

"Stupid fucking American."

He doesn't say this. At least, I'm pretty sure he doesn't.

I ease the bike forward and look for a clear patch of real estate. Fresh streams of people wander down from the proper dock a hundred yards away. Maybe another ship is already inbound. The cool kids ford the crowd, laughing a bit too loudly and smiling a little too often in spite of the current goings-on. They're not bad kids. I saw them on the ship a few times, a film crew (I'd gathered) shooting a piece on the aftermath here in Port-au-Prince for their local church. I found this rather noble, considering that not one of them looks to be a day over twenty two. It's a properly stand-up thing they're doing, and chances are they'll head home affected and changed in ways they'll (hopefully) want to sort through in the coming years. I slap a bug on my neck before realizing it's trickling sweat. I'm hot. It's not even noon.

I need a few minutes to go over the bike, but I'm distracted and having trouble focusing (which isn't exactly ideal for any preflight check). I need to calm down first. I stretch my tight legs, but find balance rather tricky as the pier rolls gently on waves that slap the wood precisely one half-measure off. I count four other piers, each one a hockey rink long and stacked with hundreds of cargo pallets, end to end and side to side. I walk the bike between two large wooden pallets overburdened with plastic-wrapped and unrecognizable contents. It's a decent spot for now and mostly hidden from those farther down the pier. Only the fellow with his green sheets can see me here.

A mammoth yellow crane lists to one side on the far end of the bay. I first noticed the derelict in the looped news coverage, and it hasn't budged since (the last thing it did was keel three degrees to the right when its foundation cracked far below the surface). I can't explain why, but as weeks dragged on and the thing appeared time and time again in hazy backdrops, I had to look it up. To my surprise, it was the lone such workhorse here, shuffling millions of pounds of cargo longer than I've even shuffled around. Maybe I saw the thing as an icon. A totem. Or maybe I just pitied the old thing. Hard to say. I've had a soft spot for honest machines for as long as I can recall. Rusty freight containers litter the choppy water around it now like aborted bites of chow.

Some part of me knew I was Haiti-bound that January day, but it took a good week to finally accept it. I'd originally planned on bringing Gerty, my main two-wheeled squeeze back home (a BMW K 1200 GT that's seen more miles than anything else I've owned). She too is an honest machine, not some random collection of plastic, metal, bang and blow. She's been my buddy on long trips, a real companion (which likely says plenty about the kind of person who abandons a successful software studio at the peak of their success). But she wasn't the right choice for this trip. Sissy, on the other hand, is a flexible machine. A dual-sport multi-tool purpose built for a place like this - perfect for the beaten path or none whatsoever. She was a good purchase, gently used and priced right, but rather attractive for such a rugged bike in bright silver and crimson red. The friend I was living with back in Portland and I fixed that one Saturday afternoon with a few spray cans of black and grey (and more than a little 47.3% encouragement). I'll never fully blend in here. I know that. I just want to vanish as much as possible.

It'll be a short ride today, maybe five hours or so. Just enough to get away from Port-au-Prince. And while that's far from taxing, I have no clue where I'll be stopping (or eating or sleeping) tonight. I need time in hand for that. I'm here to help, but not in the capital. The grinning man at the ramp waves at me.

Stupid fucking American, indeed.

I've caught my breath and calmed down enough for now, and though they shake with each squeaky step, my legs no longer threaten to give out. To my relief, the bike looks remarkably intact for being forced horizontal (twice). Somehow the right mirror has folded up. The black composite shell is a little scuffed, but the lens seems fine. I swivel it back down and study the right side to find the fairing, footpeg, and rear brake pedal all unscathed, but the right auxiliary light is pointing skyward and not straight ahead as it should. I try to swing the metal lamp back down (switching hands as my tender right palm barks), but it's bound up.

I turn the key in the ignition and toggle the riding lights. The left one shines. The right doesn't. They're handy little buggers, forming a unique triangular pattern with the main headlight when everything's lit up. The thinking is that the peculiar light pattern they create draws attention from oncoming motorists you'd rather not meet head-on at slightly rapid closing speeds. I doubt I'll get to ton-up much here, but it's best to fix it. It's why I came, after all. To wander the country fixing bikes. A 'nomadic mechanic', as my friend put it that last night Stateside. I can't very well be fixing other people's bikes while mine's messed up.

I haven't a clue how much money I'll need, so I've brought what feels like more than enough. I've folded half the bills into a waterproof wallet and stuffed the rest into secure nooks here and there on the bike (there are tons of hidey holes on a motorcycle). The wallet's still here, overstuffed and wedged sideways in one of the jacket pockets (probably the only reason it didn't fall out with the other as of yet unidentified bits back on the ramp). I pluck the passport from the other pocket…pluck it from…

It's not there.

I shield my eyes and scan the ramp. The diamond-shaped openings aren't very large. There's no way it fell through. But where the hell did it go? I had it this morning. They came around and stamped everyone an hour before we docked.

Did I get mine back?

I stare at the ship. I'm not about to leave Sissy and go back. Maybe I won't need it. It's actually been a while since I've needed one, and I was amused to discover the section marked PARENTS on the application had changed at some point. It no longer asks for MOTHER and FATHER. Instead? PARENT ONE and PARENT TWO. This doesn't bother me (some parents are neither mother nor father – there are often two of either), but the clinical nature of a numerical parental pecking order was a little depressing. Someday my five-year-old daughter Maggie will make that strange decision herself.

Maybe it's just guilt. PARENT ONE didn't run away from everything.

I tend to think about relatively trivial things like this since leaving my company. Sometimes I feel such thinking is useful. Valuable, even. I often think the sum of these innocuous little equations may yet equal a real matter of consequence. What was it that Markson said? Inconsequential perplexities have now and again been known to become the fundamental mood of existence? Something like that.

I notice that new helmet is already banged up as well. Nothing serious (they say you're supposed to replace helmets if you drop them...like bikes, I *may* have dropped one or two), but I'd tethered it to one of the oh-shit-handles with a long security cable I stupidly left far too slack and it's now dinged and chipped from the fall. The gloves stuffed inside the helmet are also new, but I wore them exclusively in Baja last month so they're broken in some (enough that flexing doesn't immediately cramp my hands). They're not yet comfortable, but sweat and time will fix that. The comfortable gloves are in the left sidecase, buried at the bottom under everything else; two spare pairs of armored gauntlets heavily seasoned with years of memories, road grime, and me. I've never lost a pair of gloves, but I seem utterly unable to leave these ragged stowaways behind. I shouldn't do this. Space on a bike is limited before you've even packed the very first thing.

I lock all three cases, which is really just an optimistic crossing of fingers in the event they happen to drop anchor once underway. Maybe they'll stay closed this way should they end up tumbling down the road behind me (luckily, I don't know if this works).

The little GPS between the handlebars hasn't acquired satellite signal yet and displays not only Portland time, but the last active route as well (the short jaunt to the loading dock back there from my buddy's house one rainy Tuesday morning). It thinks the route's still in play and dutifully clicks off the moving/non-moving minutes:seconds since. I thumb *CANCEL?*, reset the trip data, and load the escape route that will lead me out of here. I check the tires as the GPS propagates and find both still slightly over-inflated, just as I set them three weeks ago.

That hazy, fluffy feeling I get the first morning of any big trip starts to creep in. The bike's okay, and aside from a gently bruised ego (and a missing passport), I feel pretty good as well. I haven't been questioned (or arrested) and nothing on the bike is damaged beyond repair. The sky is clear blue, and just beyond the perimeter of the city I see the mountain range I'll be crossing soon. I'm all set. I hop on, pop Sissy off the center stand with a gas tank grind, and thumb the starter. She whirs slow and teases half a catch before snapping to life. I let the idle settle, don the helmet, and ease off down the pier.

I truly thought I was ready for Port-au-Prince.

I prepared as much as possible. So much, in fact, I was absolutely certain nothing could catch me off guard, but my senses are pummeled in minutes. The bright blue sky against everything else is flat wrong, mocking the misery I find myself slowly threading at a tense and unsteady pace. I expected the rubble and broken walls, but it's the overwhelming stench that threatens to murder my abilities in total. It's not even a smell. It's a toxin. A phantom. And it's not that it interferes with breathing – it impedes basic cognition.

I cross a bridge over what must've been a small canal at some point, now little more than a dry, garbage-filled channel paralleling this main road south toward the outskirts of the capital, past rows of rough wooden carts strapped to modern metal hitches, past a (no longer) decorative fountain, past a broken university. An optimistic sign advertises *Spirit Bar Resto Hotel*, hand painted across the building's façade by souls not yet affected by the shifting Earth two months ago. No glass in the windows. No door in the frame. Concrete clusters and rusting rebar are all that remain in the dark shell of the retreat and nothing more.

Even the road itself is broken in ways I can't even imagine repairing. Cars and trucks and fender-less hulks of bus/van/wrecked things dart and weave chaotically in ways I must judge, chastise, and fear in mere seconds. I pick my route carefully, watching the drivers and trying to read their erratic intentions to the best of my own crippling abilities.

Homes are split in half, slanting into adjacent structures for improvised support. Families still live in most of them. I see them walking around inside. I see them leaned up against what little remains. I'm struck not for the absurdity of their decision, but by the obvious lack of other options. It's a roof over their heads, even if the angles scream a precipitously temporary one. What do you do when it's the one place you've got? The only place you've ever had? Do you even try waking from this perpetual nightmare? Wondering if the next aftershock will strip your kids of the only security they've got (all they've ever had)?

This road is cluttered with bits of everything, but it's wider than I'd expected with two makeshift lanes in either direction. I toured the Gulf coastline in Texas years ago after hurricane Ike dismantled those unprotected communities. That timid ride felt much like this does now; long stretches of untouched life morphing to unrecognizable slop just half a mile later. I pass an old junkyard on my right, so overgrown with tall grass that most of the rusting carcasses within are fully canvassed in tendrils of yellow-green and brown. Such a place seems redundant now that the city has sadly become one giant version itself.

A dozen broken hearts scream out along every city block, each just one of thousands in this crumbling city. As much as I want to give them my attention, I need to focus on this road. Huge chunks of it are missing altogether, leaving gaping sinkholes wide enough to swallow the contact patch of either tire. Rubbish and rotting rags break crusty bonds to skitter across my path in the foul wind.

The BMW sounds utterly alien here and attracts a peculiar gaze, a gaze I've become accustomed to in smaller communities back home. No diesel clatter, this. No heavy machine grumble. It's the ballad of a boxer engine and a song I typically savor, but I feel liable and suspect right now where such functional and well-running sounds are clean spots on the blight.

The parallax of gloom against that happy sky is really just wrong - the prettiest weather for the most disfigured place I've ever seen. I don't feel okay with this, slipping through their reality in such a transitory way. I don't feel good at all, and the uninvited interloper conundrum of any such plan flops right in on. I suddenly have to focus quite a lot on basic balance. I try to keep my elbows slack, but the tension just migrates north to my shoulders. Everyone stares (*every.single.person*) and I can't help but expect it so earnestly that I begin seeking out every face far in advance. I'm not blending in. Not a bit. I'm having trouble focusing. I should ignore them.

Why? For what? For a more digestible slice of despair elsewhere?

I guess at their perceptions of me and paranoid shame begins to color my already grim outlook.

I know I'm reaching the outskirts of town, and that mountain range (foothills, more accurately, but right now Alpine) ahead isn't far now. I invest myself in those hills.

This city has all the help she needs.

I say this over and over in my helmet.

But beyond the green? Maybe I can help out there.

The rubble thins as I wander farther south, corresponding with the dramatic absence here of fractured buildings. Even the stench dissipates a little. I spot the only standing street sign I've seen so far: *Boulevard Harry Truman.* I try not to laugh for fear the foul air will trigger bouts of gagging and vomiting I won't be able to stop (this hasn't happened yet either, hurling in a helmet). I'm not entirely sure why I react this way. It isn't funny. It's not even that ironic. But I laugh a strange little laugh, much like the relieved snort I might cough up should the fire alarm blare just as my dentist reaches for his drill.

The GPS squawks through the earbuds in my helmet that I've reached my turn and I swing left down a narrow brick alley.

Damnit! The map showed a side street!

Small stands and tents fill the limited space and I just barge right through. I want to apologize to every startled face turning to my mechanical racket.

I might as well be riding straight through their homes!

The GPS dutifully ignores this little insight. I'm so out of place. My face flushes hot. After what feels like several agonizing minutes, I'm through and astonishingly haven't hit anything (or anyone). Some of them yelled out to me, I think, but no fists were raised. No angry sign language cast at my passing. Just confusion. And smiles.

At me. Right now. With all…this. How is that even possible?

The GPS squawks again and I follow her lead (after a few choice words of advice), turning down a dirt road this time, perhaps the one I was expecting back there. Everything here (homes/buildings, standing/otherwise) juts up to the edge where a shoulder or real sidewalk should be.

They're not even really buildings. More like little tin shacks, most of them still standing from a simple lack of space to fall. They're stacked together gap-less as far as I can see. There's no green here. Just pale brown dirt and tarnished rusted roofs stretched thinly over faded pastel walls. Sad eyes peek out from glassless windows, young and old alike. I want to stop and just be here a moment, but rigid habits push me on, committed to some increasingly stupid plan drafted far away, somewhere safe and warm, where walls and roofs remain perpendicular and always will.

I know I'm close. The foothills bulge above and thankfully blot a little of that cruel blue. The road intersects yet another, identical in every fashion (dirt/rust/eyes). Up and south I climb, the path cresting while the GPS does her level best to guide me on a blank screen where my marked position floats in dead space, unmapped and apparently unnecessary to record. To its credit, the GPS originally wanted me to tread straight through some of the hardest-hit areas (it wouldn't know this, of course, but I found this interesting nevertheless). I do want to see them, for reasons increasingly macabre with reflection - a need to bear direct witness to things that will undoubtedly redefine my understanding of ruin and poverty and despair, as if the absence of an intermediate LCD screen will somehow clarify the unthinkable. Still, that's not why I forced an alternate route down brick sidewalks and dirt roads. The risks were much higher in those heavily hit neighborhoods. I think. I may have it exactly backwards.

It's greener now. Spindly branches reach farther over the tin and cast hypnotic shadows on the road in the graveyard still (and presumably graveyard quiet. The cacophonous racket of the bike and subaquatic muting of the earbuds permit only presumption). Old souls cast puzzled looks my way when I'm safely past and I return their curious greetings in my mirrors. After a mile and a minute or two, I finally squeeze free of the tin alley and the dusty path shrinks in to dogleg around shallow switchbacks, growing rutted and coarse as I climb (steeply now) through broken rock and no more road until I realize I've breached the city limits. I stop at a small clearing affording an elevated view of the city sprawled far beneath. I'm only a few hundred feet up, but the temperature has already dropped a little. You tend to notice little changes like this on a bike.

I spent a good amount of time studying this next bit so I know the coming miles will be tricky. When I suck up the breath to try it, I'll be scaling a dry creek bed just a few inches wide up to another road atop this little hill. Just the perfect sort of terrain to try something this tricky for the first time ever.

I thumb the kill switch. I'm alone now. I've had somewhat predictable conditions to this point, but there's no ink for the next few hours. If I make it to (and through) nightfall, *'It'll All Work Out'*. I try to believe it.

I look down at the city. I'd watched the amazing things being done there after the quake and wished I could help somehow. In a purposeful way. Where I wouldn't just be *in* the way. It was while watching the early footage that I first noticed all the motorcycles here.

Right here? This is between. There's a reset button behind me or the rest of whatever's left. I wonder what Logan would think. I wonder if he'd follow me up. Maybe I'll just camp right here for the rest of my life in this little clearing. It's a bit breezy, but the tent just might stay put with some creative anchoring.

I crane up at the hill and look for the rut. I don't see it.
Foolhardy.
That's what he'd think.
"Let's do it!"
That's what he'd *say*.

"So, what about Maggie? You're okay just leaving her like that?"

Great. His very first question is the one I can't answer.

"And what about Scotch? Instead of vodka. It should travel better, right? You always take it neat, so no need for ice or any sort of cooling solution. Unless you decide to take it on the rocks there, but I'm not sure why you'd do that..."

He furrows his brow at this.

"However, hmmm. The *heat*. It's rather warm in Haiti, right? Muggy? You'd almost want to, if you could, but then you're back to the issue of—"

I twirl at the pasta on my plate. Logan's compressing a month of questions into our first thirty minutes together. Tomorrow morning, we will pack up a pair of rented BMW R 1200 GSs and plow south through Baja. This is a much needed vacation for him, but it's a trial run for me.

Scotch? Sure. Let's discuss. But I can't talk about my daughter just yet.

"I considered it, but the price difference was at lea—"

"Really? Cost is suddenly an issue with you?" he interrupts with a smirk. "What about bladders? Build 'em into the side panels? Behind them? Essentially occupying the otherwise empty space?"

He fiddles with the raised decorative relief around the perimeter of his plate. He's debugging.

"I thought about that too, but there's really not much space there on a GS. What little there actually *is* might be there for cooling purposes. I'm not sure. Not to mention the issue of material. I looked at resin moulds, but I'm not really interested in drinking chemically altered single malt."

I think he's heard me, but he seems to be clicking through other options already. Back in high school, he was the one kid our little group of nerds expected to go far; effortlessly smart with boyish surfer looks (blonde locks and all). It really didn't seem fair at the time. At the moment, he's focused on the matter of my little alcohol problem (so to speak). Namely, how to best stash booze on a bike for a long-distance trip. He's a fixer. This attentiveness might have irked me not so long ago, but what I see right now is Logan helping his old friend. It's silly, the effort he's putting into all this. But I love him for it.

"Wait. I've got it. Reserve fuel cell. You've seen those before, right? The boxy units those guys run on Ironbutt rallies? That should work."

"Might work. What are those? Two, three gallons?"

He stops tracing his plate. "Christ, Greg! I hope that's enough!" he blurts. "I know you're trying to drink yourself to death these days, but come *on!*"

It's a good idea. Beyond being relatively insulated, a spare tank wouldn't advertise anything other than fuel.

"Well, I was thinking about one anyhow. Maybe I can fit a larger main tank on the bike instead and use one of those for booze. Priorities, huh?" I chuckle.

"See?" he beams. "Easy!"

Our food's grown cold. It's the first time we've seen each other in nearly two years and I've forgotten just how nice it feels to spend time with someone who knows where I've been.

"Heard about the surfers?" I ask.

"Surfers?"

"Yeah. Baja's apparently a Mecca for 'em. And Canadians. And folks living out Baja 500 fantasies. And then there's us, but at least you'll fit right in with the surfers." I gesture at his blonde curls.

He laughs as I run a hand over my scalp (I started shaving my head a few years back). Riding in Texas summers with hair was like shoving a heating pad in the helmet. The only real drawback to the shorn noggin is I'm often told I look less than friendly. Amazing how a simple haircut can so completely re/shape perceptions of you.

"Heard from Shelly yet?" I ask.

"Not yet. I texted her, but she hasn't said anything yet." Logan sighs. It's still a sore subject. Shelly also rides. He twirls at his food now.

"I thought she was having trouble getting time away from the lab?"

That was several weeks ago. Hmmm.

"Wasn't she?"

"Well, yeah, but..."

"Look, you can totally blame me. I'll obviously ride with someone else if the circumstances are right," I gesture between us with the blunt end of my fork, "but three or more? Just the thought makes my skin itch. It's not that I dislike the camaraderie. You know that. I've done it before, so I dunno, lessons learned and all. Plus, you know my pace can be a little brisk at times. What did she say that day in Banff? And you know I don't make many stops. Not to mention the sleep thing..."

He's listening. He doesn't look up, but he nods.

"So, these factors—"

"Flaws," he mutters with a little grin.

"Okay, flaws. Anyhow, all these things make me a pretty lousy riding partner. Just blame me when she calls."

I suspect he already has. Most riders I've known like to hit the road pretty early (often before daybreak), but I've suffered from a sleep disorder all my life and have to drug myself just to increase the odds that I'll possibly crash before six AM. I gave up fighting what everyone else had always called it: lazy/broken/whatever. However, one day during her routine medical research, my wife Janet read about something called

DSPD*, and lo and behold, I was the spitting image of their target study. Finally! This was language where none existed before (though certainly not a coat hook I wished to overburden). I never actually went to see anyone about it, of course, as I was usually asleep during regular office hours.

"But even beyond all that, I thought this trip should just be us. We have a lot of weird shit in common. We think too much. We talk a lot—"

"*You* talk a lot."

"Okay. Fine. I'm flawed *and* I talk a lot. But Shelly's a bit more, mmmm, rational. We'll have conversations on this trip she'd absolutely loathe."

"I know. But she's not pleased, which means, well, it just means that…you know, never mind all that. Let's just leave it there."

And we do precisely that.

After paying the tab, we wander to the hotel bar for cheesecake and cognac and talk about the various movies and TV shows we've been watching (the same things, nearly without exception), car stuff and what bikes we've been joneseing for since the last time we swapped notes (also similar lists). We've known each other for decades, but we're no different than anyone else. It takes time to reacclimate. Our faces have changed, and just as all old friends do, we secretly gauge their march of time against our own.

"Nervous? About tomorrow?"

He shrugs, but it's an overly long shrug that seems to freeze a little before sloughing off.

"Yeah, I guess. I'm excited, sure. But if you believe everything you see on TV, we're going to be kidnapped, chopped up, raped, or held for ransom."

"In that order?" I cough. "Good grief! Stop watching TV!"

Delayed Sleep Phase Disorder

We giggle and drink. He goes on to tell me about a little note he jotted down before bed a year ago: '*Men of letters. They must still exist.*' Serendipitously (we suss out), I'd been writing him one that very same week, catching him up on the details of my failing marriage, spiraling depression, and all the sizzle accompanying such festive topics. We secretly agree that while it's not the proper or classic form of accepted letter writing, we'll continue to email our diatribes for fear of lost desire. It's a worthy concession, I think, as we have indeed become men of (digital) letters.

After dessert, we ride the elevator up to adjacent rooms and say goodnight for the evening. I read for a while, giving Logan enough time to turn in before quietly slipping back down to the hotel bar. I brought a bottle for the trip, but I need to ration that over the coming week. The bar isn't for fun. It's for sleep.

One of the problems with operating as a functional drunk is that it often takes incremental measures each evening to do the job. Like many alcoholics, I freaked a little at the first signs of delirium tremens, but took what I considered to be a rather unique and responsible approach to things: I researched. If I was going to continue medicating, I needed a better plan. I studied the particulars of ethanol dependence and the numerous ways it rewires the brain. I listened to anyone who'd gone too far for too long. I purchased a breathalyzer (a relatively inexpensive though reliable model, rather depressingly advertised as 'The *perfect* Sweet-16 gift!') and an accurate-to-the-cc measuring beaker to precisely monitor the amount required to get the job done. I've always had a narrow window, one that's just right for sleep and knocks me out when my head finally hits the pillow. I logged and calculated my intake over the course of an average month, determining this minimal window of mine to be .16~.19, and with regular and careful adherence, I was able to somewhat curb that ramping plateau.

In my case, the job in question has always been shutting my thinker off. It never stops. It's not stress. It's not because I worry. It's something far more obscure, like a long term fuel trim all out of whack. It's a photo album of everyone I've ever known, a sketch of everything I've ever seen, a library of every word read. All of it interleaving sinkholes of home movies and thoughts and reactions to thoughts and observations about the very nature of this queer construct, all of it stashed in messy cells capable of apparently perfect recall...a lousy, grey Plinko machine spilling memories down upon the steel minutes of every night. It dribbles uncontrollably. Every recollection of each memory is slightly different than the time before, altered by distance or flavored with new experience. Without anesthetic, I simply don't sleep before six AM. Often later. Or at all. At one point, I began keeping a tumbler of vodka on my nightstand the way many keep a revolver handy.

I once read about this calming mental exercise where you're supposed to imagine a pendulum swinging back and forth, tick-tocking, and slow it down with each successive swing until it drifts to a quiet standstill in a black room. I've tried this. But there's a problem in my attic. My pendulum's apparently fueled by a plutonium-powered reactor in the glare of a searingly bright courtroom where everything in my history's on trial each and every night, over and over and over again. The fucking thing doesn't stop, so I grab it and drown it in 40% anything until I can barely make out the liquid clicks of its murdered gears slowing to a nice, numb halt.

Properly medicated, I manage to fall asleep a little past two AM. But vivid dreams of giant rats plague me. I stand there, paralyzed, watching them drag their bloated bodies across a living room I do not know, digging gnarled, yellow teeth into old carpet to haul their disturbing hefts, compensating for skinny simian digits worn pointless and ground down to furless nubs.

Neither the anticipation of the day nor the soul sucking alarm at eight AM inspire clarity, and the wretched sensation of the dream lingers like a hangover. Still, it could be worse. My nose isn't *too* bad. There's a fair amount of discharge, and breathing is labored for the first thirty minutes as it always is. But at least it's not bleeding today.

When I've showered and dressed, I head down to the lobby and find Logan already waiting for me on a couch. He has his laptop open, likely squeezing in a few tethered minutes before we leave. We're going to wing Baja internet free, so for him this is sort of like kissing dry land goodbye before shoving off. I was the same way a few years ago, but I've undergone a sort of unplanned 'technology cleanse' since leaving the company I co-founded a decade ago. I don't use Twitter or Facebook. Not because of some refusal to embrace new technology, but simply because I haven't anything interesting or important enough to say that the need to parse down to a basic and/or limited form of communication strikes me as anything resembling a good idea. There's more to it. That's just the dime-store defense. I reckon I miss the personal connections these new outlets have all but relegated to relic status, and I'm mildly terrified we 'men of letters' are endangered (if not already extinct). I never want to simulate conversations like the one Logan and I had last night - those very real and engaged moments. Sometimes I feel like I'm not just in the minority, but actually *am* the minority (last of the Luddites, Logan lovingly calls me).

"I stopped looking up simple scientific phenomena," I'd shared with him last night. "I mean, right away. Like if I wondered about why something was the way it was. Dumb stuff, I guess. Like goose-bumps. Or why cavitation works the way it does."

"Goose-bumps?"

"Yeah. Did you know it's just evolutionary leftovers? You know, like when we're startled. Like cats or porcupines. We just don't get fluffy."

"Sure, but we get cold."

"Yup. So do animals. All that stuff popping up creates these little air pockets, like extra insulation an—"

"Okay, great. But why wonder? That shit is like four seconds away online."

"I dunno. I guess I like mulling it over. I like trying to figure it out on my own. I'm often wrong, but I still do it. Kinda' random here, but did you know the brain doesn't just shut down at death? There's some evidence to suggest that it might go into this sort of safe mode as it dies, like some long trippy dream for a period of time. Days or hours or whatever. The general thinking is that the brain knows it's a lame duck, so it does its best to ease out on a happy note. Like a unicorn chaser. There's no way to know if this is actually happening though, of cour—"

"Sound like a solipsist's wet dream," he interrupts.

"I kinda' thought the same thing. Do you remember that meteorologist? The one that shot herself on live TV?"

"Can't say that I do."

"Really? She was covering that freak tornado a few years back?"

"Nope."

"Huh. Anyhow, she tries to kill herself but she fucks it up, right? She had it all planned out. She had the right caliber gun, right spot at the base of the skull, etcetera and so on. She'd been thorough, but the bullet ends up lodged in her spinal column or something and she needs brain surgery. But there's a problem. They couldn't operate on her brain without the procedure actually killing her, so they killed her. Proactively. The surgeon actually induced death, performed the operation, and revived her some time later. What's nuts is she could recall details about the procedure that she shouldn't have been able to. She didn't make it, so she got what she wanted in the end, but isn't tha—"

"Okay, sure. That's interesting, but still," he'd admonished, "why not just save the time? Spend it doing something else?"

It's a valid point and one he's made before. I didn't push the issue.

"Call home yet?" Logan mutters without looking up from the laptop.

I haven't. Maggie would be in school. Janet would be driving to work. I think. I'm not even sure they still live in Dallas. I slip outside for a moment with my cell. Logan doesn't know about all that just yet. I plan on telling him in Baja, but for now I do the expected thing and fake dial and stand with a dead cell to my face and loiter near the curb and pretend to leave a fake voicemail as I watch vacant faces pull up and leave in dirty, neglected rental cars.

A long van with action shots of dirt bikes silk-screened down the side pulls up under the portico. The driver throws me a wave and I pocket the phone, signaling Logan in the lobby. I guess the driver's already pegged us as the clients he's picking up. I shouldn't be too surprised, given how often he must shuttle guys like us here for their 'Big Adventure'.

He helps us with our bags and tells us his name is Jim with a firm handshake. He grills us the moment we drive off. For some reason, I feel the urge to assure him we're proper and experienced riders. I don't know why this is so important to me. It shouldn't matter at all.

"First time to Baja?"

"Yup."

"Going all the way down?"

Nervous chuckle.

"Gonna try to."

"Cool. Cool. Where you guys from?"

"Dall-uh, Portland. And Seattle."

"Longest ride yet?"

"Nope. Well, not for me. For him—" I look at Logan. He's thumbing at his cell.

"Yeah, longest trip," he mumbles. He's still working. He belongs to a rather elite group of programmers, a position many at his company refer to in hushed tones as 'totally black-ops' in their selectivity and protocol. It's a big deal. A *really* big deal. Which means he doesn't get to leave work behind. Still, I don't think it's his longest ride.

We're able to paint a fairly accurate picture for Jim of our riding pasts as we thread slow traffic on I5 North. I feel like a kindergartner at circle time excitedly telling my teacher what I did over spring break (which is just fine as I tend to quite like anything that makes me feel like a kid these days). I ask Jim if he likes the area and he tells us that he's lived between San Diego and 'TJ' for going on thirty years. He says anytime he takes a trip anywhere else he's reminded why he keeps coming back here. 'Yeah, it's hot. And the dust and sandstorms fucking suck, sure. But it's home.' He's worked a dozen pit crews for the 500 over the last twenty years and does so not professionally, not for pay, but for kicks. Most people wouldn't consider crewing a grueling race like the Baja 500 for any reason, but I get that. If I was coming back from Haiti, I'd probably want to volunteer sometime, too.

After a few short miles, we pull into a small converted used-car lot now operating as the *Baja Bike! Adventures* home base. A number of bikes line the front lot - trial bikes, customer bikes, unintentionally disassembled bikes, and there, behind the rest, our pair of BMWs. They're much newer than I'd expected. And taller.

"They're too shiny!" I blurt.

Jim laughs. "Well, they are right now. We more or less rebuild 'em each time they come back. They always need something fixed or painted. Or extracted."

They're purposeful machines, side by side on their center stands like a pair of mechanical Clydesdales. I turn and give Logan a 'Can you believe this?' grin that he doesn't return.

They go over the bikes with us in detail, but it's a half-hour whirlwind of knowledge transfer and giddiness (a terrible combination) that all but guarantees any attempted recall of this semi-important data will trickle forth not as anything useful, but as the wah-wah voice of all adults in Schulz's world. Still, even though the details are muddy, the main objectives remain clear. Where? Baja. When? For the next five days. How? On these behemoths right here. Why?

Fuck me. Why indeed.

We snake out of the city and onto the interstate, Logan in tow as I lead left. The short jaunt to the border doesn't take long, and though the bikes are huge, they slim right down the way large bikes always seem to with passing miles. The BMWs are equipped with a bike-to-bike intercom system, something we've both been riding long enough to know not to overuse. They're useful for keeping each other amused more than anything else, handy for random cracks about funny billboards or shared opinions on sailed through scenery. That sort of thing. Otherwise, they can be a real distraction at exactly the wrong moment.

Traffic's light heading South on I5, but it's incredibly heavy the other direction back into the US. It's a Thursday afternoon, but I've never been here. It might be like this every single day for all I know. I'm prepared for the border crossing to take a while, but once again I'm surprised. The thorough bike inspection I'd anticipated doesn't take place. We're not asked to dismount. We're not even subjected to the usual battery of questions ('Why you trying to enter the country and How long you intending to stay and You got any A,T or Fs and Why you eyeballing me, boy'). Logan and I peer at one another through open visors. His shrug echoes mine.

Traffic in Tijuana, however, is absolutely snarled. The roads are all crammed together and immediately twist around on themselves in increasingly confusing ways. But the GPS doesn't indicate a change of direction, so I remain on the spaghetti loop we're on and check now and then to make sure Logan's right behind me. He is, and I see him check his own GPS every few seconds as well. When we finally bust free of the clutter, I look back and see him visibly relax before I do. Contrary to expectation, this is a pleasant sensation on a bike and one that really doesn't translate well to other forms of travel. There's this precise moment when you break away from everything and everyone else around. You're suddenly less vulnerable and the very liberation makes the chaos of traffic (almost) worth the stress as it all fades in your mirrors.

The day wanders on, and the wind picks up the farther south we ride. I'm somewhat familiar with the Santa Anas and know that if you must wonder if it's Devils Breath, it just ain't. Strong wind is a fact of life in day-to-day riding, and it took several years to grow comfortable riding in sustained winds exceeding twenty or thirty miles an hour. On a fully loaded bike, eight hours of that can be flat out exhausting. The trick is to do something completely converse to what every fiber in your body's already doing; if you can go (and remain) slack and just flow with the machine, things actually do settle down. You'll still clench at those sudden gusts that send the bike rocking and changing lanes, but it does help. The other thing that works is good old MPH. The gyroscopic effect of a motorcycle's wheels act to stabilize it, so the faster you ride, the more stable things become (there's a point of diminishing returns with this, of course, and convincing someone else to speed up when they're far past terrified is like asking them to inhale deeply while they drown).

Logan lets me know over the crackling intercom that he's not particularly fond of this latter trick, and I bring the pace back down. The gusts aren't terrible, but the mini sand storms we punch through every so often are brutal. Even with my visor completely shut, determined bits of sand and grit find a way past the seal to rocket against my face with alarming force. I crack the visor an inch in hopes the wider gap will reduce the venturic velocities.

Something very hard smashes into the corner of my left eye. I try (unsuccessfully) not flinching with the entirety of my body.

"Need to stop?" Logan's voice sputters over the intercom.

I turn my head to the side and nod *YES*.

I ease off at a wider stretch of shoulder half a mile up the road. The pavement is slick with windswept sand and I slide to a sloppy stop, not yet familiar with the grabby nature of the front brake (this, of course, being what I'll tell Logan later). I fetch neutral, straddle the bike and remove my helmet. The pain's gone, but something is firmly lodged in the corner of my eye. Everything's blurry.

Logan walks up beside me.

"What happened?" he shouts through his closed helmet.

I turn my face to his and look skyward, pointing to the damage. He pops his visor and furrows his brow. He doesn't react with alarm (which I read as good news), and I lean forward to peer at my eye in the mirror. It's red and swelling. I do my best to flush it out with a little vial of artificial tears (that I always keep in the breast pocket of my riding jacket), but the wind makes this a particularly frustrating exercise and I end up doing a better job of flushing Logan's entire face. I still don't know what hit me. Not sand. More grape size (whatever's lodged in there is but a part of the larger thing). I've ridden through Junebug swarms before, but I doubt they have February versions of those winged morons here. The odds of something that size navigating the short windscreen just to rocket through the gap at the bottom of my visor seem staggeringly high to me (and to hit me up top, near the eye, not smack-dab in the kisser.

Another inch to the right and I'd no doubt be spending the next few days in some questionable Tijuana ER).

I don the helmet, give Logan a thumbs up, and head back out. That wonderful chilling effect as fresh sweat dries under ventilated mesh thrills me like it always has. Our route today shouldn't take too long. I wasn't sure when we'd actually leave San Diego, so I kept the miles low and easy at just over two hundred total. Today's all terra pavimentum. We'll leave the beaten path tomorrow and put what little off-road experience we have to the test.

A little road on the GPS catches my attention. I thumb the intercom button strapped to the left grip.

"Gonna make a quick detour."

"I see it," he crackles back after a second. "Good call."

We swing towards the coast and right into the suddenly overpowering scent of the Pacific. I spoke to a few people before the trip that knew Baja. Most of them portrayed it as an arid desert, but the number of gas stations, specialty shops, and small homes here all suggest something very different. It feels like we're straddling old Bradley tanks on Rodeo Drive. I'm sort of surprised we haven't seen a McDonald's.

The number of small shops selling knick-knacks and ice cold beer doubles in the final mile. We pull into a narrow parking lot close to the beach and kill the bikes. I peek over at Logan as he pulls alongside, and we both shake our heads in mild disbelief. I'm really not sure what we were expecting.

We wander towards a railing where a group of tourists watch the surf crash against the rocks below. They coo and yelp as the spray washes over them. They lean far over the bars and take pictures in unnatural poses.

"Feels like we haven't left yet," Logan says.

We saddle up and head back towards the highway. Those pleasant feelings I experienced moments ago have vanished. I just want to be smack-dab in the middle of nowhere. Disappointments like this (even one this insignificant) can keep you from exploring such roads, and I make a little promise to myself that it won't.

Why am I upset to see people here enjoying themselves? This *is* a vacation destination, after all. I'm not sure why I feel this way. Perhaps my heart's already in Haiti and I'm dumbfounded by the sight of happy people doing anything at all.

And what do I call this? Isn't this my own strange version of happy?

I sigh, peering at Logan in the mirror, wondering if the intercom transmits more than it should.

Not ten minutes after rejoining the highway, I spy another little road on the GPS leading to the coast, shorter and twistier than the one we explored.

That's the one we should have taken.

I imagine what it looks like as we sail past.

We arrive at the little no-name motel a little after four o'clock. The place is clean, but feels more like an old apartment complex than a cheap over-nighter. I wonder if anyone else will even arrive as we plop ourselves into a pair of cruddy plastic chairs in front of our rooms. The bikes tick as they cool in the late-afternoon shade. It feels too early to be stopped like this. I had more miles in me. I suspect Logan did, too.

"I'm learning French," I mumble in the middle of a full body stretch.

"Oh yeah? How's that going?"

"Well, I should say I'm *trying* to learn French."

Logan chuckles. I glance over and see his phone balanced across one knee.

"They don't all speak French, exactly," I continue. "It's Creole. Or their version of Creole and some mix of the two. I wanted to start with a good base of French, but I think I'm just going to have to wing it. I figure if I can get some of the key phrases down, I can at least stammer through. I know salle de bain and merci beaucoup. Basic stuff. If I hear blanc, it probably means someone's talking about me."

"Have you studied any Creole?"

"Not a bit."

Logan looks up. I think the very tangible nature of language has suddenly crystallized this whole nutty thing as real.

"Okay, so how did you decide? When? Did you just wake up one day and say, 'Screw it? I'm going to Haiti?'"

There actually was a singular moment. I inhale slowly. I've only told one other person what I'm about to tell Logan and it didn't go very well. I want to get this right for him, as if the correct words spoken in the precise order with perfect rhythm will strip away all the crazy.

"The day after the quake, I was making lunch and had CNN on. Their Breaking News thing flashes up. You know, the full-screen deal? They're cutting to an aerial shot over Port-au-Prince. Now, remember, they'd been covering the quake nonstop for twenty-four hours, so breaking news seemed like a big deal at the time."

I pause and look over. He's pocketed the phone. I sip smelly ice water from my plastic cup and continue.

"The banner thing across the bottom read 'Rioting in Haiti' or 'Protests in Port-au-Prince'. Something like that. That bag of hammers anchor what's-his-face is stammering and stumbling through his copy all excited and nervous. It was hard to tell what was going on. The chopper kept circling, so the camera guy was all over the place. There *were* a lot of people there. I guess it did kinda' look like a protest from the helicopter, but I didn't really get a rioty-vibe. Even if they *had* been rioting, I thought they were totally right to be upset. Supplies were arriving but stacking up. Volunteers were showing up in droves and scrambling to figure out who the hell was in charge of what. Of course they're mad, right? But they weren't rioting."

Logan doesn't seem familiar with this story. Not many people are.

"They were singing. Dancing. It was like a parade. A celebration. They were happy and thankful to be alive. CNN doesn't know what to call it, so they just nuke the banner. As soon as they had audio and a better shot, it was completely apparent it wasn't a group of angry people. Some of them were crying. Others were singing. But everyone was dancing. It was fucking amazing. *That* should have been their on-screen banner: '*Fucking amazing scene in Haiti*'. It floored me. I actually had to sit down."

"I can imagine," he offers quietly.

"So they cut to commercial and when they came back, they moved on to other stuff. Just like that. They covered it later as a feel-good moment amidst all the shit, but that was all I ever saw of it. The thing is, I wasn't seeing the same reaction in people that I'd had. I couldn't figure out why that was. They had every reason to riot or protest or loot and scream at the top of their lungs. That's what we do here, you know? I think that's what got to me. But what they did? I think I felt very ashamed."

What looks like an old police cruiser swings around the corner across the street and vanishes down the main road in a belch of black exhaust.

"Ashamed how?"

This is where the connective tissue of my reasoning falls apart. The idea forms so perfectly in my heart, but seems to lose all definition aloud.

"It's— well, *we* jump to that conclusion. When we see something like that? It absolutely must be something awful. It can't be anything else. It's how we operate because it's what we expect. It's what we know. Hell, I did the same thing. It never occurred to me that it might be a celebration under those circumstances. I saw a group of people marching and jumped to the same conclusion as those reporters. I'd never seen anything like it. But that isn't why I decided to go. It just confirmed some important groundwork taking shape."

There's more I want to tell him, but I'm suddenly very hungry. I slap the arms of my chair.

"Let's get something to eat. I'm starving."

We lock the rooms and check the bikes for anything we might have forgotten. The dirt parking lot leads back to the main highway and we wander out towards the din. The dust in the air is so thick it's impossible to avoid breathing it in and the handkerchiefs I've seen wrapped around so many faces here suddenly make perfect sense. I tell Logan we should look for some after dinner.

The narrow highway is crowded with a bizarre mix of vehicles. Dump trucks fly past while single cylinder dirt bikes dart in and out of side streets at speeds that make us both cringe. I point at a guy on a little scooter barely getting out of its own way.

"You know, bravery is just a fancy word for calculated stupidity!" I yell to Logan over the din.

He shakes his head. "Sometimes it's just stupid!"

We demonstrate it ourselves and rush across the busy street. Tecate and Corona signs blink out at us from every angle, and while it's nice not to have to worry about where we're going to eat, it's once again far from what I'd expected. We pick a decent looking taco joint with a fenced-in patio along the side and order huge slushy margaritas, chicken tacos, and salsa hot enough to peel paint.

Logan puts his palms on the table and leans forward after we've inhaled our first few bites.

"Alright. Get on with it. You were getting to some point back there."

I sit back and fold my legs with a heavy sigh.

"Right. So, I was paying my property taxes for the place in Texas. I guess this was about two weeks after the quake.

Anyhow, I'm in the post office parking lot. It's really late, like three AM. I'm the only one there. I'm sitting on Gerty, pulling my gloves on, and it just hits me...I hate all of this. I hated that expensive bike. I hated the property taxes I was about to mail off. I hated the big house I was paying those taxes on." I rub my face. "Okay, hate's a little strong. It was disgust. I think. I dunno. I had an episode. Something. I really couldn't put my finger on it. I just had too much. It didn't seem right to own so much...*stuff*. Sure, I'd worked to buy these things, but that in itself was another problem altogether. During my last year or two at the company, it didn't feel like the owners had to work very hard at anything if we didn't want to. We had a crew of a hundred people at that point. And you know what? Most of them were younger and smarter and far more talented than the four of us had ever been. All we had to do was keep the lights on. I'm oversimplifying here, but you get the idea."

"I'm not really sure I do."

"Okay, let me give you an example. I was riding the elevator one Friday night and it stops like two floors down. This girl gets on, and I did the usual thing and made uncomfortable small talk. Typical bullshit about the coming weekend. Stuff like that. She said it didn't really matter because she had to work both days. 'That's not right!' I say. 'Your boss sucks!' She agreed and we both laughed. Turned out she worked for us. For six months. I didn't know her, and she didn't know me."

Logan watches me. I know he's perplexed by all of this. I'm describing problems most people would love to have.

"So you have to pay property taxes yourself?"

"No, that's not— I mean, sure. A bank isn't submitting property taxes for you every year when you own your home outright. You get a bill from the city and a bill from the county and you pay them by the first of February. Anyway, I guess the point I was trying to mak—"

"No, I get it. I wouldn't want to write those checks."

"It's not that," I sigh. "I don't mind paying taxes for the things we get to take for granted. My daughter goes to a great public school not a mile from the house. I'm happy to pay for that. What I felt that night was something else. No one thing in particular set me off."

This is a tricky thing to make crystal clear to anyone, like explaining sarcasm to a kid.

"Seeing the parade, that celebration or whatever? It was a catalyst. Like a fuse was primed. Days later, putting stamps on those tax bills at the post office at three AM? It finally blew up. I wasn't mad. But something snapped. I just didn't know what it was that night."

Logan chews his food slowly. I sense he wants to challenge me on this but isn't sure how to do so.

"I don't think there's any question I was pretty fucked up when this all happened," I continue. "I was, shall we say, already susceptible to sadness. You remember how bad it was there for a while. I sort of went numb after the quake. Look, I know this all sounds really melodramatic."

"Nah, I hardly ever watch the news and it bothered me, too."

"Right? I think most people were affected by it. It's safe to assume everyone feels a little guilty about how easy we have things here. And I considered that. Maybe it was a really bad flare-up of Western guilt. That's normal. We feel a little selfish and realize it's not so bad here. Like we're almost relieved this horrible thing happened to grace us with a reminder. As if the point of the thing was to remind us of how awesome we have it here. So we donate some money or we volunteer. And most people feel really good about helping out. Right? They move on. But I wasn't moving on. Something about that damn parade stripped away my perceptions of what or who I'd become. A few days later, I finally realized what I'd felt watching them. It wasn't guilt. It was envy."

He nods. Maybe something's clicking.

"You ever watch jellyfish swim? Like in those documentaries?"

He stops nodding. "Huh?"

"Never mind. Anyhow, I mailed the taxes and rode back to Alex's, but when I got bac—"

"Oh." He stares at the table. "This happened in Portland?"

"Yeah, I think I got there back in, Jesus, late November?"

He doesn't know this.

"I thought you said you got there last month."

"Well, that's, yeah. That's a long story. Longer, I mean. I'll tell you later."

He regards me with a new kind of furrow.

Christ! In the middle of all this heart-to-heart honesty, I've lied to him about something so trivial!

I can't even remember why I didn't tell him back then (then again, the past few months have been rather hazy). I sheepishly continue like everything's cool.

"So I rode back there and thought about all of my stuff still down there in Texas. All the cars and motorcycles. They suddenly felt like empty trophies. I had all this...stuff. I had an entire closet full of DVDs I'd never even opened, rooms crammed with gadgets and a million kids toys. We had two whole rooms upstairs we kept shut because they were junk rooms the way people have junk drawers in their kitchen. I'm glad I was in Portland that night. If I'd been in Texas, I just might've burned it all to the ground."

Logan chokes on his drink and we both laugh.

"I don't know if I could do it," Logan begins, "but you have the time to. It'd be easier to consider with that kind of time. Hell, I have trouble even getting a few days off. This little trip? I thought I was going to have to promise them my firstborn!"

I smile, but there's truth in the cliché. You do promise them your firstborn. You promise away all the children you'll ever have. Just not in the way we joke about.

"To be continued?" He peers at me over his sunglasses.

"Of course."

We pay the tab and head back outside. The sun is low in the west now and the winds have calmed, but the traffic's picked up. We exercise a little full-tummy caution and wait to cross the highway.

"So how long you gonna' be there?" Logan yells over the trucks thundering past.

"Dunno! I guess I'll know when I'm done!" I yell back.

It's a rehearsed line. It's a lie.

Logan taps my shoulder and points down the road.

"Look! McDonald's!"

I step out of the tiny hotel room to find a crisp morning air has replaced the mugginess. It's perfect riding weather and already so bright I can't look directly at the shiny bits of the bikes. Logan's door is cracked open a bit, which has always been our shorthand for 'I'm up'. I hear him brushing his teeth inside. *Christ. He's almost ready. All I've done is stumble outside.*

I sit down in one of the plastic chairs and pull out my cell phone. No messages. Logan steps out. He's already geared up. His riding boots thump the dusty causeway next to me with heavy implication.

"You just waking up?"

It's not really a question.

"Yeah. I'll skip a shower this morning. I need to better get used to that for there. For over there. Might as well now start stinking."

My brain always struggles this early in the morning.

"I just need to pack the bike is all."

This seems to satisfy him and he thumps back into his room. Neither of us are big morning people, but I see he's become much better at it than me. There was a time we both crashed around dawn and woke up when the sun was good and hot. Seeing him awake and ready to go at this early hour makes me feel like he's the guest of honor at some party I wasn't even invited to.

I hop up and slip back into my room. Unlike yesterday, my sinuses are bad this morning. Really bad. Packed and bleeding.

The morning remains cool as we bisect Baja on a dusty ribbon south. In the direct rays of the sun, the temperature is nearly ideal and offsets the slight morning chill. Neither of us brought any cold-weather clothing to wear under our gear, though it might not be the temperature that has us shivering our way out of town. He's using the intercom much more today.

"Did you bring a gun?" he crackles through the earbuds.

"Now listen. Just 'cause I lived in Texas thirteen years doesn't mean I've gone all outlaw or whatever."

He's quiet a moment.

"So? Did you?"

"Of *course*."

Our first turn of the day comes up after a dozen miles of relatively smooth pavement. We fueled up back in town and managed to score some of those handkerchiefs from the cashier (though we decided to figure out proper fitment under the concealment of camp later and not right in front of the smirking locals).

I'm thrilled not knowing what the rest of this day will bring. I've ridden on dirt and gravel roads before. Sometimes it's unavoidable. However, those had always been slow and cautious jaunts for a few hundred yards at most.

A large dust plume rises to the sky half a mile ahead and I pull over for a second to gap what I presume is the car or truck kicking it up. Logan's voice squelches over the intercom.

"Everything okay?"

"Yup," I radio back. "Just giving them a head start."

I gesture ahead at the curling cloud, but he doesn't say anything. Seconds later an old pickup rattles quickly past, kicking up another huge plume which envelopes us immediately.

"I think we're just gonna have to go for it," he says. "Maybe it's not a bad thing to have folks around, you know, just in case?"

He's got a point. I check the mirrors and head off behind the old truck, carefully maintaining a healthy distance to keep the dust cocktail to a minimum.

"What did that sign say back there?" Logan crackles.

"I'm not sure. Wanna' go back and see?"

I assume this road is okay for us to use.

"Well," he sighs, "I'm sure it's fine. Doesn't look like a long stretch on the GPS. I don't think it even has a name! How cool is that?"

We know we're not really off any beaten path here, but to admit this would suck some of the magic from the day. Right now we're boys with toys. Our pace grows braver with each passing mile and we begin seeking out both larger ruts and broken surfaces to test the machines. The GS is doing all the work here. In just minutes I'm trusting the bike completely, feeling ready for whatever Baja throws our way. But this is dangerous thinking.

"These bikes are almost too good!"

He doesn't respond.

Maybe he thinks I'm babysitting.

The road grows twisty as we climb and a shallow cliff begins forming to our right, one that grows more and more eye opening with every other turn. We pay so much attention to the sudden edge that we don't even see the cars above us right away.

"What the *hell?*" Logan screams over the intercom.

My earbuds clip with the sudden volume. I'm too dumbfounded to respond. I ease to a stop in the middle of the shallow rut I'd been tracing. I switch the bike off. I raise my visor. I look over at Logan who's done the same. Cars, above us on the highest bluff. All parked in tidy rows. Next to a pool house. Next to stables. The more I look, the more I see.

"It's a resort," I sigh. "It's a goddamn resort."

Logan just stares. He doesn't know what to say. He grunts a glove free with his teeth and whips his cell phone out to snap pictures. I stare south.

Barren. We should be out there.

"I wonder what it's called," Logan murmurs.

I slam my visor shut and start the bike.

Really? Is he suggesting we go up for mimosas?

He starts to stash the phone, but stops to tap at it some more. I can't tell what he's doing, but it's quick he indicates with a raised finger. *Uno momento.*

HOOOOOOOOOOOOOOOOONKKKKKKKKK!

We jump, startled and scrambling to keep the bikes upright. A massive delivery truck has crawled to a stop just a few inches off our rear tires. I have no idea how long we've been blocking him. I hadn't heard a thing.

"Come on. Put that shit away."

The hair on the back of my neck bristles at my own tone. He shrugs and throws the phone in his tankbag. We ease to the right, towards the cliff, so the truck can squeeze past. I hate how dangerous this is, but we have little choice right now. The driver grinds into first and swears loudly out the open window as he bounces by. I don't blame him. He probably thinks we're staying at that ritzy joint.

"Hey," I begin, "I just didn't expect to see that. We're out here trying to get away and *tada!* It's not what I expected. It just caught me off guard is all."

"I just don't understand why it's such a bad thing," he finally replies.

I start to thumb a response.

Broad spectrum analysis of this eyesore? Nope. That's an all-night kind of thing.

"It's not, I guess. I don't know."

Before long, we're descending the other side of the ridge. The ruts have vanished and the road is smooth, like it's maintained. Soon our little dirt road becomes paved, then populated, and without much warning we're suddenly deposited onto another southbound highway. I know from studying the maps that this will gradually wander to the other coast in an hour or so. It's silly, but I'm eager to see water on this side, too.

An awkward funk has settled in. I wait for Logan to chat over the intercom about the area. The resort. The weather. Anything. But he doesn't.

"I don't know if I mentioned this before," I cave, "but some of that road back there was part of the Baja 500 a few years ago. They seem to change things up every year, but some of that was used at one point."

"Oh yeah?" He pauses. "Any more roads like that on the route?"

"I think there's one little stretch coming up before our turn. I'll point it out when we get there. Provided I see it."

His tone's friendly. That's good.

But the sky has grown overcast and the funk doesn't lift. There's little chance of rain. It's just low, slow moving grey that renders everything dull. Even here. The world shrinks in. No shadows. No depth. Just static and dead.

"You hungry at all?" I thumb the com.

"I'm glad you asked first!" I can hear him smile in his helmet.

"Me too. Looks like there's a town up here in a bit. If you see anything, just holler."

The road is cracked from the year-round heat and sand fills the webbed striations like dusty spackle. These are lonely roads. I love this kind of road. There are desolate highways like this back in Texas where I can pretend the world begins and ends between my horizons. Any stretch where I won't see another vehicle for hours is my kind of road. I've ridden with people who find such solitude unnerving, but I never want it to end.

As we near San Felipe, the vibe quickly morphs from solitary slab to manicured development. Flower planters dot the median, interleaving perfect little palm trees. The gas stations and shops appear new and clean. I start to wonder if we've wandered into an honest-to-god mirage.

"There. Right side," Logan crackles over the radio.

It's not even a restaurant. Just a stand.

Perfect.

We pull in and kill the bikes. It's our first stop of the day, and we're both happy to be off and stretching muscles not yet familiar with these saddles. My gas gauge hasn't budged much from full. I'm not sure it's accurate, given the hundred miles behind us, so it's either a pleasant surprise or a new concern. I settle on pleasant when I see that Logan's reads the same.

We order flour tortillas and fajita-style steak wrapped up in steaming tin foil. The side of the stand provides the perfect place to eat, and we plop down in the dirt with our backs against the warm, painted wood.

"Why didn't you pass that truck?"

"What? The old dually?"

"Yeah. The fumes were *horrible*. You couldn't smell that?"

"I did, yeah," I nod, "but I'd be breaking my locals law."

"Your what?"

"Locals law. If I know I have a turn or a town coming up in, oh, say the next five miles? I just fall into formation. Hang back. You ever get caught at a red light after blowing past someone at a buck twenty?"

"No, not recently."

I suspect he has. It's not something you freely admit.

"I had the mother of all fucked up passes a few years ago. In fact, it was on the way to Lake Louise to meet you and Shelly. Not too far past the border. Anyhow, I'm not really paying attention to the GPS and I end up stuck behind this beat to hell truck. Slow as balls. It wasn't even *that* loaded down, but he was just dragging his ass and swaying all over the lane. I have this semi coming up behind me, so...*fuck it.* Right? Blew past him in no passing zone. And I mean with spirit. Like I was doing him the service. Like *he* needed a reminder. I get a half mile up the road. Not even. BAM. Major four-way stop at the edge of this little town. Like, ten seconds later."

"Oops."

"Big time. I can't really zip through the stop and everyone's being polite, just taking their sweet time, and here he comes. He's got all this metal shit strapped to the front grille. Badges and signs and shit. I can't really make him out, but I can clearly see that the gun rack behind him is empty. Which, at first, was like this huge relief. You know? But then I realized he probably had some fucking cannon already laid out across his lap."

"Did he?"

"I don't know. I think he realized he didn't really need that. Though he did edge right up on the back tire, but I kind of had that coming. Anyhow, yeah. Locals law after that. As long as I have five miles or more to make hay, sure. I'll pass. But I'm in their backyard. I'm sure you have stuff like that. Little ridecraft rules you've developed over time."

"I never used to cover my brake through intersections. Until I got hit, I mean. Like that?"

"Sort of. That's a good one, but it's also part of that big, cosmic ridecraft bible. Like the wave. I'm almost certain that started as a universal reminder to keep an eye on oncoming traffic. It's just propagated out as this brotherly love thing for decades or whatever."

"Huh. Hadn't considered that."

"Listen," I offer between bites, "I'm sorry about that back there on the hill. It was unfair of me. I was disappointed to see that place all of a sudden and I let it bother me."

"It's fine," he sighs.

It's not, though, and I wait for him to continue.

"I just, well, it doesn't bother me like it does you. I see a place like that and the first thought I have is 'Wow! This would be a great place for Shelly and I!' That would be nice, I think. Something like that would make this kind of riding worth it for her. If you had a place like that to look forward to at the end of the day? You know? A nice soak? Good food? If it meant she actually did the trip because of someplace like that? Don't you think that's a good thing?"

I can't argue with him. Sometimes all you want after a really long day is a nice place to call home for a few hours. Setting up camp, starting a fire to cook your meal? That can satisfy or crush your spirit. It depends on the day you've had. For him, a place like that means a shared trip with Shelly, one they can enjoy without compromise.

"Speaking of the girls, what do Janet and Maggie think of this Haiti thing?"

My mouth's full, which is just as well. I haven't told them. I shake my head 'no'. The food is good. Really good. I'm tempted to go back for more.

"What?"

I swallow too fast. "They don't know," I cough. "I told my folks, though."

I take another large bite and wash it down with a gulp of flat soda. He watches me, waiting for eye contact I won't grant.

"We had one of those typical grey weekends in Portland a few weeks back. I woke up feeling down and broke my no-booze-before-dark rule. Had a few doubles. Which was dumb because it always leads to a Broadway binge."

"Huh?"

"Yeah, you know. Five, six, seven, eight!"

Logan's head slumps practically to his chest. "Wow. That just might be the lamest thing I've ever heard."

"*Anyhow*, I called my mom and dad and told them what I was planning to do."

"And they didn't freak?"

"Oh, she freaked. She was fine at first, but it turned into twenty questions. And the more she asked, the scarier it sounded. I told her I was going over there for a while to help out. No, I didn't know for how long. It wasn't going to cost a lot, no. Yes, I'm aware I'll need a passport. And like that. She didn't seem too surprised by it. Just confused. Scared. It looks scary on the news, but like you said at the hotel, *everything* looks scary on the news. I did my best to explain things, but it just made her nervous."

Logan shakes his head and stares at his food.

"But you're going to tell Janet, right?"

"I don't know."

I hate how it sounds. But it's the truth.

"I'm trying to picture having this conversation with Shelly," he says.

"Yeah?"

"Yeah. My guess is we wouldn't make it past dinner. She'd tell me how nuts I was for even considering it. I'd totally be sleeping downstairs."

I chuckle and take my last bite.

"Well, it *is* nuts. Calculated stupidity, right?"

"Well..." he begins, but trails off.

"Yeah. We'll talk more tonight."

We head out after lunch and once again I'm happy to leave cultivated perfection far behind. We trace the coast over the next hour in rich air ripe with the overpowering scent of the ocean, slipping through pockets of cool damp air now and then that leave me wanting to turn around just to do it again.

The asphalt looks more like a wide, black chalkboard than any road. Delicate wisps of sand snake and switch along either side like snow in the evening sun, threatening to close in and seal off our escape.

It's nice watching another rider. It's more than just a change of perspective. You see shared habits, developed together or independently. Other times it's the reverse and you see things you should be doing.

Logan stops and hesitates at our exit. It looks more like a hiking trail than anything we should be venturing onto.

"Keep your legs out and don't grab any brake if you feel it slip. Let it slip some," I coach over the intercom.

Like I know. Christ.

We take it very slow at first, allowing the bikes to fish around a bit as we make steady, careful progress. I'm nervous, but the bike is utterly unfazed. It seems to have things all figured out without much input from me and the trust that's been building all day helps loosen my grip some.

"Having fun?" I thumb.

"Fucking *A!*" he yelps back.

We have just a few hours of daylight left, but there's no particular end point for the day. The plan was to exit back there and just head inland to the middle of nowhere. That's it. We'll know when and where to stop when we get there. The little trail we're on begins to fade, leaving us no choice but to forge our own. No path, no idea what's coming. In a few moments the uncertainty ends at a rutted road well worn in from a variety of machines. We blend down into it, the long suspension travel soaking up the transition without drama.

"Why haven't I done this before?" I yell into the intercom.

"I know!" he bellows back.

Why indeed? I used to justify *not* doing this sort of riding, whining that I didn't have anywhere to do so back home or that I didn't really see the point. We expect a route ahead of us at all times. There must be a path. But this is great! No road? So what?

"Why don't you pick our camp site tonight," I suggest over the intercom.

Logan looks down, wanting to thumb a response. He waits a bit and crosses a seriously deep rut first.

"You sure?"

"Yup. I'll be in a tent. It won't matter where."

He starts looking for a spot almost right away. We don't have to stop just yet, but I wouldn't object. He swivels in the saddle, one way, then the other, trying to talk back to me through his open visor.

"Use the intercom," I thumb.

"Sorry. What about over there?" He points to our right, towards a flat clearing among the ocean of rolling dunes that define this area. The sage is much taller (and thicker) everywhere around the clearing.

Good kindling. Dangerous kindling, but good.

I watch him reach back and tug at the left sidecase. It's not open, but it moves a bit when he wiggles it. He leans back to thumb the radio.

"Hold on a sec. I think this thing's coming off."

He starts to put the bike down on the kickstand. But the kickstand isn't down. He fights it, locking his leg and leaning wildly over to the right. But the bike is far too heavy. It chucks him out across the ruts and wobbles to a stop on its side.

"FUCK! FUCK FUCK *FUCK!*"

"Are you okay? Hold still!" I hastily kick my stand down and run to his side.

"I'm fine. God*damnit*. I'm fine," he sighs. "I can't...*fucking*...believe it."

"It's okay! I've done the same thing. Thought the kickstand was down and *bam!* Last time was in my garage. I mean right in front of the girls. Maggie needed therapy."

He doesn't laugh. He shakes his head in frustration. The bike looks fine, but we won't know if anything's broken until we get it upright. Somehow the damn thing's still running.

"I kill the bike with the kickstand now," I offer gingerly. "I know my timing's lousy here, but just heel that bugger down and the safety switch kills the ignition. Good feedback loop, right?"

I can't tell if he's heard me. He's sitting up in the dirt with his arms across his knees.

"Don't worry," I assure him. "They're made for this."

He's still shaking his head in disbelief. "Think they charge for cosmetic damage?"

"In your case? It'll be double when I tell them how it happened."

I walk to his bike and switch it off. I pop the key in the right sidecase and twist until the latch mechanism securing it snaps free.

He walks over and watches me.

"I'm sure the two of us could lift her, but this'll make life easier," I explain. "Try to release that other case."

I toss him the key and lift the grips to remove pressure on the trapped pannier. He twists the key and opens the case. The release handle moves, but we don't hear the telltale pop indicating it's free to remove. He jiggles the case as he tries, but it doesn't help.

"Well," I offer, "I'd say your bike has picked our campsite for the evening."

I smile. He tries to. He's taking it hard (I always have, too).

"Thanks," he sighs as we hoist the BMW back up. "Christ. I am so disgusted right now."

"Don't be. Seriously. I drop bikes like it's my job."

He laughs. For real this time.

"Are you sure you're okay? Sometimes you won't notice things right away."

"I think so, but ask me again in the morning."

We start the bikes and angle them carefully up the sandy dune bracketing the road. Both of us nearly lose control as the tires scramble in the soft stuff, but we manage (feebly) to throttle through. We wander into the brush, looking for that clearing, but eventually just stop. It all looks the same for miles in every direction.

"Home sweet home," I mutter.

We set up camp quickly, and despite me using several of the collapsible posts in several wrong spots, the two tents remain upright without assistance.

"I haven't cooked over a fire in, god..." Logan trails off.

Come to think of it, I don't remember him ever telling me he's camped.

"Stew or chili?"

"Huh?" I turn and see he's pulling out the various little tins of food we've brought along. Stew sounds pretty good and I tell him so. I dig a wide moat in the sand with the heel of my boot and prepare a quick pit in the center. Spongy branches from the sagebrush separate easily under a fold-away saw and the fire lights off angrily, hissing and popping immediately. We're surrounded by more than enough tinder to bring our trip to a rather spectacular end should the wind pick up, but the flames relax after a moment, billowing thick dark smoke before settling to a slow, even burn.

Logan tells me about the new job back in Seattle. It's only been a few months since he landed the gig and he seems to truly love it. It sounds rewarding and incredibly challenging in every possible way. It's been four years since I left that world, and hearing some of the intricate and technical details of a normal day for him has my head spinning.

"Do you ever miss it? That kind of work?" he asks.

"Yeah, some things. I miss working with a small team, sorting out some random issue at three AM. That sort of thing. There's still more that I *don't* miss, which is why I've not really wanted to go back."

Logan stirs the stew we've placed on a grate over the fire. The metal fork clicks brightly against the cheap tin pot. I'm not sure why the sound is so comforting.

"That was always hard for me as our company grew," I continue. "The size of a team, I mean. If we had too few people, everyone was swamped. But too many and the personal bonds blurred. There was a sweet spot for me, back when we were

small enough to all get together in the foyer at the end of any
given day and just spitball. I guess we had somewhere between
fourteen and twenty people at that point. Now that I think
about it, it's amazing we got anything done with such a small
team. This was ten years ago, but still. These days something
like that would take—"

"Double that," Logan finishes. "I can't believe it either. We
have that many IT peeps supporting just one team."

It doesn't sound fun to me, but I don't share this with him.
"When did you know you were done? I mean, how exactly does
one know it's time to check out?" he asks.

I laugh, but it's uncomfortable and forced and I hear it just as
clearly as he does.

"I never told you?"

He smiles at me behind the flickering flames between us. He
looks devilish as he shakes his head slowly 'no'.

I stand up to stretch. "Wow. Okay. Let me get a drink
first."

I don't mind sharing this story with people I know and trust
so I'm surprised I haven't told him before.

*We rode together in Canada a few years ago. Certainly I told him
back then?*

Maybe he just wants to see how I retell it a second time. I'm
not sure. I suppose it doesn't matter either way. I plop back
down in the sand, carefully gimballing the tumbler in my palm.

"I came home from work one night, I don't know, about the
same time as always. Maybe a little late. Maggie had a temp of
a 102. Which was a little high, but not crazy. She'd had worse.
You get used to fevers as a new parent. But this was different.
Her whole body was really hot, like, head to toe. She was sitting
there in the rocking chair on a big bundle of blankets just
shivering uncontrollably. I had Janet on the phone with the
pediatrician's office, and between being on hold with them and
me yelling at her that she should have fucking called me
sooner—" I take a deep breath. "It wasn't fair, of course. I

wasn't fair. But it felt like something she could have acted on earlier in the day and I lost my temper. I don't know. I was *incredibly* overprotective back then. If Maggie so much as burped weird, I totally freaked out.

"Anyhow, we're trying to get a real doctor on the phone. It's getting a little late, probably nine o'clock or so? Late for a kid doc, I mean, so everything is after-hours service by this point. But they can't find the pediatrician. I'm checking Maggie's temp, over and over, hoping to see it drop a little. We'd already given her the maximum dose of cherry flavored whatever, but her fever kept creeping up. 103, 104..."

"Fucking hell. How old was she?"

"Oh, this was early '05, so ten months? Right at ten months. But when I saw 105, man, we were in the car and flying into Dallas a minute later. There's this hospital there that was supposed to be the best place for kids about twenty minutes from the house and I just flew down there with the hazards on. Janet was quiet. I was yelling. Maggie was in her car seat just shaking away. I don't know how or why she wasn't crying."

I take a long, slow sip.

"They didn't know what was wrong. That's what really sucked. That sounds obvious, I know, but when a doctor tells you *they're* stumped? When it's your kid? Anyhow. They blasted her with this huge dose of antibiotics through an IV needle that barely fit in her hand..."

I try and block that image of her, forever burned to memory. Her face frozen in a silent scream. Her huge pleading eyes begging me to help, to rescue her, as I hovered just above whispering *it's okay...it's okay...*her hand squeezing mine, my hand squeezing the gurney far too hard. It wasn't all fucking okay. I felt helpless. I was helpless. Something delicate in her died that night. A primal instinct shattered and vacated the instant it saw the façade of all parents fall away: *I cannot protect you from everything.*

"They didn't have anything to go on.   Blood work was inconclusive. She didn't have any other symptoms, which is why they were really concerned. After a few hours of this IV drip, they told us to go home and get some rest. Her fever had broken. She seemed fine. I remember easing her into the car seat like she was thin glass. We grabbed some fast food and got home around four AM or so.

"So I go to put her down in her crib, but there was this mockingbird singing its head off outside. She'd been up almost twenty-four hours with all this drama and here she is, finally able to sleep. And this fucking bird. Over and over, screeching loud as hell. It was in a tree five or six houses down the block. I finally cracked. I walked down there and threw whatever I could get my hands on, but the little bastard would not stop. I couldn't believe it. Like I wasn't even there.

"Anyhow. Maggie's pediatrician calls us in the morning to tell us she'd like to see her. She'd had the paperwork faxed over from the hospital. I'm upset, of course. She's available early Saturday morning, but not the night before? When it mattered? Whatever. I stayed in bed and Janet took Maggie in. A few hours go by, I guess. I don't know. Janet wakes me up. She's trying very hard not to cry. She says we need to go back to the hospital and do some more blood work. Blah blah. It sounds routine. But Janet's really upset so I know something's up."

I sip.

"The phone rings as I'm getting dressed. It's the pedi again. Wonderful bedside manner, this broad. She actually says to Janet: 'Feed Maggie one last meal and bring her in. They're calling in the infectious disease team. She might be there a while. Pack some clothes.' So, I'm reeling. Trying to gather stuff up, just trying to stay focused."

"Janet?" Logan asks.

"Unglued on the closet floor. I was so mad at her. The doctor, I mean. She could have said that just a little differently. But the way she said it set this tone that had us both flipping

out. Neither of us had slept much, and now we had to go
through it all over again.

"Anyhow, we were in the hospital a week. They stuck
Maggie in one of those plastic E.T. bubbles. She was actually
the one that made us laugh, not the other way 'round. She
seemed completely okay with it in there, like living in a giant
balloon was totally normal. I was a mess. Janet was way past
that. The nurses were inconsiderate. They'd walk in and flip the
lights on in the middle of the night. Which sent Maggie
upright every single time. Which hurt her hand. She had
another giant IV buried in it and the line wasn't quite long
enough so it'd yank, and she'd cry, but we couldn't comfort her
in the bubble.

"Damn. I bet that wa—"

"See, if those first ten months had been it? Months I'd
wasted with her? If she'd died? That's when I decided to leave."

Logan watches me very carefully.

"It wasn't the first time I'd thought about it. Leaving the
company, I mean, but it was the first time the conditions were
just right. Sometimes I had some random thing in the company
bugging me enough to want to leave, but I never really felt
anything *pulling* me from the real world. You know? But I had
both that week. I knew it was time. It was suddenly very easy
to see what mattered."

"Man, I don't even know what to say. I can't imagine it."

"I hope you never have the pleasure. During that week in the
hospital, I'd head home once a day to check the mail and grab a
shower. I just needed to get out of there. But I felt so *lost*. All
of these roads I'd been driving on for years looked foreign.
Everything smelled different. Every song on the radio had
somehow been written for my little girl. I was seeing the whole
world without her and I hated it. I hated me. I had enough
money to take care of us for a long while and Janet wanted to go
back to work anyhow, so it all just kinda' made sense."

"How'd you do it?"

"Easy. I stopped buying so many goddamn cars. After a while, I—"

"No, no. How did you leave? How did you actually walk out?"

"You remember where my dad used to work? When we were kids?"

"I think so. The bread place?"

"Yup. Well, they got swallowed up a few years ago. You know, that same old song and dance cliché dismantling of the smaller fish. Anyhow, that's not really important. My dad was pretty unhappy there and had been for a long time. Voices on the phone, people he'd never even *met*, were telling him to fire folks who'd worked there as long as he had. Thirty years? Some even longer. He wasn't unhappy. He was absolutely fucking miserable. I called him from the hospital one night to give him the daily update on Maggie. I could tell it'd been a particularly lousy week for him there, so I made him an offer."

"And?"

"And I told him if he resigned the next day, I would, too."

Logan hasn't heard this story. I can see it through the smoke.

"And you know what? He agreed. He actually agreed. He had a rough idea of what he wanted to do with the hot-rods he was building on the side. He'd been fantasizing about doing that full-time for years, so even the idea of not working at *all* was better than one more day with those parasites. So, he agreed. We each went in the next day, dropped our respective bombs, and that was that."

"Is it like you always imagine?" he asks. "A big middle finger as you kick the door in? Like when people win the lottery?"

I finish my Scotch.

"Nope. Well, not for me. I think his exit had that sort of pomp to it, but for me it was like going through three divorces at the same time. It was completely out of the blue to my partners. I was just about to take on this big project. One I'd been looking forward to for years, actually, so I think it seemed very strange for me to be leaving. Things were great! Right? We'd had our biggest year ever. And I was about to check out? They supported me, but they didn't really understand it. Hell, I didn't really understand it at the time."

I stretch back.

"And now, here I am, all run dry in the middle of Baja."

Logan hangs his head. The fire snaps and shadows dance over his blonde hair.

"What does your dad think?"

"About quitting?"

"No. About Haiti."

"We haven't really talked about it much. He knows I've been down for a while so he wasn't totally shocked by it. But, yeah, he's concerned of course. He thinks I could do the same sort of work right here in the States."

I gesture over my shoulder. "Back there, I mean. He doesn't see why it has to be Haiti."

I've exposed a loose yarn. He doesn't tug at it, but I see the question form before he changes his mind.

"I'm sure he's just worried about you. He'd probably feel like he should've talked you down if something happened over there. Not that he's right for trying to, but I know that's what my father would most likely do."

He stands up and walks to the packs. The desert is absolutely black beyond the fire's reach now, the velvet nothing far above pinpricked a million times through. It's a little cool, but not uncomfortable.

"What time is it?"

"Time for a refill," he says. "Continue, good sir. Continue."

"Christ! With what? I'm tired of talking. That's all ancient history. Maggie's healthy, my dad's still building hot-rods. He seems to do okay. He's happier. And here we are, under this sky."

"Well," Logan begins. "Ancient history to you, but news to me. I didn't know a lot of that stuff."

He hands me the bottle.

"I do have some questions about Haiti. I wouldn't be much of a friend if I wasn't thinking ahead."

I stand up to grab a smoke from the packs.

"Fair enough. Shoot."

"Well, you could start by telling me why you're really going."

"I already told you," I say over my shoulder. "I'm going to help. I have time on my hands, so, you know. It feels like the right thing to do."

He watches me pull a cigar from the travel canister.

"Greg."

I cut the cigar and light it. New smoke obscures our views.

"Stop fucking around."

I don't answer for a moment.

"It's not bullshit. I really am going to help." I take a long draw. "Sure. I'm fucking depressed. I can't seem to get motivated about anything. The things I want to do lately are held hostage to this...this expectation of normalcy, or, like, *servitude* to these things I tried to get away from. Some new twenty-year plan. It seems like everybody's more worried about the financial element than what's become important to me."

"You're talking about those bikes you've been restoring, aren't you?"

"Yeah. Not many people our age do that. And that really sucks, you know? It'll be a dead language before too long. I love working on those machines. Learning new things and solving all these little problems I have to actually dig into and figure out. Learning to paint parts, for instance. I didn't know a thing about the process. I spent a year learning, painting a single swingarm until I had it just right. But I learned. I stuck it out and I learned through trial and error, no differently than anyone who's done it before. I guess working with those old machines feels like, I don't know. They're older than me. Hell, some of them were built decades before we were even born! There's this inherent respect in just touching them, let alone performing open-heart surgery. But mostly I love doing it because it makes me happy. It's new and singular and I get to think in these fresh ways. It doesn't remind me of anything."

He's listening.

"Look, there's no one answer that's just gonna work and sum everything up here. I know nothing I say will suddenly justify these weird motivations. One thing has become clear to me, though. I was only happy, like *truly* happy, when everything was a little uncertain. When I had a sort of need. You know? Once I caught whatever I'd been after, I didn't seem to care anymore. And man, for a few years there we caught plenty. *Everything* was certain. And you know what? It sucked. And then it sucked to even think that, to even *feel* that it sucked, which just compounded it all and made everything far more difficult to sort through. I felt like a spoiled fucking brat who got all he ever wanted and somehow it still wasn't good enough. Does that make sense? It was very strange to feel that way when there are folks out there that would've murdered me for a chance at what I had."

I take a deep drag and pause.

"Listen, I'm going over there because, Christ, maybe it'll wake me up. Maybe I'll feel good about doing something. A reason to keep getting up in the morning and all that."

"Alright. Then tell me why you haven't told Janet."

"I left Texas five months ago."

He doesn't move. He doesn't say anything.

"She filed for divorce and I cracked. I knew I wasn't going to survive that, so I signed everything over to her one morning and left."

"Jesus, man. I didn't know. For Portland?"

"No. I wandered around for a while. Listen, I didn't want to go through it. I didn't want to put Maggie through a custody battle. I'm not completely nuts. I see what divorce does to everyone else. The last thing I wanted was some lawyer whispering in my ear and launching an all-out assault on my best friend. I never wanted a divorce. I've always loved her. But somewhere in the last few years, I dunno. She gave up on me."

I draw long on the cigar and let the smoke slip lazily from my lips.

"Don't get me wrong. I'm not blaming her," I continue. "I'm not the same person. I thought I was getting back to this better version of me, but you can't expect someone else to change in the same ways."

I need more Scotch.

Please don't ask about Maggie.

"Well, okay, so what about the bike?" he blurts. I can barely make out his face across the dying fire. Maybe he can see mine.

"Huh?"

"Are you shipping the bike back here when you're done? Or is it cheaper to sell it? Or store it? Or...?"

"Don't know yet. I asked for a shipping quote back, but the transporters needed a return date for that."

I can't tell if he understands yet.

"Well," he sighs finally. "It sounds exciting. And nuts, sure, but how many people get a chance like this? I think it's cool. Not many would even consider doing it."

Exactly. They'd remain catatonic and happy.

"It's going to be something. You'll have some amazing stories to tell when you get home."

I smile and snub the cherry out in the cool sand below.

We knew it would cool down a little in the mornings, but the brisk desert air still takes me by surprise.

I enjoy the quiet moment, shivering shirtless and exposed as the sun creeps up. The bikes are damp with condensation. I stare at them in the low light and wonder how my mornings will feel over there, waking up like this with my bike and the sun at strange new angles.

Logan stirs in his tent, but doesn't come out. I'm oddly proud of him. I want him to sleep in. I want him to forget the chaos back home for a while.

I quietly tear down my tent. This is always a low point for me on trips. Not staying, but not yet gone. After a while, Logan emerges from his. He's quiet. And dressed.

"Sleep okay?" I ask. This is always a dumb question. You never really sleep well in a tent.

"Eh."

"You want something to eat before we head out? I can light a quick fire," I offer.

"Nah."

"You okay?"

He sighs. He tries to busy himself with his own tent. He doesn't answer for some time.

"So, I get this email this morning. I called back in when you were sleeping. I must have been too loud. Sorry."

He hadn't been. I sleep with earplugs most nights. This is rather unsafe in an unknown environment, but with my sleep issues it's the only way I get a few restful hours.

"How did you—"

"Sat-card."

"Oh. So?"

"So they need me back. Like, yesterday."

He'd mentioned last week there was a remote possibility of this happening. I thought he was merely underscoring the importance of the new position.

"Well, you said it might happen," I sigh. "It happens. Is it big?"

"Yeah. I'm not even going back to Seattle. Straight to Kentucky. It's an issue we've been dealing with for a while, but apparently the client pulled rank and it's all falling apart. I'm heading there tomorrow morning."

Tomorrow morning. Our trip is over. Right now.

It'd be good practice to stay out here by myself on the GS, but the thought of Logan riding back alone and distracted prevents me from considering it.

"Pretty roads. You'll like 'em."

"Huh?"

"Kentucky. The roads up there. Nice. You should keep an eye open for the Hayden brothers out training."

We pack up in silence. I try to pace him as we do, but can't. He's in dirty-clothes-suitcase mode and cramming stuff anywhere he can.

"Sorry," he sighs over his shoulder. "I had a feeling this might blow up. It's not fair to you. I'd totally understand if you want to yell at me."

Yelling at him is the last thing I want to do. It'd be like yelling at someone for being terminally ill.

"You know there's always a chance of this sort of thing happening. Especially when you're plugged in the way you are. You're integral there, right? You said so yourself last night. You're black-ops."

It's sincere, but it's not what I want to say. What I really want to say will do nothing to help him or the situation. He knows this, too. I think it's why he's upset. He thinks he's let me down. He's stuck between important/validated back there and free/adventurous here in Baja.

We load the bikes with much less effort than I'd anticipated. When he steps away to check his phone, I'm able to slip the letter I've brought for him into his luggage. He shouldn't see it for a few days. I even manage to get him to eat something. If we're booking it straight north to the border, we have a long day ahead of us. A quick bite now will save valuable time later. He's too quiet. I want to comfort him in some way. But I also want to grab him and shake him from his coma. He spends the majority of the quick meal staring at his phone. I spend the majority of mine blowing my nose.

"You okay there? Catch cold overnight?" he asks between bites.

"I wish."

Guess I haven't told him about that, either.

"Huh?"

"Candida."

"What's that? Like bad sinusitis or something?"

"Fungus. Too much of it," I try to avoid direct eye contact. "It's this happy little perk for drunks."

He purses his lips, as if he's going to ask something else, but stops. He's asking himself instead.

"Alright," he sighs. "Let's go. Gonna' be a long day," he tries to sound upbeat. He's resigned himself to what's ahead and that's as good a first step as any.

This is my least favorite kind of riding. When there's an absolute deadline or destination to reach by nightfall. Days like this tend to invite trouble. But the traffic isn't bad, the weather is pleasant, and we make incredible time. Today proves the exception. A single stop halfway up the peninsula provides a quick respite from the tension of the morning, but we say very little and keep our banter to the various oddities we've seen.

We reach the border a little after four o'clock in the afternoon, and as expected, the traffic heading into the States stretches back forever. I ease the bike onto the kickstand at the back of the line and try to relax. Logan's pulls alongside me, shocked at what he sees.

I raise my visor.

"I think it's gonna be a while," I yell at him.

He doesn't respond. I repeat it over the intercom. He nods very slowly, scanning the sea of cars ahead. I think he's looking for a solution. He's debugging traffic. After a few minutes, he relaxes a little and kills his bike. He yanks his gloves off and fetches his cell phone from the tankbag only to drop it on the pavement. He swears and instinctively begins to set the bike down on the kickstand. Which isn't down. Again.

"*STOP!*" I shout. A number of caged faces turn to stare at me.

He freezes and locks his leg in time. He angrily stamps at the kickstand over and over, trying to catch the edge of it with his dusty boot. He finally gets it down and lets the bike wallow over heavily as he hops off the seat.

He grabs the phone, shaking his head, and thumbs at it like he hates the thing. I hear several cars fire up ahead of us, and the telltale show of red taillights tripping white tells me we're about to move. Logan still has his helmet on and doesn't hear them. I fire up my bike and blip the throttle a few times to get his attention, gesturing gently ahead.

He throws the phone in the tankbag and tries to push the bike forward, but the asphalt is sandy and not quite level so he's forced to hop back on and ride the ten short feet. I wait for him to look my way when he pulls alongside.

"Let's keep the bikes running a little. The batteries won't like all the stopping and starting."

He agrees.

"What about that line over there?"

He gestures far to the right. There's a walkway for foot traffic, fenced off beyond the car lanes. It's actually moving much faster than we are.

"How?" I shrug.

He looks down at his bike. He's already so mentally wrapped up in the next few hours (the flight, the calls, hotel, shower, food, laundry, the actual job ahead of him in Kentucky) that all of this around him now isn't real anymore. It's a speed bump he'd rather not deal with.

"Do you think there's someplace to leave the bike? Maybe they could come and get it tomorrow."

He already knows the answer. All of the obligations ahead of him are nibbling away at his common sense.

"Something tells me you'd get a bill for that GS in the mail. Even if you could find a place for it."

He peers ahead. We have daylight left, but this will take at least another hour. Probably more.

"Think we could lane split?"

I chuckle. "Go ahead! Call me when you get to the front and let me know how that goes."

He sneers, but almost looks tempted and ready to try.

"I'm *kidding*. Don't do anything stupid."

"Stupid? Like trying to sneak a gun across the border? What the hell are you going to do if they find it?"

"They're not going to find it."

He's not mad at me. I just happen to be the nearest target. He slumps back against the bike and makes a call. He's probably calling Shelly.

After a very long wait, it's finally our turn. They question us this time. Dogs sniff the bikes. Flashlights scan our packs in the dusk. Having been through a few border crossings, I know to remove my helmet before being addressed. Logan doesn't do this, and they shine their flashlights through his visor a lot more than he'd like. I'm worried a barrage of profanity will explode from his composite helmet, but he keeps it together. Some selfish part of me hopes that he *does* lose it so we'll be detained and tossed into some tiny Tijuana prison cell, where he'll awake in the morning with a distinctly bohemian mindset that has him screaming 'Fuck it! Back to Baja!'. But he calmly answers all of their questions. He even smiles at the dogs.

We cross the border and fly straight to the rental place in San Diego, arriving just as night falls. We unpack, separate our gear, retrieve our clothes from the on-site lockers and just like that, it's over. I'm wearing sneakers again.

Logan phones a cab and asks me over the covered cell if I want to share one. I decline. I'll probably head back to the same hotel we met up at, but some part of me suddenly wants to rent the GS again and set out for Texas. Right now. Middle of the night.

Just go. See them one last time...

"They're on the way," Logan sighs. "So strange to have to call a cab from downtown. Usually I have to get out of their way."

The uncomfortable silence we've been dreading finds us. We know it's goodbye in this little lot, under a humming street lamp that struggles to light unsuccessfully every thirty seconds while staring strangers drive past just a few feet away. This trip was my way of saying farewell but I never really did.

"Look—" he begins, but his voice isn't right. "It sounds like you're probably not coming back. Anytime soon, I mean. But anything can happen over there, right? So maybe this turns things around for you. Not that you need turning around, but who knows? Maybe you'll start importing bikes into Haiti, for crying out loud!" he laughs. It's slightly louder than it probably should be. "I don't understand everything that's led you to this point. But I like to think I understand you and I can tell that you're invested in this. I know it's what you want to do."

I try to say something but can't. I drop my bag and wrap an arm around him instead.

"Thanks," I whisper. "Don't drown. In Kentucky. Or back home."

We're trying very hard to remain strong, confident young men.

"Tell me about this client. When you get home. Write me a letter?"

"I will."

"I'll do the same. I'll find a quiet spot there and write you about all the bikes I've already ruined."

We try to laugh some more.

A cab pulls near and stops twenty yards away.

"Airport? Airport?" the driver yells out a slowly dropping window.

Logan nods yes and stares at the bags at our feet.

"I'd be there, too. If I could. Right? You know I'd want to."

He might. In a different life, he just might.

"Write or call when you get there. Okay?"

"I will."

He's resisted the urge to scorn me or correct faulty code he must view as absolutely bug-riddled. Even if it means this might be the last time we see each other.

He's my friend. And I love him for it.

Sissy fires up the instant I thumb the starter. It's always a nice feeling when she does this, a sort of expressed mechanical trust. She's ready. Even if I'm not.

That dry creek bed isn't here. Rather, it's not here in the way I expected it to be. What should have been a shallow, dusty channel is trickling and anything but dry. I scan the hillside for a safer route up, but it's all too overgrown to consider.

I might as well head back to the dock if I'm not going to do this.

It's not that steep, but there, seventy yards up, a gentle undulation obscures everything beyond and I'm left wondering if my research was really all that accurate. I stand on the pegs and try to relax as I start the climb, transferring my weight forward as the angle increases. I'm expecting the bike to slip and fishtail the whole way up, but the rear tire bites in, helped in part by the extreme weight bias of the packs. Before I know it, I'm halfway up.

The slight rise is hardly noticeable as I crest it and I have to look in my mirrors to even acknowledge its passing. Another channel (dry and dusty and most likely the one I was originally expecting) branches off from this muddy rut and I slot in to navigate it to the top. When I reach the real road, my heart's racing and I'm grinning so stupidly wide that my cheeks ache in the tight helmet. It's just rough dirt, but it might as well be slab right now. It's a boost just being here as I know this leads to my real destination for the day, the main highway that will take me to the southern coast and points farther west. I crack my visor and listen for signs of anything other than the knock of my own pulse.

The corners are blind at times, which is exciting in a somewhat nerve-wracking way, but a bus or pickup roaring around one such bend would require evasive action onto terrain at angles I'd rather leave untested. I click at the GPS to zoom in. There's still no road to correspond it with on the map. I'm not far from the city, maybe a mile or two, but it's strangely quiet here and I realize I haven't seen anyone in some time.

The view below me opens up and for the first time I'm able to get a real scale of Port-au-Prince, enormous and sprawling beneath me to that hazy sea, dotted here and there with green clumps and black plumes. Broadcast images haven't accurately conveyed what this view instantly does.

The road narrows to little more than a footpath before vanishing altogether and I'm left to slip and slide in a general direction through trees and brush, buoyed on by the GPS that the road will reappear soon (but worried the damn thing's just wrong again). The growth is incredibly dense and everything's wet in the heavy air. I duck under low-hanging branches and flinch whenever they whack the windscreen.

I'm startled by the sight of several men through the thick vegetation fifty yards to my right. I try not to pivot my head, instead watching them from the corner of my visor. They've heard me and stop whatever they were doing to watch me pass.

Why are you way out here?

I counted five, but when I look back in the mirror to verify this, they're already gone.

Right on cue (and much to my relief) I pick up the narrow road again and follow it west. It feels nice to crack the throttle and I fetch a higher gear to rush some air over the hot cylinder heads. The bike gently surfs and pogos over the rough stuff and I relax my arms to compress and flow with her. I round a gentle sweeper at a quick clip, enjoying the momentary bit of speed, but what I see ahead forces a handful of front brake. My right foot slips from the rear brake pedal, now wet with slippery vegetation. Several men stand in the middle of the road. Facing me. Like they're expecting me. They don't speak. They don't gesture. They just watch as I rein in my speed and bring the

bike to a stop. They're standing next to the remains of some old
tree blocking the road. The whole thing is snarled and leafless.
I don't see any others like it here.

I quickly dip my head and check the GPS, like it just might
have magical advice about how to best proceed. It's an
involuntary defense mechanism. I've done it before. *Relax.
I'm the odd duck here and they're just trying to place me.
Nothing more. Relax.*

I'm hidden behind the tinted visor. I lift it and click into
first to ease towards them.

They whisper. One of them breaks rank to approach me. I
bring the bike to a halt a dozen yards short. He's a stocky
fellow, dressed in a sleeveless denim shirt and crusty lemon-
yellow shorts. He smiles at me and somehow manages to appear
authentically friendly, even with the swinging machete dangling
from his wrist.

"Vous - s'arrête là. Arrêtez-vous et attendez-moi!"

I have no idea what he's saying.

"Pourquoi avez-vous ici? Qu'est-ce que tu fais ici, hein?"

I slowly flip the kill switch with my right thumb.

"Hi there!"

I don't know what else to say.

"Vous voulez aller vous avez besoin de me payer. Payez-nous.
Arbre mort là-bas, pas de mouvement sans salaire, vous voyez?"

"Umm, any English?" I ask, gesturing at him. He doesn't
respond. I nod towards the men behind him.

He yells something back that makes them all laugh.

"Vous retournez si vous ne payez. Machine à Nice et de
nouvelles. Vous journaliste? Soldat?"

He enunciates every third word with the machete as he
speaks.

"I'm American," I say, slowly pointing to my chest like I'm
from outer fucking space. "I'm here to help. Repair bikes.
Motorcycles. Fix them," I mime like I'm riding a motorcycle,
stupidly blipping an imaginary throttle inches above a real one.

He shrugs. The other men chuckle. His volume increases and the friendliness wanes.

"Peu importe. Tout le monde paie. Vous payez."

He points the rusty blade back at the tree, but his eyes remain glued to mine.

"Vous payez dès maintenant à aller!"

He holds out his palm.

Ahhh…right. Idiot.

I nod quickly and fetch my wallet.

"How much?"

"Qu'est-ce?"

"Uh, bills? How many bills? How much money?" I mime a stack of short to tall bills with my hands.

"Il suffit de payer, vous baise stupide!" he barks.

I thumb the bills trying to remember the exchange rate.

What was it again? Does it even matter?

I give him everything I have from the wallet. He seems pleased. Thrilled, even. I'm just happy he's lowered the knife.

He doesn't say anything as he walks away, waving the wad overhead to the delight of the other men. They laugh. One of them buries his face in his buddy's shoulder as they drag the tree aside just enough. I've clearly overpaid for whatever this is.

I start the bike and ease forward. They're all smiling at me and they hoot and gesture as I pass. One of them even pats me on the back. I wave over my shoulder when I'm completely through, though I'm not sure why I do this. I'm waving thanks for the mugging.

I just helped out with a charitable cash donation. Sure! That's how I'll look at it.

But the inevitable analytical circus cranks up as I ride away and I spend the next several minutes cross-examining the encounter in ridiculous and unnecessary detail.

I reach the main highway without further issue. This is the one I've dreamt of these past two months. That rutted road before hadn't been graded into the mountainside at all, leaving travelers to deal with a constant camber shift towards a long fall.

I pass under towering metal radio antennae and follow curves around and down the other side of the ridge. High above me, an enormous house silhouetted against the clear blue looms into view. I assume it's a church at first, but see elaborate metal fencing and gardens and carefully placed security lights as I ride near.

Class structure exists everywhere and to expect its absence here is naïve and hypocritical.

It's not as if I sold everything when Katrina hit. For all I know, the owners of this opulent maybe-home/maybe-church are doctors saving lives in the capital this very moment while I tsk-tsk.

But it looks just as out of place here as I do. I try to ignore the gated driveway I pass.

I have a bad habit of over-anticipating new sections of twisty blacktop. There's no traffic in the fantasy, as if it's my own private circuit. I'm always hoping for that perfect two laner, and a great deal of this has to do with the very satisfying, very emotional nature of riding a motorcycle. You fully experience the road. If it's rough, you feel that through your arms and backside. When it flows, you feel it through every inch of your body, leaned far over, gradually dialing in speed and guiding the machine through winding, smooth trajectories with the merest shift of weight. Good roads are fun in a proper car as well, but it's magic on a bike. It's low altitude flight.

This road, however, isn't one of those roads. I dodge gaping craters uncannily plastered at every apex. There are no marked lanes or designated rules of engagement and the traffic seems to obey a 's/he who was here first' rule. Still, the people aren't impatient. In the States, most drivers are absolutely committed to the clock and driving anywhere is usually done out of necessity, squeezed into minutes we've scarcely allocated. As a result, everyone seems to hate everyone else. Like we're all just wasting each other's time. We plead for one another's acceptance as we cut each other off and say truly awful things about every living relative they've ever had. The worst part is that we all just seem to accept it as a normal way of life. What else can we do?

But here, at least so far, the pace is different. Maybe because there're no conference calls to be five minutes late to. No expensive reservations to fight towards in the hell of rush hour. But it's not just the pace of traffic. It's the pace of life. It affects everything. The rules of the road are loose but friendly. Brightly painted bus/taxis (or tap-taps, as they're called) swing around blind corners while occupying every usable inch of pavement, but there's zero malice in the act. Everybody waves. I might be a stranger, but I almost always get a giant smile or friendly wave before I have time to process or return it. This lifts my spirits and keeps me on my toes (the tap-taps are quite large and feel very out of place on this very narrow road).

I have a little over seven miles before the population thins enough to even consider looking for a place to camp. It's not advisable to do so anywhere in the country, according to officials, so I'm officially choosing to ignore good advice. The larger of the two national parks in Haiti occupies the central region of the island and it's there I've conjured up a sort of hideaway for this, my first night, someplace hopefully away from the buzz and uncertainty of civilization. But I'm not sure I'll reach it by sundown at this pace. I need to stop early enough to repair that riding light. I knew plans would be a bit ad hoc out here. I need to remain flexible.

I know the sprawl will recede in the coming miles. It's a crush of homes, bazaars, tiny restaurants, tin homes, churches and missions all crammed into too little space. This is their suburbia, I guess. I try not to focus on the hours ahead and settle into the slower rhythm the traffic dictates. From time to time I'm forced to stop as large trucks plod around the tighter corners. In some places, there's so little road they must perform three-point turns.

I approach a tap-tap that's stopped at the peak of a slight hill. The driver's letting gravity roll him back a few feet to make room for an even wider cargo truck rounding the bend. It's glacially slow, and just as I'm preparing to slip the clutch and move out, the oncoming truck stops alongside the bus. Both drivers kill their engines and engage each other through open windows. I can hear them way back here. Their tone is friendly and playful.

The truck driver can't see me, though the bus driver probably could if he'd look back. Children cluster together in the rear of the tap-tap with their little faces pressed against the dirty windows to point at, observe, and dissect me through the glass.

This is where I am right now.

I kill the bike. I could use the break. I snake the blue tube free, open the modular face of the helmet, and take long draws of warm to progressively cooler water from the CamelBak.

I smile at the kids who turn to one another and exchange unknowable secrets with big giggly grins. I wave to them and get excited waves in return. I want to perform magic, but I don't know any.

The drivers laugh loudly and wave farewell to one another. I throw one more toodles to the kids, flip the visor down, and fire the bike.

The bus starts up slowly and creeps forward around the bend. I wait a bit, gapping him enough to allow a more ride-able pace. I check my mirrors every few seconds out of habit, happy there're no irate drivers behind me clueless to the dynamics of stop-and-go riding and incensed I'm not moving inch for inch with the bus. I begin to ease ahead, but see movement in the mirror. I angle down and see a reflected group of kids running after me, young, with bright smiles and little threadbare bodies. They must have been standing there in the periphery the entire time.

I slow a bit. Then a little more. They give chase until I roll to a full stop. A little boy no older than five pushes his way to

the front, suddenly bashful now that he's assumed point.   He
stares at the ground and fidgets as the others crowd past.

I swing the kickstand down and remove the helmet to reveal
a real person. They surround me, grabbing hold of the bike and
my mesh pants.

I'm a UFO. I'd probably touch one, too.

Some of them stand back, little hands outstretched with zero
ambiguity or shame. This is a way of life. It's not a chosen one
and dignity isn't a privilege they're afforded. I dismount, being
extra careful not to kick anyone with the booted foot I swing
high over the seat. Seven little bodies surround me without a
shirt or shoe between them.

"Hey there," I say. "Let's see what I have."

I pop a sidecase open and two of them immediately start
rummaging through the zippered liner inside. I don't stop
them. The others crowd around and dig, a hive mind searching.
They must be looking for money. Maybe shoes.

Food, you moron. They're looking for food.

It feels presumptuous to think, but they seem unsatisfied
with all of the tool kits.

I pop the other one open as well. The youngest boy stands
just behind the bike now with his fingers in his mouth. I wave
at him to come closer, but he won't. The kids rifle through until
they find what they're looking for. They back away and reach for
the prize held high by the tallest boy. It's the bag of hard candy
I always bring on long trips. I sigh and they bolt with it the
moment they see my shoulders slump. I wave 'so long' but they
don't look back. The little boy, however, stands his ground. He
totters on bare feet behind the bike, staring up at me with fear or
distrust or something very much like both in his eyes. He
doesn't return my smile. He slowly turns and shuffles off after
his friends.

I watch them vanish into a maze of homes beyond a tree line I
hadn't noticed before. The cases are no longer carefully packed
and the lids won't close until I lean my weight against them. I

swing into the saddle and thumb the ignition, smiling at Maggie's picture on the tach. I used to take this picture of her with me on long bike trips just to have her close, but she also became a safety measure of sorts. I wasn't banging off the rev limiter as often with her smiling face blocking the rapidly swinging needle. One frigid December night in the Texas hill country, I slipped out to put Gerty up on the centerstand for the evening. I set the alarm on the bike and was touched to see the flashing red light pulse behind her photo, an LED heartbeat pitter-pattering away in the stinging sleet. I've taken that picture with me on every bike trip since.

I catch the bus and wave to the kids as I pass. Unsuprisingly, sitting stationary there behind them has only amplied the heat. I'm really sweating now.

Just as well. It tastes the same.

The traffic remains random and slow, but it doesn't bother me like before. The number of people walking along the side of the road certainly does, however. They seem to go about their business more than a little oblivious to the danger mere inches away. A thousand interesting things fight for my attention along the roadside. There is already so much to think about. Whenever I'm able to stop behind a waiting tap-tap or pickup, I look around and study earnestly. I'm about ten miles out from the capital now and the physical damage from the quake still branches out in all directions. Everything's been disrupted in some way. I wonder if it's worse to have survived the quake with little damage.

Does that almost assure that you'll get bumped down priority lists, over and over again? For even the most basic supplies?

I'm not seeing many motorcycles. Lots of little scooters though, often overburdened with entire families somehow pulling it off like the little buzzbombs were made for it all along. But to my conflicted dismay, every single one I see is running. To be fair, most of them are dead simple and just about anyone can fix them through trial and error. Chances are they're gonna sort it out, even if they don't understand what they've done in the end.

I creep through long lines of smelly trucks in this stutter step progression before the pavement gives way to loose dirt again and the cramped tin shacks give way to spread out farmland. I can stop now. Any little path leading nowhere in particular will do. I crest a particularly steep hill and scan the dense areas below.

There!

A few hundred yards down. A little grove. But I don't see a path or any easy way to reach it. I circle around and head back down the road to look for some other way down there. Another decrepit truck peeks its front bumper around the approaching corner and I resume a normal pace, returning their friendly wave as they pass. I slow and watch it lumber up the steep hill in my mirror, waiting for it to belch smoke at the summit and disappear down the other side.

Good. Hurry.

I flip around and fly back up the road, stand on the pegs, and guide the big BMW over the edge and down the side of the slippery hill, trying to angle shallowly across as I do but the hill's much too steep and it's all I can do to keep Sissy from sliding out from underneath me in the slick grass and the more brake I use the faster I slip and the faster I slip the farther away this stupid stunt puts me from where I need to be on the other side of that goddamn cluster of— *fuck!*

I come to a hard stop at the bottom and kick my legs out to keep from falling. I look back and immediately wish I hadn't. It's a long way back up. And steep. Really steep. I know there are farms peppered in this area, so I'm likely on someone's private land.

Great. This is just fucking great.

I back the bike up to the tree line. If I have to make a quick getaway, I might as well be facing that goddamn hill. I'm hungry, but I need to fix that riding light and set up camp. It's much darker down here. I can wait for food. It'll be a cold meal anyhow.

The tiny tent goes up quickly. It's the same tent from Baja and loose sand trickles from the folds as I lay it out. It's a small bugger, just large enough for me in my sleeping bag, but it weighs next to nothing (very beneficial on a bike) and I've had it for years. It's a bit like the old spare gloves, I suppose. Lots of embedded memories.

The hundreds of little bugs flitting around my face do a fine job reminding me that I've lost daylight. I don a head-mounted flashlight and slip into repair work I've done many times before. The harness inside the light's metal shell must have chaffed when the thing rotated up, exposing enough bare wire to short out against the mounting bracket at the caliper. I remove the plastic side panel on the bike where I've tucked the fusebox for the lights and find one blown. In a few minutes, I have the fuse replaced, the exposed wiring stripped and re-soldered (with a little battery-powered iron from my assorted repair kits), and the fresh joint wrapped in electrical tape. A quick flick of the key verifies the fix.

When this first happened years ago, I'd suspected the fuse and replaced it. The light would work for a while, but the fuse would eventually pop again. What bothered me about the repeated shortage wasn't that it was happening. It was that some part of me *knew* what the real problem was, even though I insisted on the quick (and incorrect) fix over and over again. Why? Why would I spend more time on the temporary patch when the real fix took less?

I slice some mini-bagels I grabbed from the boat earlier this morning, yank the pull-tab on a can of chunk chicken, and make quick little sandwiches. I'd like to prep the bike for morning, but it's already too dark. I feel around in the top case and carefully unwrap the single frivolous luxury I've brought along: a proper glass tumbler for the Scotch. It's a small indulgence until I lose or break the damn thing. Unfortunately, my usual dose isn't one I can trust here (the third or fourth measure is typically my hundredth sheep). But not tonight. Tonight it's shallow drowned.

The evening air is lovely and fragrant, surprisingly so, and I yank the sleeping bag from my little yellow cave and smooth it out flat in the grass. I lie back and stare up at a sky just beginning to sparkle.

I don't know that anyone ever truly understood what happened all those years ago. It wasn't just Maggie getting sick. Life was growing still. Status quo, I think they call it. Like a lukewarm bath. Not so hot you need to jump out, but not cool enough to bother heating up. Some people refer to this as 'just right'. Most people strive for it, in fact. But 'just right' is the same as stale in my eyes. Nothing's dynamic and life slows to a crawl. If it remains just right, it rots.

I know I should be home with my little girl. She took life from my hands at one time and I've taken that away from her. A few years ago, I returned home from a long bike trip with a curious little bell I found (I remember really liking a bumper sticker on the way out of the little gift shop that sunny afternoon in Big Bend. It was on the sagging ass of an old beat up Volvo and it read: *Have moment. Will Fleet*). The bell was a scale recreation of a sunken relic recovered from the wreckage of the infamous pirate Blackbeard's *Queen Anne's Revenge*. A garish placard on the crowded sales counter worked an overtime sales pitch of myths and rumors surrounding the (surmised) history of the bronze original. It was interesting stuff, no doubt, but secondary to two far more important reasons for my purchase. The first being that it was just really cool and unlike any other bell I'd ever seen. But second, and perhaps more importantly, it was my last chance to secure the routine and expected souvenir that I'd utterly forgotten about to that point in the trip.

I told Maggie it only worked when I was on motorcycle trips. If she missed me and truly needed me to come home, she could ring it. No matter where I was I'd hear it and whistle right home. Just like that. She was so worried about breaking the spell, so utterly terrified she'd accidentally ring it when I was still home, she began hiding the bell from herself, often burying it in the back yard while 'Just making mud pies, daddy' or squirreling it away at the bottom of her backpack, wedged under Early Reader books, 'borrowed' bits of this and that from friends at school (including polished rocks, various lip balms, headless dolls, and an old lunchbox, her favorite one, that had seen far better days). The bell began to take on a sort of proxy patina of its own. But after temporarily misplacing it under the old Weber in the backyard, she finally decided to keep it locked away in a little treasure box on her bookshelf. It really didn't matter that it'd been lost for so long. I was drinking far too much in those days to even consider a bike trip.

I rest the tumbler on my chest and watch the gold flutter with my heartbeat. She's a thousand miles away now, wondering where her daddy went. I wonder if she flips that little princess pillow over in the morning so mommy won't worry too much.

I want to drink. Really drink. But I know that's a bad idea. Probably not as bad as digging out that little plastic bottle of Oxy, but I shouldn't give into negotiating on the very first night here.

"Don't underestimate this shit," my friend had warned. "These are the 160mg nukes they can't even fuckin' sell anymore. Pace, man. Pace."

I open my eyes and stare back in time. Diamonds to coal in that lonely void.

Shoot me a star. Tell me I'm right.

I close my eyes and wait for sleep I know will be long in coming.

I've repositioned myself in the tent so I can feel Sissy's rear tire through the fabric with my foot. It's not a matter of security. Here, as in places past traveled, there's only so much I could even do in the event of a hostile takeover. It's more for comfort. To reach out and know she's close.

I let my mind wander. I try not to think of the girls or the home I ran away from. But it proves pointless. I think of Maggie. I think about that very first letter, four short years ago.

My dearest little Maggie,

At this moment, I am waiting to board an airplane that will fly me back to you and your mother. This being your first birthday, I wanted to start a little tradition for you: on every birthday, I intend to write you a letter telling you a bit about our lives at the moment and of our year together since the last letter.

As you read this, you are turning eighteen (!!!). For the next eighteen years, you will receive a letter on your birthday that was written some eighteen years before, until your thirty-sixth birthday, at which time you will be the same age I am right now.

A bit corny? Absolutely. But you will have a very unique gift every year that will hopefully provide an interesting perspective on things during that time. A sort of time-defying spyglass for you to peek through and see the goings-on way back when.

This past year has been such an amazing one for
me.   The day of your birth was, without
question, the happiest day of my life.   It was
actually -me- the nurses kept checking on!   I
simply   could   not   stop   weeping   tears   of
overwhelming joy and love for my beautiful
little girl (yes, daughter, you are permitted
to puke at this point).   I have never looked
forward to meeting someone as much as I did
you.   I will never forget your perfect little
face that morning, your eyes fixed on mine, and
the cute little kissy face you made whenever I
gently blew against your face.

Things have been amazing in other ways, too.
As I type this, it has been just one month
since I left the company I helped form nearly a
decade ago.   A lot of people in your old man's
life are having a heck of a time understanding
what's going on.   Hell, I am too!   Maybe this
isn't such a bad place to explain what's going
on in my head right now...maybe see if I can't
sort a few things out.   But where to start?

Well, it was our second company, actually.   Our
first had gone under the month before, a two-
year venture we referred to as 'practice'.
Your poor mother had just moved in with me a
few days before that first one closed up.   That
she even stuck around is no small miracle.
There were five of us back then, all dirt broke
(or damn close).   We truly had nothing to lose.
We'd meet up every day, working in our homes
and apartments, and over the course of a few
crazy weeks a little company took shape.   Our
timing was perfect.   Not only with each other,
but in the market, too.   It was still possible
back then to produce a good title with just a
handful of people.   Of course, it didn't hurt
that our first deal was a big one (big enough
to grow the company without fretting over more
projects right away).   Our first office was a

single 'war room' we all shared, but we grew rapidly. We occupied the tenth floor of a tower one year later, some fifty employees strong.

It was an incredible time, Maggie. We were young, we were doing what we loved, and we complemented each other in our respective skill sets. As owners, the five of us wore several hats. We'd take care of the business stuff by day (payroll, bills, managing teams, interviews, publisher/producer soothing, scheduling, blah, blah, blah - all the mundane details) and by night, we jumped in the trenches with the other programmers and artists to flex our (admittedly aging) creative sides. We endeavored to hire people more talented than ourselves and over time, we became a strong little studio.

There was a period of time when I was really happy at the company. Not mostly happy, Maggie. I mean a creatively satisfied sort of happy I'd never known before. It wasn't because we were making tons of money (we weren't) nor was the future clearly mapped out. But there was this vibe in the company back then, when we didn't quite have it all in our grasp. Where every single day truly mattered. Every one of -us- mattered. There wasn't anywhere to hide. But perhaps more importantly, none of us wanted to. The dream had finally become this tangible reality for us. It was tremendously exciting stuff, simultaneously scary and beautiful every single day.

But something wilted in me over the years. I can't pinpoint a time or a single reason, but something quietly changed along the way so gradually that I never even noticed it. My definitions for happiness had changed. And as

days became years, we all quietly developed
different (and often conflicting) long-term
goals. A few years in, one of the other
partners decided to take a sabbatical but never
returned. From then on, it was the four
partners and we would continue this way another
five years until I left as well. They were
very good years. Busy and rewarding. We made
good money, more than we could have ever hoped
for a few years earlier, honestly. We'd all
been middle-class kids who'd fantasized about
this kind of life for years. I'd dreamt of it
while delivering newspapers on freezing
mornings back in junior high. But it was
actually very numbing for me when that all
happened, like I'd crossed some invisible
finish line. I'd believed for years that such
a thing was a 'real measure of success'. A
lofty, dreamy thing. But when I crossed it, I
desperately wanted to go back. I didn't
realize this at the time. I was over the moon
and thrilled to even be there.

Our employees seemed happy early on. Our
salaries weren't the highest in the industry,
but we all shared equal royalties across the
board. For those first two years, all of us,
partners and employees alike, enjoyed a
satisfying parity that sadly wouldn't last.
Sure, as owners of the company we shouldered
greater risk, but this was always cold comfort
for me. It's the natural evolution of any
company, I suppose. But new folks (who were
doing more and more of the heavy lifting) were
oblivious to the supernova experience of those
early days and would know only a diet version
of the fantasy.

I have to be honest here. I never really felt
our financial success was fair compensation. I
wasn't sure -what- would've been fair exchange
for that kind of money. Other forms of

entertainment make big money for often
unimportant work. What's the harm, right? It
was the dream we'd all had as kids! But
something didn't feel right. For everyone else
it seemed like the beginning of something
bigger. The first bite of an even larger pie.
But I was discovering I wasn't all that hungry.

I'm struggling for an answer here. One as
crystal clear to everyone else as it is to me.
A lot of people don't really understand. 'Why
do you feel this way? You worked so hard for
everything!' they say. 'Success?   Comfort?
Independence?   Aren't those desirable and
wonderful things?' I'm asked these things on a
daily basis.

Other things changed, too. The relationships,
for instance. As partners, we'd always found a
way through whatever we faced. But it felt to
me that the larger we grew, the less concerned
we became with the individual employee. It
didn't happen overnight, so we didn't seem to
notice it. Also troubling was that by the time
I'd decided to leave, it almost felt that it
didn't really matter if the four of us even
showed up every single day. Maybe that was
true. Maybe not. But such a thought would've
never crossed my mind just a few years earlier.
At one point we'd all contributed equally.
Weekends, late nights, early mornings.
Whatever was needed. It didn't matter. We
were all integral and committed ourselves to
the same trenches. There'd been no fat in the
company, but I think success slowly gave us a
gut.

At my last Christmas party, I stood at the back
of the huge banquet hall and just watched
everyone. Your mother had to take you home
early (you were just a few months old at the
time and had one helluva' meltdown). I

imagined I was leaving that night. What if I
was saying goodbye right now? This was my
second family here, keep in mind. I loved
them. I'd worked with many of them for ten
years or more. It was painful to look at that
happy room and imagine a life without them.
Something's screwy in my wiring, I told myself.
I was wrong. I was still happy.

And you know? Things actually ramped up in
good ways after that. We took over another
floor in the tower. We signed more deals.
Things seemed really good. But we kept making
what felt like poor choices in how we treated
our employees. The profit split underwent
creative tweaking. We'd subdivided employees
into these groups based on their time with us
(hell, I'd even voted for it myself!) and only
certain core individuals received the bulk of
the perk. It made sense at one point. But the
groups continued to split and we sliced that
pie thinner and thinner. And guess what?
People noticed (gasp!). They were rightfully
vocal. We hear you, we'd tell them. But we
know what we're doing. We're doing the right
thing. We don't want to grow a batch of
millionaires every four or five years just to
lose them. How ironic.

Over the last three months, it became difficult
(and eventually impossible) for me to even wave
the corporate banner. Some unseen
metamorphosis was underway. We'd grown large
enough to justify the hiring of full time
attorneys, executive office managers, and other
'corporatey' positions. I truly felt I was
treading far deeper water than I was qualified
for. A lot of us were. Any number of these
seasoned professionals we were hiring could
have run the business side of things that we'd
handled for so long. In fact, this had been
the point of hiring them initially — to

shoulder the day to day stuff, so we, the partners, could get back in the creative trenches. But even so, the four of us never felt comfortable handing them the keys. We remained in the executive branch. We created redundancy. What was it like to work for a bunch of young guys who'd been winging it for years? Guys who thought they had all the answers? Can you imagine? Sure, we had a vision for the company, and people looked to us to lead. And we did. Deep water or not. Many successful companies are piloted this way, after all, by young and intrepid people learning on the job. But I wouldn't perform root canals just because I have teeth, you know?

Maybe most taxing of all was the simple fact that I missed most of your first year. Several times a week I'd get home well after you'd already fallen asleep. I knew I'd see you sometime during the overnight hours for a feeding or to comfort you, but it wasn't much of a relationship. This might be difficult for you to understand, but this is all-too-familiar territory for every father. We're expected to force scripted time into these fractional spaces between everyone and everything else. Most guys find a way through. They find a way to cope.

But Maggie, I hated it. I wanted to really be there. Not just present and accounted for. I wanted the bad with the good, all unscripted. Your grandfather (my dad) was in a bad way at the time as well. The mental and emotional toil of clocking in for a company that no longer valued his sacrifice was tearing him to shreds. We spoke several times a week and I could hear that the walls he'd hidden behind for years had all but crumbled. What I heard

over the phone was the echo of a hollow life
caving in.

And when you got sick?   That was the real
catalyst (you won't remember - ask your
mother).   It was clear what I wanted.   I
gathered the three other partners in my office
one afternoon and told them I was leaving.
They didn't know what to make of it.   To be
fair, they were incredibly understanding and
patient with me.   I was struggling, even on
that very first day, for a crystal clear
explanation.   I sent them a long heartfelt
email I hoped would somehow allow them to truly
see and understand my motivations.   I don't
know if it ever did.   I'm not even certain why
that was so important to me.

I want to spend real and meaningful time with
you.   Time I could never simulate or fake.   And
someday, maybe even now as you read this, we
will know if this time together has been more
important to you or I (ha!).   It's not just
you, dear.   There are other reasons I wanted to
leave.   My personal sense of right and wrong
already feels simple again.   Maybe a little
less indexed with clauses or exceptions.   I'm
already self-analyzing more.   I see the
mistakes I've made and I want to own those I
make now.

There've been a couple of unforeseen
consequences, however.   Nearly everyone close
to me thinks I've walked away from a good thing
empty handed.   I don't see it that way at all.
I was resolute in my decision to leave.   It was
unfair to ask for my twenty-five percent
ownership in the company.   It was like those
radio station contests, the ones where a number
of people place their hands on a brand-new car
for hours, maybe days, and the last one
standing wins it (you might have to ask me what

this fabled 'radio' is of which I speak). Anyhow, if someone takes their hands off and walks away, they don't get some percentage of the thing. That's it. They forfeit.

It's disheartening beyond words to watch those you trust refer to the manifest creation of your sweat and love as common carrion. It would have harmed the little company helped grow in fortunate soil. Something so selfish would have harmed the employees. It's something I would never have done.

It's been tricky in other unanticipated ways. This too may be difficult for you to understand, but our culture absolutely intertwines men and their jobs. Maybe it's not like that there where you are right now, blowing out eighteen candles. But here, in this reality, it's one of the first things we ask (or are asked) when making introductions. I'm so-and-so and my job is blah. Our jobs define us. We allow it. Hell, we -expect- it. Our very identities are often forged in the molds of these chosen occupations. Some lucky few find purposeful work in life that aligns perfectly with who they truly are, but I think it's pretty rare.

It hasn't all been bad, mind you. For instance, I feel like the idealistic and passionate 'kid' I used to be. Between you and me and this time capsule? I don't see this a poor transformation. But I can tell that others don't necessarily agree. It's already a bit of a social liability. Like I'm contagious or something. 'What will you do with your time? How will you earn an income? What will Maggie think? Aren't you afraid of growing bored? Blah blah blah!' I've tried to explain, but the answers I offer only seem to invite further grilling. Sometimes it feels

like people have already let me go. Like I've
passed away. I guess to them, I have. I don't
know. I'm not the same person they once knew.
It was an unforeseen risk and one I hope won't
confine me to some solitary and confused
existence, wondering where everyone went. You
tell me, daughter. How'd I turn out?

Something pretty cool happened two weeks ago.
Your mother and I took you down south for a few
days along the Mexico border. You were
actually in my arms when it happened. I went
out to the car for some reason and found myself
under the most brilliant view of the cosmos
I've ever seen. I scooped you up from your crib
and snuck out of the hotel room so you could
share it with me. I had you bundled up in all
these blankets...you looked like this little
baked potato. Anyhow, without a lot of fanfare
or pretense, something just quietly rewired
itself in my brain. Nothing is black or white.
Nothing is really right or wrong.

Maggie, I didn't jump from the raft. I tossed
the oar behind me in the wake.

A fine rain begins to fall. It's almost silent, a whisper on the
light fabric of the tent. No pitter patter tonight. It will be over
soon, but for a moment the sound soothes and sleep finally finds
me.

I'm awakened by the alarm clock screech of a bird I've never heard before. It's far too early. Through bleary eyes I can just make out the heavy beads of collected condensation on the other side of the tent. I sneak a hand from my snug sleeping bag and rest my palm against them, ushering them together in quick, cold rivers.

The volume of that mystery fowl is astonishing and I'll be shocked if the damn thing's not perched right on Sissy's handlebars. Mornings are tough for most people, but they are particularly hard for me. When Janet discovered that DSPD diagnosis years ago, I felt a little vindicated and somewhat understood (though it didn't help our relationship much). Knowing it wasn't by choice helped her accept it a little more, but it remained a major disconnect. Which is perfectly understandable, really, given that most women detest sleeping men.

I slip from the bag, struggle with the zippered door, and stumble into a damp world I barely recognize. My head's pounding, but my nose isn't nearly as bad as I'd feared it'd be (paradoxically to my lay understanding of the condition, moderate to heavy measures the night before seem to keep the Candida sated, which almost certainly means I've snuck another drink or two overnight).

I know the routine, but I'm dulled and unable to get going. The anxiousness I typically feel before a big ride simply isn't there. Maybe because there's no destination. No script. My small cocoon flutters and drips behind me in the morning breeze. The bike, too, is beaded up with its own perfect glistening coat and some of the bugs and dirt from yesterday will sadly be washed away in it (I'm quite fond of the hieroglyphics of travel). I stand there a long while, just absorbing the shapes and colors around me.

I hear the clatter of the small displacement diesel long before I see it. I freeze and scan the hill high above. That main road is the only place it'd be coming from, but I don't see anything. It drops out only to return slightly louder a moment later. It must be coming from the fields.

The racket fades once more and is suddenly here, a sun-bleached red pickup, an old compact with an ill-mannered lump clack-clacking under its dimpled hood. The driver stops a dozen yards away. My gut yanks the chains, screaming at me to flee like some hobo tumbling from a stationing train. The message will surely translate: 'I'm sorry. I'm leaving.'

But the driver doesn't fly from the cab. He's alone. I watch him kill the engine, ratchet the parking brake, and squeak the creased door open. He's a tall young man, lanky and lean, all tendon and cocoa skin. He smiles. I try to.

"Bonjour! C'est un beau matin, oui?" he says, but changes his approach when he sees my hesitation.

"Morning is good, yes? I am happy to find you still here!" he booms. He seems genuinely happy to see me.

"Yes, it is pretty nice," I call back as he slushes through the grass.

"I notice you last evening, yeah? I see you here. From there." He turns and points somewhere I can't see. "I watch you and see you alone. We wonder some for you, yeah?"

He points at my boots.

"You news?"

"Nope. Is this your land?"

"Yes, our farm. I wonder if you trouble? Or lost? Maybe you hide?"

Ding ding ding!

"My name of Remy," he grins and walks right up.

"Greg. I'm Greg." I shake his hand. "I'm traveling here. Helping people out. Making repairs," I thumb at Sissy over my shoulder.

"You fix?"

Why yes, yes I do fix them! I know precisely what it takes to make them perfect!

"I try."

He looks deflated and studies the ground between us.

"You make better, oui?"

"Usually."

"We have, mmmm," he mimes something this tall by that wide, "back there, yeah? It good, but old. It not staying start. You know of them usually, then?"

"I—"

"Okay! I tell them you help! You on one! I see a light and one light and tenthouse. I know it!" He pauses and stares over his shoulder. "Maybe yes? For looking?"

"Sure, I can do that," I stammer. "What kind of motorcycle is it?"

He laughs. "No, no. You see! Ride with me, yeah?"

I still need to pack Sissy. I can't leave everything out like this.

"Let me get everything cleaned up. I can follow you or meet you there. Is that okay?"

"Water near. You cross in truck, no problem." He sees my confusion. "Deep."

I usually pack everything back into the limited space of the panniers just so, carefully distributing the weight in a particular manner. But not this morning. I just cram stuff wherever I can. Remy leans against a tree and eats an apple while he watches me.

When I'm ready, he pops the tailgate free and lets it crash down, yanks a wooden board from the bed, and slaps it into place. He must be joking. The approach angle is ridiculous.

Second drop, coming right up!

But somehow I manage to skitter up the beam and wedge the front tire against the back of the cab without falling over. The GS doesn't just feel massive in the back of the little truck. It is. The whole ass of the truck sags to what must be a foot off the ground.

"You stay on, see?" he yells up to me when I start to dismount. "Steady, yeah?"

I've never tried what he's suggesting. I shrug and prop the bike back up to straddle it. I leave the kickstand down and first gear engaged. He fires up the truck and drives off in a rushed single motion without a hint of a pause for the poor lump to even fully cough to life.

The struts are completely shot. It's less a ride and more a wavelike waft with the lazy rebound several undulations behind. He drives too fast, like he's eager to get back before I change my mind. From higher up here I see that I've been on the outer edge of what is indeed a working farm. I can't tell what the primary crops are, but it's all neatly groomed in tiers that climb the hilly terrain in tall, tidy pyramids.

The water crossing he referred to is little more than a large puddle. The truck scrabbles through, slipping left and right on balding tires in sickening lateral sways that have me wishing I hadn't agreed.

I can't believe how humid it is. I've spent the last decade in humid environments, but this just redefines it. I slapped my helmet on back at the campsite so it wouldn't roll around the bed (or out), but the swampy air is so thick and difficult to breathe that I must keep the modular face flipped open to cope.

The path Remy's treading is little more than a pair of ruts trenched in between rolling green hills. It meanders on farther than I'd ever have guessed it might.

What if there's no farm?

I don't wonder long. Just about the time I'm contemplating a brazen escape, roofs loom into view. I count five structures half a mile ahead. Homes. A barn. A farm. Okay. Okay.

Remy's yelling something out the window.

"How's that?" I lean down on the tankbag.

"You listen? I *say* this here where we come! I show you that bloody bouzin! But first to meet others."

"Sounds good to me!" I holler.

Remy pulls in between two of the buildings and slides the little truck to such a dramatic stop that I must lock my legs around the tank to remain sitting.

He hops out, smiling and whistling under his breath.

"You still there!" he chuckles with feigned surprise and knocks the tailgate free with a balled up fist. I ease the bike down the board and tiptoe it around the side of the truck. Remy yells out to several kids behind the barn who immediately come running. One of the curious boys asks Remy if he can sit on the bike and I hoist him up on the seat.

"Come! Meet others, yeah?"

We leave the kids to explore and clamber up on Sissy (whom I place on the centerstand). Remy leads me across the little courtyard, up a few simple steps, and right through the hinged screen door of the nearest house. Eight pairs of curious eyes flick up to study me from a kitchen table a few inches in. I fight the instinct to step right back out.

"C'est le gars qui campait là. Il dit qu'il est américain et s'appelle Greg. Il dit qu'il ne peut fixer la pompe!"

He turns to me. "Greg, this my family."

"Goo, er, bonjour," I stutter stiffly.

Some of them kind of nod.

"Très bon, Greg. Please. Eat with us."

I don't have all of my riding gear on, but the mesh pants and boots I am wearing leave me feeling embarrassed and alien and strange in their kitchen like this. They size me up, unsure of what they're even looking at.

We sit and Remy speaks excitedly to his family in French, stopping to verify bits and pieces in his retelling. We eat a lovely meal of rice and beans wrapped up and steamed in large banana leaves with chunks of juicy pork. I try to eat politely, but it's easily the tastiest thing I've had in some time and I fight the urge to inhale it all in gulping swallows.

I gather from the bits and pieces of French I do understand that they've rigged an old motor to drive a well pump for irrigation purposes or drinking water or something I don't understand. They seem just as eager for me to look at it as I am and before I can even finish my delicious lunch, Remy leaps to his feet and leads me back outside. I try to offer my sincerest thanks to everyone in fragmented French, and even get a few smiles in return. Some of the older men stand to follow us.

The motor isn't just dead. And it's not just a motor. It's the leftovers of an old Honda, maybe an early '70s CB. The frame, gas tank, and engine all sit crusted together on a warped board. The wheels and bodywork are absent, as is the seat, exhaust and suspension bits. Instead of turning the rear wheel, the chain is now rigged to drive a chunky gear-set that mates up to an old bilge pump on the rim of what I'm guessing is their water well. I can't believe that it ever actually worked. The air cleaners are missing, allowing the carburetors to snorkel dirty air (and anything else for that matter). The clutch cover is cracked and missing half its face. Yellow, dry grass has grown up and through the cooling fins on the cylinder heads and how the whole mess hasn't caught fire is a complete mystery.

I ask Remy if he'll try to start it for me. A faded battery sits on a caved in oil drum next to the whole mess with long, twisted leads connecting the two. He snaps rusty alligator clamps to the battery, shuffles to the kick starter, and gives it several full body thwacks while holding the rotting frame still. The motor actually turns, to my surprise. That's good. It means the filthy thing's not seized. But it doesn't catch.

"That battery. Is it good?"

"I think?"

"Fuel?" I ask.

"Petrol? Yes."

"Choke?"

"Yes. We try most choked, no choked. No change," he sighs.

I lean down and pull a crusty spark plug wire free with a pop-*click*. The plugs are barely finger tight and I'm able to thread one out.

"Give it another kick," I tell him, snapping the plug back in the harness. It sparks. I check the other plug in cupped hands and find the same result. The old men whisper against the wall a few feet away.

I hit the dirt and look up under the tank. The fuel hose is still attached to the petcock, but the screw clamp is worn and loose. I wiggle it free. The pickup screen is still in place, but it's no longer a filter. It's a solid plate of rusted filth.

"Let me grab a few things. I'll be right back."

I walk back to Sissy and find two kids still straddling the seats, pretending to ride her with supplemented motor noises and enviable lean angles. The taller one pilots, reaching for the distant grips over the tall tankbag, his passenger just behind with her little arms wrapped tightly around his waist. Maggie used to do that with me in the garage.

"Where you two headed?"

They turn and giggle shyly. They whisper something to each other and toss their heads back laughing. It'd be easier to bring Sissy to the old Honda just to have everything handy, but I'm not about to ask them to hop off mid-adventure. I yank the left liner from the case instead.

The elder men watch me quietly from their posts along the wall as I rifle through the large bag for my assorted toolkits. The day is really warming up now and trickles of sweat stream freely down my back. Thankfully, I'm able to remove the carburetors without snapping their weathered mounting bolts. I dismantle the first one, carefully parsing out the pieces onto an old towel Remy's laid down for me. The bowls and jets are packed with nastiness I don't even try identifying. The channels here are quite small and the gunk has plastered in like scale. It's likely been dead for some time.

Remy kneels next to me. One of the old timers stands behind us now, looking over our shoulders and whispering down in Remy's ear from time to time.

"What's he saying?" I ask.

"He ask is okay now? Is okay?"

"Not yet," I smile. "But I'm working on it. How've you guys been getting water from that well?"

"Ah, that hard job. That for youngers. Take turns, switch all day. Work okay, but slow. Slow."

I clean and reassemble the carburetors while curious eyes watch my hands. I tell Remy what I'm doing and why. He nods, and even repeats some of it back to me, but I can't tell if he really cares or not.

With everything back together, the motor starts up on the third kick. There's no muffler to speak of and the angry twin shakes the air in heavy *whump-whump-whumps*. I tell Remy to kill it and he does so by holding two blackened rags over the exhaust ports until the shaking lump sputters out.

"So good! I knew it fix!" he says.

I warn him it will die again unless they start using air filters (and screens for the fuel petcock), but he seems unconcerned. It works, he says, and that's all that matters for now.

The kids have gathered around us. I stand and dust myself off as they wait with covered ears to see it run again, but Remy shouts something at them and they run off instead.

"You stay here tonight?" Remy asks me.

"Is it okay?"

"Of course! You guest now. You free time for lessons. Big debt. So, you guest!"

"Remy, how exactly did you see me last night? From here, I mean, like you said?"

He laughs. "Ha! I tell them you not so muet! I see because we check for dem bloody pas de voleurs enculé bonne. Each night we check. Our crops? They take! But I see you instead. If they get you...?" he trails off with wide eyes.

It seemed so calm and quiet back there.

"Maybe next time you next hide, you just sleep on the road, yeah?"

I spend the next few hours walking the grounds with Remy as the children orbit us like eager little moons. They aren't afraid. Only curious about me, fascinated with my odd look and strange words. The men seem perfectly happy to kick back, content to waste the day blissfully unburdened, while the women shoulder the bulk of the work load and move with a sort of effortless grace and purposefulness. I am helplessly smitten with each and every one of them, their inquisitive and careful gazes quickly averted with shy little smiles whenever I catch my own lingering a little too long.

I learn that three families live here and work this land. Remy isn't a blood relative to any of them, but he's been here nearly seven years. It's a peaceful place. Everyone's friendly, and beyond the occasional question regarding the big city 'Gwo vilaj', I'd never know a nightmare shook this country two months ago. Remy doesn't speak much of that day. There's really not much else to say.

He tells me that their main crops are coffee and sugar, and even though neither is doing particularly well, they are lucky to have anything to grow. The biggest problem, he explains, is that so many people need so much. They need everything, and stolen crops often provide a respite. It's a tricky tangle of emotions and I see the dichotomy of this pains him greatly. He loves his country and those who call her home. He understands their motivations in these desperate acts and truly struggles to damn them at all.

The evening gently melts to twilight as we wander. Remy appears pleased to have a new audience. I feel incredibly lucky to be here at all. He's an enthusiastic storyteller and I envy his spirit. In spite of everything, he's still happy. The evening insects serenade the hazy air as we dawdle back to warm smells of another meal at the farmhouse.

I'm treated once again to another hushed and slightly awkward gathering around the kitchen table. To my delight, we dine on barbequed goat. It's not trimmed or cut into what Westerners would consider personal portions. Rather, the animal has been cut into eighths and served on massive plates.

Maybe I'll just stay here and repair that old Honda. I could break it now and then to justify my stay.

After supper, Remy leads me out behind one of the homes where a large bonfire spits and crackles and the women dance with the children, twirling and happy, their lively shadows flickering on the dirty walls all around.

"Nightly fire. This family time," he explains.

I sit with him and listen to everyone talk, bicker, and giggle about things I can't understand. I catch a reference to me from time to time, but it never sounds mean or critical. I feel a forceful nudge at my elbow. The old woman next to me is pressing a wooden bowl into my arm. Remy leans over.

"Clairin! Drink it. You like!" He winks.

Never one to waste booze, I drink freely from the bowl to the delight of seemingly everyone.

"No! Not all! We take turns, yeah?" Remy laughs, slapping the top of my head.

I hand him the near empty bowl and swallow. It doesn't burn much and the flavor is that of cheap bourbon sun-warmed in a soapy glass. Remy excitedly tells my story again to those around the fire, this time without any input from me. He does so in animated Creole and speaks rapidly to much giggling all around the fire. I wish I'd spent more time learning the language. My time was already split between other preparations, but it's still a massive regret. I sit quietly and nod or shrug at what I feel are appropriate times.

So many regrets.

My eyes glass over in the blaze while I listen. My mind wanders to her as it often does.

We met in high school. We were friends at first, best buds who had one another's back for years while dealing with our own relationships and breakups. I truly knew her, and I feared I'd spend the rest of my days hopelessly looking for her in other women if we ever split up.

But what felt like a return to my former self looked more and more like giving up to everyone else. Including her. With this change underway, her love flickered and would dim with each passing season. One day, it simply went out. I reluctantly agreed to a divorce and tried to put on the bravest face I could. I didn't fight. I didn't want to torture her or Maggie with a custody battle. I wanted her to be happy, even if it was in direct contrast with my needs.

It took me less than two weeks to realize I wouldn't survive the process. I pretended I was fine. For her sake. For Maggie. But the equation in my head remained simple. I loved her, and this choice to tear along our dotted lines would not improve our lives. I still wanted to be her husband. I suffered dark nights alone in what had once been our bedroom. Losing Janet was an amputation, and I often felt like the only one who saw the absurdity of it all.

So, two weeks into that funeral procession of lawyers, experts, and so-called friends, I signed everything over to Janet and I vanished. I left the keys to the bikes and cars. I filled the bank accounts with investment cash and retirement funds and I ran away. There was a day before and a day after. On that day between, I pretended to wake up early for a glass of water as they got ready for their day. I strapped my daughter into her car seat and kissed her goodbye for the last time. I groggily told Janet farewell. I stood there in the kitchen, motionless, waiting for the heavy garage door to slam shut before slumping to the floor. Maggie's confused cat circled me. I was worried about riding in that state, worried I'd be unable to face the rest of the day (let alone the rest of however long I had left in me), and it was in the grip of this paralyzing uncertainty that I left my shore.

I listen to the easy voices against the hissing crackle of the fire. I swallow hard and close my eyes for a while. Remy's hand is on my back. I'm not sure how long it's been there.

"Your motorbike. We need get ready, oui?" he exclaims louder than he needs to. I appreciate the gesture and follow him from the bonfire, offering my gratitude with clumsy nods and a smile not quite like the one I mustered earlier.

We walk through the dark courtyard, barely able to see a thing through bonfire dilated eyes.

"You have family?" he asks.

"I do. Yes."

I want to explain everything, as if it may exorcise the ghosts or waylay some of the guilt. It feels like a debt I should repay him somehow. But I'm unable to. I wouldn't even know where to begin.

Sissy's exactly where I left her. There are still a few clean spots that shine in the sparse moonlight.

We'll fix that. We'll get rid of those tomorrow.

I fish for the key in my jacket pocket.

"What?" Remy whispers.

"No key—"

I walk up alongside Sissy and feel for the plastic lump I already know is there, indeed switched far to the right. I yank the key free. There's no real point. The battery's already dead.

Remy swears loudly. "You have charger?"

I didn't bring a charger or the converters for one to even function here. But I do have jumper cables.

"Can you bring the truck over?" I ask quietly in the dark.

"No. How I saw you last night. Jehk out tonight with truck."

"That pump?" I ask slowly. "Does it have a stator still attached? An alternator?"

His momentary pause is the only answer I need.

I grab the small flashlight from the tankbag, squeeze it between clenched teeth, and rummage through the sidecases for my multi-tester.

We walk over to the old Honda and I apologize that we need to start the loud thing up this late at night, but Remy seems unconcerned and goes about kicking the mess to life. I search for the old battery in the flashlight's meager splay, tracing the leads up from the frame. The terminals are neglected and crusty, but when I tap the leads with the tester I see greater voltage than capacity. I push Sissy over with Remy's help and position her close to the clattering derelict. I wipe the flashlight clean on my shirt and hand it to him. I should have waited to start it.

"You think kids? They do this?" Remy asks over loud, cracking thumps.

"Nah, I'm sure I did it. When I went back for my tools."

I uncurl the jumper cables, remove the seat, and strap Sissy with a small spark. We sneak around the side of the barn and lean against the wood, happy to escape the racket.

"Is there enough fuel in that tank?"

"Oh yes. We fill. Soon as you fix, we fill and get to pumping. Much faster. Not so much yelling!" he chuckles.

"I'm glad it worked out."

"You have kids?" he asks.

Can't escape it.

"One. Maggie. She's five."

"You have wife?"

"Sort of."

"Sort of?"

"Yeah."

"Then why you here, hmm?" he asks wryly.

"I already told you."

"Yes, but do I believe? I ask, Remy? You think this blanco honest?"

He leans over and taps my chest.

"You no say what you mean. I know something in there no good."

"I can't talk about that, Remy."

"Why not? What price you pay? To tell? Who I am? Who I know?"

"It's not that. Just talking about that stuff gives it life. Which means it never goes away."

"Okay," he says quietly. "Okay."

After a little while, we walk back to the Franken-cycle transfusion to check Sissy's voltage. It's better, but it's going to take longer for a full charge and I don't particularly feel like riding around in the dark to top it up.

"Thank you, Remy. For today. I think I needed that."

"Ha! You need? You fix! We be thanking you, no?" he laughs.

The beat-up pickup is back now, parked alone in the dark. We didn't even hear it over the clatter.

"Come. Let me show how I see you."

Remy drives out on what I presume is the same route we took in, but it's impossible for me to tell as the headlight's feeble yellow wash barely cuts the dark. I try to keep from clutching up in a frazzled ball as we veer off and climb some hill, slipping and crabbing sideways as the old tires scramble for purchase. Somehow the damn thing finds a way and Remy lurches us to another skewed stop at the summit. He kills the truck, leaps out, and clambers up on the cab to let his legs dangle against the pitted windshield. I climb up and carefully sit alongside him.

"There," he points. "I see you there. I out early, come here for de fumée, yeah?" he mimes a cigarette. "Sometimes do.

Quiet place. Watch the sun. But last night? I watch you. I think, what this crazy do? I see that motorbike and see that tenthouse and ahhh! I know! I think he some real crazy!"

"You just watched me?"

"No, no. I watch you some and think you not far off road. People see you. If they want? They see. But at farm, I ask and nobody care. So I come. I get you in morning if you still there."

I find the battery topped up enough back at the farm and put the poor Honda to sleep. The sudden silence is enormous.

Remy sets me up with a simple cot in the corner of the old barn and bids me goodnight. For the first time all day, I'm alone again. I sit down to write Logan, but I just don't have the words. Not tonight. Part of me wants to write Janet. I could tell her what's going on. Where I am. Everything I've seen.

And then what? Tell her I miss her? Like nothing ever happened?

I want all of these things. I want to kiss my little girl goodnight. I close my eyes and fight for sleep while Maggie rings her bell.

To my relief, I somehow sleep all night without dreaming. I might have slept longer, but a distant braying, an overzealous rooster, and the boundless force of children's laughter have all conspired against such plans. It's the orchestral chorus of this working farm and far from a gentle alarm. The early daylight doesn't really correspond with my internal clock. It's a problem that should self-rectify in the days to come, with the toll of the long days seducing me to sleep earlier and earlier. That's the hope, though I doubt the reality will be so kind.

I'm scarcely out of my sleeping bag when Remy slides the barn door wide open. How anyone over the age of ten has this much energy is just beyond me.

"Ah! You up!"

I'm not dressed. My face is little more than half slack. And I can't even piece together a sarcastic response. I stare back blankly.

"No bother. You wake fast. Come. I lead you. Back to road up there, yes?"

"Sure. Um, give me, uh, five minutes?"

Five hours?

"Yes, yes. You hungry?"

"Nah. Thanks though. It makes me sleepy. I'll snack once I'm on the road."

He smiles broadly and bounces out, leaving the door wide open. Giggling children stand there in his wake and stare at my pale bare skin. I give them a sheepish grin and slowly slide the door shut as they laugh and scatter.

I shake my head and sigh.

Poor things. I've probably traumatized them.

I convinced Remy the water crossing wouldn't be an issue for Sissy (it wasn't). He's led me back to my campsite with such vigor that he almost seems anxious to see me go. He slides the truck to his usual slippery halt, pops free from the cabin like it's on fire, and tosses me a huge red apple before I've even heeled the kickstand down.

"I no like goodbye. So, I say see you soon."

He grasps my hands in his.

"Thanks, Remy."

He squeezes tight and lets go. I sit there straddling the bike with the apple in my hand, watching him slither the old beater away. I don't remember the last time I had an apple. I take large bites and stare at the hill still looming between me and the highway.

I should've asked Remy about a better way out. But to my delight, the impromptu hill climb goes okay. I practically fly up the damn thing at a pace I didn't really intend. It feels good, confident even, and I crest the top with such speed that my stomach volleys in momentary weightlessness.

I'm nearly halfway south across the country now. To my left, the capital city some miles back. To my right, everything else. If I had two clear objects to glass, I could probably calculate the deviated angle that's led me all the way here. It's quiet. I shouldn't be surprised. Midpoints often are.

Years ago, I read about the founder of Kodak, George Eastman, and his decision to end his life. I had a very sympathetic reaction to the details surrounding his choice. His suicide note simply read: *'To my friends, My work is done. Why wait?'* He was the victim of a degenerative spinal disease which shackled him to a life of daily pain, a life he chose to cut short with a single gunshot to the heart in 1932. To me, his wasn't a sad or tragic tale. It was merely the end of his puppet show. No more, no less. There wasn't anything left to endure days of agony for. He'd had his fill. When we're full, we stop eating.

Why is the notion of a full life so very different than a full tummy?

The lack of traffic here does feel a little strange. Surely another truck will roar by at some point, but for quite some time I ride the backbone of this ridge all alone.

An hour or so into the day, I finally do see someone else. A group of older, military-spec Jeeps speeds by, the lead driver's ballcap whipping in the wind as we pass and wave to one another.

Like roads, I have a tendency to pick spots I think will be the highlights on any trip, and the La Visite National Park just ahead is at the very top of the list. I have no clue what to expect. In this present seclusion, it's mine to experience in a very pure way. I slow and roll to a stop along the shoulder. It's so quiet. Just a whisper of wind in the towering pines ahead. I remove my helmet and listen a while.

It's as good a spot as any to see if my phone works. Part of me hopes it won't, but I told Logan I'd check in. I've never liked cell phones (*hate* is rather strong, I suppose). It was a cell phone fight three years ago that would became the final coffin nail for Janet and I.

Still, I did promise him. I set the bike on the stand, fish the phone free, and switch it on. It actually connects, but no new messages stream in. No voicemails. No texts. Nothing. I send myself a text, just to test things, which immediately appears in my inbox.

Pathetic.

I sit in the grass and lean back against the sidecase. I dial Logan and wait. I realize I haven't even considered the time difference as he answers.

"Hey! It's Greg!"

"Hey man! Where are you?"

"On a mountain. I'm here. You wouldn't even believe what I'm looking at right now."

"And your phone works!"

"Right? I'm shocked, too! What time is it there?"

"Almost 8:30. Just got to work. Christ, man. Wow. How are you? How is it?"

"I'm okay. Getting here wasn't as hard as I thought it'd be. The bike's fine and hasn't let me down. I might've let *her* down, but we'll talk about that some other time. I can't tell you how amazing it is he—"

"Where exactly are you?" he interrupts. "I'm going to pull you up on a map."

"I'm about a hundred yards outside La Visite National Park. Figured I'd call before I head in."

I hear him type.

"So, you're not in Port-au-Prince?"

I suppose I never went into detail about that. It's a fair assumption, after all. If I'm here in Haiti, why wouldn't I be there?

"Nope. That's where I docked, but I'm a ways out here now. Heading to the southern coast. Look for Jacmel. That's where I'm going."

"Ah, okay." He pauses. "So? How bad is it?"

"Port-au-Prince?"

"Yeah, well, everything."

"It's...it's bad. It was pretty bad. I felt terrible that I wanted out of there so quickly."

"Huh."

"It's kind of hard to tell if the destruction is from the quake, or how it's always been. You know? Which in itself is sad."

I start to ask him something but he's already speaking.

"Hey listen, I know this is shitty, but I need to let you go. I was just heading to our morning SitRep when you called."

"Hey, no problem. Listen, email me tonight if you can. I think data's working here on this thing, so I should be able to get it."

"I will. Take a pic or two, okay?"

He covers the mouthpiece for a moment.

"Alright man. So, be safe!"

"Will do. Hey, if yo—"

But he's already gone.

I stash the cell. Not a single passer by this whole time. Not a sound beyond the slow wind and tic-tick-ticking of the cooling exhaust.

The cell phone fight with Janet three years underscored just how strained our relationship had become. We were both home with Maggie every single day and had been for a little over one year (which shouldn't drive you or your spouse slowly nuts but has a sneaky way of doing precisely that). Janet was growing bored. Maggie was fully engulfed in the terrible twos. Bickering was expected. But the cell phone fight reflected differently. It verified a number of things we'd not yet put into words. Perhaps most importantly, it cast bright light on the simple fact that I was losing my fucking mind.

I'd flown back home for a week to help my dad with his new business. Building hot-rods was something he'd always done as a hobby, but after quitting his job he was finally able to do it full time. It was exciting for him. There were tons of new and daunting issues for him to worry about, but the thrill of being in charge and getting to do it all his way was enough to power him through the stress.

I flew up to lend advice (if he wanted it), but I was mostly just there to spend some quality time with him. He'd recently finished his first car and was drumming up a little exposure by entering it in a local show. The car did well, winning first place in its class.

The day after the show, the security company that monitored my home in Dallas called me in my hotel room a little after seven AM. The alarm had been tripped. I gave them the password and told them I'd call Janet. False alarms happened from time to time, so it didn't seem like a big deal. But Janet didn't answer. The alarm company called back and told me the police had been dispatched.

I kept calling her with no luck. It was a weekday. She and Maggie would be alone in the house at that early hour. An agonizing thirty minutes passed before the alarm company called again to tell me the police had 'left the scene and had issued an all clear.'

"Okay, so what does that mean?"

"Sir, they saw no signs of forced entry. They knocked on the doors, but nobody answered."

"What about the gates? Did they try the gates? The back doors? What about the garage?"

"Sir, I don't have that information."

"Why not? What good is this if you don't even know that kind of thing?"

"Sir—"

I hung up in anger. I was sick. I couldn't breathe. In my fragile state, I'd pressed myself hard into the corner baseboards of the little room. I tried calling her again. I texted. I emailed. I called Vincent, my buddy and partner at work. I begged him to drive over to the house where I could get him in with the garage code. He agreed and brought a few of the other guys from work with him.

"Just in case," he assured me. "Just in case."

I kept calling her, but I'd forgotten to charge my phone overnight so I had to tether myself to the wall on this short charger cable and dial from my knees, pressed up against the wall for support.

Vincent got there fast. I gave them the code. I heard the garage door creak open over the phone. I was having trouble swallowing. It'd been two hours since the first call and I had no idea what he'd find.

"Uh-oh."

"Uh-oh *what?*"

"That interior door is wide open," Vincent said quietly.

"What do you mean?"

"That door leading into the kitchen? From the garage? It's wide open."

"Then go!"

"We are," he sighed. "Relax."

"Her car! Is the wagon there?"

"Nope."

"Okay! That's good! Right? That's a good sign?" I pleaded.

"Sure, I guess."

"JUST GET THE FUCK IN THERE! PLEASE! *Please.* Sorry. I'm sorry, but please."

I could hear them muttering to one another. Snickering. I couldn't tell who was there with him or what they were saying.

"Holeee shit," Vincent whistled as he stepped inside.

"*WHAT?!*" I screamed.

"It's a fucking mess."

"As in give-us-all-your-fucking-money mess?"

"No. Just messy. Toys and clothes and shit everywhere."

I was relived. I was pissed/shocked/embarrassed, too, but relieved. The cleaning crew must have heard me yelling and called management, who then came to my door knocking and asking if everything was okay.

"It's fine," I yelled back. "I stubbed my toe in the shower. Sorry. It's fine. Really."

The voice paused. Long enough that I froze, preparing for that unmistakable keycard rasp-*click*. What I sight I would've been.

"Alright, sir. Please let us know if you need medical attention, alright?"

"Sure, sure. Will do."

Vincent walked the house. The doors were locked. The windows were intact. Nothing was broken.

"Dude, I think that door blew open is all," he concluded.

"I think you're right. Is it humid there today?"

"Huh?"

"Is it humid there. Today. Right now. *Where. You. Are.*"

"Man, you need to get a grip. Yeah, it's humid. Why?"

"That frame swells up when it's humid so you have to really pull that door shut. She knows that."

"See? There you go. Nothing to freak out about."

Vincent didn't yet have kids. He was married, but he'd never felt real parental panic.

"Do you want me to reset the alarm?"

Janet still wasn't answering. I paced the room, redialing every three minutes from the floor. Fear had melted into an endorphin-rich overload of numb relief, but it was all quickly giving way to hostility as the minutes ticked by.

Finally, three hours after it all began, she called me. I answered without a word.

"...hello?" she asked.

"Where. The FUCK. ARE *YOU?* Where is our daughter?"

"Umm, we're just leaving the mall?" she replied, confused.

"The alarm went off at the house. Three hours ago. Do you even realize what I'VE BEEN GOING THROUGH HERE?"

"Oh god. I'm sorry. Shit. I had no idea, Greg."

"Of course you didn't! You didn't answer your goddamn phone! Again! How many fucking times is that now, hmmm?"

"I—"

"Why are you fucking retarded when it comes to your stupid phone?"

Silence.

"*Hello?*"

"What."

"Most people carry their phone with them. Why are you unable to do this one simple thing? Huh? The way I see it, you're one of two things: you're either stupid, or you're malicious. I don't think you're *that* stupid. Who knows? Maybe I'm wrong. Which means I'm left wondering if you do this shit on purpose. Is that it? To fuck with me?"

I knew I was off the rails. I hung up and hurled the phone across the room. But it was still tethered to the outlet by that short charging cable so it snapped back and came apart in four distinct pieces against my right cheekbone.

I went to bed early that night, staring at two doors (well, I *tried* to sleep, which means I swallowed a sleeping pill or two with my nightly double measured four times. I'm told this is lousy math). Not one. Two doors. The split, swinging doors of the hotel bathroom where I'd left the light on (but fuck if I was about to get back up to kill it) and one of them was dark, the other backlit in the meager beams behind it. Two doors. It was in the black shadow of the darker door that I washed the rest of those pills down with Buckley looped in the background.

Apparently, the will to live manifests itself as the voice of a needy thirteen-year-old girl. I texted Janet from my taped-together phone:

**pleasepleaseplease tell my
littlegirl that I loved her so
vert muxh. PLEASSE**
Sent: 7:51PM

Janet called her stepmother. Who called my dad. I think. I'm a little fuzzy on the exact sequence of events and I didn't really think to ask either of them about this when I eventually came to in my father's arms, the both of us lying on the floor in a pool of my toxic sick. He stayed a while. I'm not sure how long. But I do remember the old man's calloused fingertips pressing hard into my wrist several times before he left.

The elevation change in the park has led me into a thick, grey fog that suddenly has me and everything else here wrapped up in cellophane. I've always sort of liked places like this, places that seem to cause claustrophobic reactions in other people, and the dense trees and thick fog (and heavy riding gear and closed-up helmet) have me feeling a bit deep-sea diver. Maybe too deep. I open my visor a little.

My fantasy of the park and the reality I'm finding really don't jibe.

Great. This may be little more than a fifteen-minute jaunt through the woods.

I slow, pop the bike into neutral, and roll to a stop in the middle of the road. I open the visor fully to the soupy haze. It's cottony and comforting in a slightly suffocating way, like those first few involuntary seconds trapped under a heavy pile of thick blankets as a kid. Before the panic.

I round a gentle sweeper and spy the mouth of a little path to my left. I brake quickly and look back. It's not much, more like a hiking trail. I fetch neutral again, amble straight back, and angle in.

I need to see more of this place.

It's not a path at all. It's a muddy rut wandering through the trees. The fog collapses my depth of field to a smoky pancake and grabby branches suddenly pass a little too close on every side. My arms compress with the uneven jolts. The rear tire slips in the muck. I'm riding too fast.

It's not like I have to be anywhere.

I ease up. I don't know that this path even leads anywhere, but I feel compelled to follow it. I'm not sure what I'm hoping to find. The GPS shows me treading uncharted space again and I can't even tell how far in I've wandered. A mile? Less?

The elevation drops and the fog thins a bit. It's not a huge improvement, but I'm able to see more than four seconds ahead, enough to see now that many of these trees are scarred in a curious fashion I hadn't noticed before. The bottom half of nearly every other tree has been stripped several inches in and all the way around.

Without much warning, the rut cuts left and end in a hollow no larger than a swimming pool, a clearing of dead, dark stumps in a rough semi-circle just wide enough for me to clumsily turn around.

I kill the bike and hop off. It's entirely silent here. No wind. No birds. Nothing.

Where the hell am I?

The fog isn't nearly as thick here. I can almost see the tops of the trees. I slip my gear off and plant down on a dirty stump. Those trees are so strange. I can't imagine the creature capable of doing this. I walk the spongy clearing to study a few up close. It's a deep cut on every one, like they've been lathed and replanted.

Ahhh. Tool markings.

Rough and imprecise, but definitely blunt metal. I look around the underbrush for signs of the harvested bark but find none. Every one so cut is dry and sick looking several feet up.

Something flutters behind me, like a hundred birds lighting all at once. I turn fast, too fast, catch the toe of my boot in gnarled roots and crash awkwardly to the ground.

I sit up as best I can.

When's the last time that happened?

My palms bark red, and I'm layered with mud up one whole side. I try to scrape it off, but end up pushing a lot of it through the patchwork of my mesh riding pants instead. It's always such an out of body experience, falling as an adult.

I clean myself off, gear back up, and straddle the bike. The motor fires right up when I thumb the starter, but dies almost immediately. I try again with the same result.

I check the obvious things. The kill switch isn't bound up. She's in neutral. I jostle her side to side and hear the full gas tank slosh reassuringly. I remove the key, count to five, slip it in, and thumb the starter with a bit of twist. The bike lights off angrily and responds to throttle blips with sharp and rapid snarls, but dies the instant I relax that right grip. I ease her back down on the side stand.

This clearing? Those butchered trees? This is all one big curiosity trap for morons like me.

I strip out of my riding gear again and stack it on one of the stumps. I take a deep breath and sit down to stare at the big bike. With a little patience, many mechanical issues can be sorted out before you even turn a wrench. Not always, of course, but you can at least get yourself in the right frame of mind before you waste your time.

I have spark. I have fuel. The bike starts and continues to run with a bit of throttle, but dies the instant it's left to idle on its own. It's been started three times now.

I should have stopped after the first start. I won't be jumping the battery way out here. Normally this wouldn't matter, but the damn thing's been drained already. I pop the seat and check the voltage with the meter. It's a bit lower than I'd like, but it should be enough to fire her up again.

Maybe the throttle cables have gone slack. I check them and find the lock rings tight. I slowly twist the throttle open to closed with the ignition momentarily on and listen. The whirrrr-*click* tells me throttle blades are opening and shutting just fine.

Fuck.

I remove the sidecases, crack the right one open, and fish out the tumbler. It's not a bad spot for a breakdown.

I'll fix the bike and the day will play out.

It doesn't matter how I feel. That's irrelevant.

I'll have a little drink and it will play out the way it does.

I kneel behind the bike and feel for the fake fuel line leading to the booze tank. It looks like any ordinary clear fuel line, drooping a bit under the rear seat assembly and leading to a little levered tap, neatly coiled and velcroed up high and out of the way. But it's no longer secured. It's just dangling now, low enough to drag along the rear tire. I tug the line free and crack the tap, but it spurts and gurgles.

Just air in the line. Nothing to worry about. Just air.

I rock the bike a little, but the waves cascading through the hose in caramel color burps don't last nearly long enough. I set the glass aside and remove the rear seat. I twirl the fill cap free and peer inside. It's nearly empty, with just a trace of color in the bottom of the white basin.

The words form like some flashing fucking billboard I absolutely will not look at.

I trace the line, feeling for a leak with shaky fingers, but find it dry.

Just like me.

I close my eyes and grit my teeth.

One swill...

I slump down on the stump hard enough to force air from lungs. Nothing is beyond repair at this point. It's a chance to think it through. This approach used to only take place well after becoming truly stuck, when I had no other choice. It's taken a long time to flip it around.

I sit a while and enjoy the quiet before I hear the voices. I can't place them. The volume shifts, carried on the wind in unpredictable ways. I turn slowly in place, waiting for the whisper in the trees to lull as sunlight paints dappled shadows on the ground.

There.

I press past twisted old trees and stamp grass flat with my boots. The ground slopes ahead of me and there, fifty yards out, the tree line simply vanishes.

I stop and listen. What if I'm trespassing?

Of course I am. I was trespassing the moment I stepped off that damn boat.

I glance back at the bike. It's certainly not going anywhere. I take measured steps ahead, scrabbling over slippery rocks and squeezing past sagging branches. The trees here haven't been stripped like the others, and they do vanish, but not how I'd expected them to. It's the edge of a cliff. A decent drop down, too, probably two hundred feet or more. Dead scrub and dark stumps dot the dry acres expanding down there before me in butchered brail. And there, in the middle of it all, bent to the earth and working in neat orderly rows, children sing.

I lose all track of time as I watch them. Standing a while, then sitting, completely entranced with what I see. I drift into a voyeuristic stupor. The growth behind me was so dense it was actually difficult to pass between the trees, but there below me in what I presume is land just beyond the limits of this protected park, it's completely barren. A whole forest razed. A sharp dividing line with no attempt to mask it.

I watch them work. These children are planting trees, writing new history and nurturing back something many of them have likely never known. But that's not why I watch.

The songs are pretty and joyful in the way that only children make them. I'm able to pick out the repeated choruses I like most as I watch and I try desperately to burn them to memory. I make up names for the kids and imagine the connections they might have to one another. It's a great range of ages. The older ones instruct and watch over the youngest, working in teams of three.

I wave at them from time to time, initially just to see if I'm visible. But as time passes, it becomes something else entirely. My waves aren't returned. No little pointing fingers or giggles. And the longer I watch, the more I ache for it. Eventually, they gather up in a small group at the far end of the field and leave.

I scramble up the incline through the darkening woods, stumbling more now than before. That calming wind has blown the sun too far west, leaving a colorless and monochromatic maze for me to navigate back to Sissy.

I usually look forward to repair jobs.

What happened?

I already know the answer. I just don't like it very much. Those kids were a trigger. A momentary relapse straight back to a reflection of another person in another time, forever trapped in a fucking mirror I've never been able to break. I've spent the last few years shedding the unsatisfying viral values of a life once constructed to measure up to empty expectations, but the damn thing still reflects and I haven't any alcohol now to dull it.

Several gnats have committed a sublimely painless suicide in the tumbler on the stump. I sit down heavily on the ground, my eyes blurring the bike. I swirl the last swallow, watching the tiny black dots spiral in currents of gold before swilling it down, bugs and all.

I'll write Logan. Maybe I'll start an ongoing letter. A diary. The blow by blow account of everything here. I'll work on the bike tomorrow.

```
Dearest pal,

I love the GS. Really. Sure, I wish I had
Gerty here from time to time, but Sissy is far
better suited to this environment (as you
already know). But man, I'm starting to lose
my patience with this German whore.

I'm here to fix bikes, right? So why can't I
get my shit together and fix my own when she's
in need of medical attention? I've lost
daylight, so I won't be getting after it
tonight. It's an almost comforting feeling,
being stranded like this. I know that sounds a
bit off, but consider, good sir: it
relinquishes further decision making for the
evening. Tell me you cannot see the comfort in
such a predicament.

I do believe I'm going to use you as my
unwitting diary. I'll send this bugger when
```

it's fully baked (sorry, no episodic updates
for you). Or maybe I'll send it later, as it
rots. Time will tell. But look on the bright
side - when you get this, you'll have one more
trick up your sleeve for inducing slumber.

I suspect it's one, if not both, of the idle
control valves. She won't start. Rather, she
dies the moment I release the throttle. So I'm
stranded in this perfect patch of nothin', a
clearing in the middle of the woods. I fell
victim to an interesting looking trail about a
mile back (you would have done the same damn
thing). Anyhow, it led me here, so I stopped
for a while to soak up the peace and quiet of
this place...and now I'm stuck. And the Scotch
is gone. Not gone as in I've already had a
bender or three. Gone as in I have no idea
where it is. Yes, your poor correspondent is
sans drink. Surely I'll discover another
suitable poison soon, no? Perhaps that's my
new mission. I'll fix bikes to breadcrumb mah
way to booze what chase off demons and such.
Ayup. Also, I got mugged. Envy me.

So, what's Haiti like? It's amazing and
beautiful and broken (which makes me very sad,
actually) and I realize that's a lazy way of
saying a whole lotta' nothin'. If I'm struck
by one thing so far, it's that the sheer beauty
of this place may not be surpassed by the real
beauty of the people who call her home. What
little I saw in Port-au-Prince was the
heartache I knew it would be. And I shot right
through there on this overpriced (now stranded)
rocket. I'm not very happy with myself. I
somehow conjured the salt to make the trip, but
I lack the constitution to help where it's most
needed? Stupid fucking American, indeed. 'Tis
the mood I'm in.

Night is falling and the bright laptop screen draws eager, confused bugs. Long shadows have given way to nothing but. I still need to set up the tent. I need to eat something. I should do these things.

```
Last thought for the day:   Everyone in life
walks forward, cradle to grave, tracing the
longest distance possible between the two.  We
all carry a little sketchpad to record it upon.
Future plans, worries, dreams, and everything
else we see ahead of us.  I march forward like
everyone, but I think I do so spun about.
Walking forwards the wrong way 'round.  Like I
only care about everything -behind- me.  So, my
sketches end up blurry and out of focus for
months.  Years, even.  They seem to develop
very, very slowly.  Far too slowly.  But then,
voila!  They materialize.  And then they're
always here.  Permanently, vividly, painfully
right here.  Maybe the pebble in everyone's
shoe is that I never really peek over my
shoulder at the road ahead.
```

I snap the laptop shut. I set up the tent in the dark. I fire up the small gas grill and heat up a little can of chili that I don't really eat.

Something still burns. Something unsaid. I flip the laptop open again.

```
My dearest Maggie,

You were my tinder.  Just the faintest ember.
As likely to whisper out as you were to ignite
the very air around you.  I cupped my hands
around your tiny, fragile face that first
morning and gently blew what life I had into
you.  You awoke.  You caught fire.  And oh, how
you burned...
```

For years, I saw you this way. My tinder. At
some point, your flame danced without my
sheltering hands.   The wind no longer
threatened you.   It fed you.   And you grew
bright.

I watched in awe.   Your heat warmed me and I
finally understood how cold I'd always been,
without knowing how cold I'd yet become.   But
for a brief moment, you were the temperature I
always sought.   For a little while, I knew real
comfort.

I still feel your warmth, but it's far from me
now.   I still cup my hands around your tiny
face.   Less to protect you.   More now to warm
me.

I try to fight the panic of a sober night. I'm alone now in this
little yellow cave in the middle of nowhere. Nobody in the
world knows I'm here. I ignore it at first.

*This is the solitude I've sought. To be this alone. To discard it
now? To fear it?*

I try. But I'm unable to stave it off and it sets in like a slow
frost. I lie awake most of the night, listening to the wind in the
woods. I lie awake. Terrified and trembling. I lie awake and try
not to think. I try to ignore that little pill bottle.

In the moonless hours, the frost finds soft parts of me I've
exposed in the reflection. I force sleep. I dream. I dream of my
Maggie, sullen and songless. I watch from below. I watch her
plant black trees in the dead soil of my heart.

I wake early, unusually alert and rested. I roll over on my sleeping bag I've wriggled from and watch dew race circuitously down the outside walls of the tent, taking curious comfort in predicting the marriage of these narrow rivers before they merge. An easy finality, this atmospheric collection formed and completing the intended journey. Not simple, but a process. A transformation. But somehow still the same.

I've no idea why, but my mood is much better this morning. There's a semblance of clarity and the weight of the task ahead no longer seems otherworldly. In fact, there's more to it than that.

Yesterday? Last night? Something registered seismic activity.

After a small breakfast, I yank the laptop out for a quick note to Logan before committing to the day.

```
Wow.  I actually slept.  And WELL!  I refuse to
chalk it up to a sober evening, so don't you
even start with me.  Maybe it was the early
turn in.  Or perhaps 'talking' to you in this
manner is absolute magic.  Whatever the case
may be, I'll take it.

Good mood or not, I do desire a shower.  And a
drink.  Though not necessarily in that order.
Not a full-on affair.  The shower, that is, as
I do desire the full-on version of a drinky-
poo.  No, just a quickie to rinse the sleep
off.  It's been a few days and I think, though
I may never actually admit this in person, that
my, um, stink is rudely waking me up in the
middle of the night.
```

```
I'm about to get after Sissy and sort her out
but good.    I've no reason to believe that
whatever's wrong with her is terminal.   Given
that, I should be back on the road before the
sun is good and warm.   If not, well, I suppose
my legs aren't broken.

I may yet edit this, but I think there's still
spark here.   It ain't much, but maybe that
casts everything I've lugged with me here into
a whole new class of cargo.   A blip isn't  dead
space...
```

I wander over and sit cross-legged in front of Sissy. I suspect the problem might have something to do with the idle control valves. Gerty had one seize up like this a few years ago. It's a guess, but it's not much work if I'm wrong. If there's an issue in the airbox, however, that isn't simple.   That's exploratory surgery.   The time commitment doesn't bother me.   It's the black hole my gumption will be sucked straight into if it's not the problem.   Plus, it will take a few more hours to button her up just so I can find the wherewithal to reassess another blank slate.

Shrinking shadows dance with the wind and frolic over Sissy like eager little gremlins scrambling to slither in and interfere. They dance left with the breeze and for a split second, I see it all lit up in a flash of momentary sunlight.

The intake snorkel's torn in half.

I fight the urge to leap up and rip the side panel off. I know what I'll find, but what I can't fathom is the culprit responsible for what I'm glaring at right now.

The kids.

The stock snorkel on a GS routes air to the motor through a filter behind the side panel, somewhat low against the fuel tank and above the cylinder heads. This works fine most of the time, but a truly deep water crossing can be rather risky with this stock configuration. Thankfully, there's an easy hack: cheap, flexible tubing. Before the trip, I'd rigged the snorkel to breathe through just such a length of tubing, much like dryer hose, tucked up high under the front fairing. But it's no longer tucked away. It's just dangling along the upper forks, jaggedly ripped in half. Not only that, it looks stretched open. Like something's been forced in. But why? And what?

What would I put in there? Were I a kid?

I start to chuckle.

Anything I could find.

The interior of intake snorkel is sticky and slightly damp with something I confirm as the missing Scotch with a scientific sniff and digit lick. I start to laugh. Loudly. Loon-like. I double over and shake my head. If my theory's even half right, the kids were just trying to start her up. I'd have done the same thing.

The air filter is also damp, and I find the bottom of the airbox awash in a shallow silt of the wasted single malt. They must have found the hooch hose, drained it into a giant watering can or funnel or something, and thinking it was fuel, force-fed Sissy through her lungs. I'm more than a little impressed with their industriousness. Maybe they took the cue when they saw me working on that mess of a Honda. They worked on mine. Tit for tat. Or maybe they just wanted to fire this spaceship up and scoot off to anywhere else.

I work carefully, the early-morning sun slipping slowly up my back and warming me from the outside in. I try to predict the noon hour where I might find my latitude measurably discoverable. It's a pleasant way to work. This is the mood I was struggling to force last night that wouldn't come. I remove both idle control valves and find that one is fine, but the other is bound up and sticky enough to have partially seized. I clean them both with gasoline wicked from the tank and replace them. I don't have a spare for the flexible intake tubing itself and use a few long zip-ties to secure what little snorkel remains.

The afternoon sun is far overhead when I finally finish putting her back together. My back and thighs ache from the awkward sitting position and I walk around the clearing to work some life into them. It's almost three o'clock. If I leave right now, I might be able to ride another two hours before sunset. But it's not enough time to reach the coast like I'd planned.

I repack the bike in a careful manner, watching my hands fly through the practiced routine, pleased to finally have everything back in place after the last two days. The laptop rests in the sun on the stump where I'd left it this morning. I crack it open to finish my earlier entry.

```
Sissy's back to good.    You'll never believe
what it was, but let's just say I know where
all the Scotch went.    I'm about to fire her up.
Here goes something...
```

I'm not worried about the repair. I know she'll idle just fine now. But I *am* worried I've drained the battery with the failed attempts at starting her yesterday. If there isn't enough juice to turn her over, I'm truly stuck.

I line the key up, take a breath, and slide it in slow. I rest my thumb on the starter button, ready to hit it the moment I turn the key, ridiculously timing this to try and salvage every last electron. I close my eyes. I turn the key. Thumb the starter. A slow whir-whir. Whir-WUMP. I slowly release the right grip. She doesn't die, but I collapse headfirst on the tankbag.

The path looks entirely different as I ride back out, like I wasn't even here just yesterday. It's much earlier. Maybe that's why. Whatever's changed, this is just another escape route now. I keep the bike in first gear and force a nice, slow pace, trying very hard not to rip straight out of here. Before long, just one short mile back, I'm right where I was before the curiosity trap first caught my eye. I head south and fight the urge to flip that rutted path the finger in the mirror.

I suppose there's some good in what happened. That idle issue was going to rear its head sooner or later, either back there in that quiet grove, or here on this main road.

People who don't ride often tell me that they just don't get it. They don't understand the appeal. It seems so dangerous, or it looks like *sooo* much work. To be fair, it's nearly impossible to clearly convey the feeling of pure elation an open road brings after anything else. It's like you're finally free from the back seat on that long road trip with your parents, or a little like the panic-tinged elation every ten-year-old feels halfway down steep hills on anything with wheels.

The road dips and in brief peeks through the trees I see some twisty stuff ahead of me. I'm flying now, free of those butchered woods and eager to lean. The GPS shows a little mountain village, Marche, not too far ahead. A little farther on, Macary. The upcoming pass is more a tangle of knots on the GPS screen than useful topographical data. Which is perfect, actually; a little late-afternoon fun with just enough evening light to find somewhere to camp. I crank up the pace as the music in my earbuds serendipitously interplays with the rhythm of the road and it's as close to outright glee as I've felt in a very long time.

It doesn't last. It never does. In just a handful of miles, the rough pavement gives way to dirt once again. It isn't nearly the thrill I'm seeking and even the relatively smooth dirt gives way to even more goddamn washboard. I roll into the second little village more than a little tense.

It's a village in name only, a collection of people living nearer to one another than a few miles back is all. More shacks, rust, and sad faces all blurring together. Another shoe box of slowly developing photos to tip and scatter when I fight for sleep in the coming days. I bring the bike to an unsteady halt and watch the

mirrors at the other side of town. A few faces have rolled to
watch me leave, but slowly turn back, one by one, when I don't.
I didn't see anywhere to stop for the night. I'm losing daylight.

Maybe I should have stayed in the hollow.

I arc around in the narrow road and ease back through town,
nodding at those closest. Some of them squint at me. Some look
straight through me. There's a turn-off to the right that I hadn't
seen before.

*I did the very same thing yesterday and I ended up swearing some
lots.*

Still, I haven't many options. I swing the bike right with a
deep sigh and head down what begins to look more and more
like someone's gravel driveway. It'd be difficult to turn around
here in the loose rock, so I scoot along and look for a better spot
to try.

Without warning, the sky opens up.

There's no buildup or graduation from sprinkle to storm. It's
just suddenly raining. I fumble the visor shut in disbelief.

Small pits in the gravel quickly turn to water filled traps and
the road no longer reads. I have no choice but to carry on to
wherever this leads. I follow the damn thing as it twists about
on itself, right, right, right, so dramatically right that I fully
expect to find myself back with the squinters. But after a few
more bends, it opens up into a sort of parking lot for what
appears to be a church, one that people are running to for
whatever temporary shelter they might find in the sudden storm.

I'm not sure what to do. I just want to turn around and leave,
but it's absolutely bucketing down. I cave and beat a hasty
retreat to the church as well, towards a jutting overhang that
several others have already tucked themselves under. I lean the
bike over on the side stand and dash for my own square foot of
dry.

'*Church of Christ Welcomes You*' it advertises in carved English
above the door. I didn't expect a drive-thru for Western

Holiness here. I guess I shouldn't be surprised. I saw the same thing in Fiji a few years back. Still, it's the first time I can recall ever running *to* a church. I lean back to catch my breath and bang my forgotten helmet loudly into the stone wall.

I turn to a couple of robust elderly women farther down who study me with genuine concern. Or dismay. It pretty much looks the same.

"Crazy!" I yell, gesturing wildly at the rain.

They just stare.

I remove the helmet and plant it upside down on the ground. This church doesn't look very old, but the little tin shacks circling the lot look just like all the others. I can't tell if they're twenty years old or brand spanking new.

Little puffs rise from the back of the bike. Just steam from the hot muffler in the rain, I think, before realizing I've accidentally left her running. I jog into the downpour to switch her off and trudge back to a dry spot that no longer matters. The women down the wall whisper and shake their heads. One of them leans over to dribble something thick and black from her pursed lips, something I hope is just tobacco. I close my eyes. The rain sings against the stone and runoff waterfalls freely a few inches away. I cup my hands in it and wash my already soggy face.

Someone's yelling in comfortable English.

There. Across the lot.

A weak, yellow lamp slowly flashes atop a truck. There's a tall camper over the bed. I think. I can't really tell what I'm looking at through the rain. I think someone's yelling '*Hurry!*'

The storm continues another ten minutes and a fine mist trails afterwards in the slowing down dripping of wet everything all around. I gather my helmet and unsnap the liner, now little more than a big sponge, and wring it dry the best I can.

"Hey!"

I glance up and nearly drop it.

"What blood type are you?"

"Huh?"

"What. Blood. Type. Are. *You?*"

She walks right up to me, stamping through puddles in what were probably very nice and very expensive sandals at one time. She's short, really short, with big shades pushed up over black hair snapped back in a long ponytail.

"Uh, A? A-negative. I think."

Her lips curl.

"You think?"

"Ha! I mean, yes. A-negative. I just don't think about it much. Like being American."

Her head slowly cocks to one side. I can see my soggy, nervous self reflected far too clearly in her sunglasses.

"Um, that's what they ask you. When you stop. For those crossings. Near Mexico. At borders, I mean. Right? They ask if you're American? When you're crossing?"

"Okaaay..."

"I just never think about being one, so it stops me."

I'm already beyond nervous. She slowly shakes her head and smirks.

"C'mon. You're the wrong type, but you can't be all useless."

Her name's Beth, she tells me, a volunteer doctor with some group of other such doctors that I promptly forget the acronym for. In fact, I promptly forget most of what she says as I follow her back to that blinking yellow light. She walks fast and I have to half-jog every few steps just to remain close.

"You walk with tremendous purpose!" I bellow.

She turns her head to peek at me without slowing a beat.

"And you talk with tremendous weirdness."

I laugh. She doesn't.

I'm finally able to make a little sense of what's going on when we reach the truck. There's a small team in the back of what I surmise is a makeshift ambulance, all of them huddled over someone on a cot laid out in the back of it. A scruffy fellow looks at Beth as we approach.

"Nope," she shakes her head.

He swivels back to the patient without a word. She hops up on the tailgate and points a few yards away.

"Stand over there with them. We're in and out of this thing a lot."

"Absolutely, sure"

My pitch is a good octave higher than it should be. I shuffle over to stand with the others.

Children run back out, free of their temporary shelters to jump in puddles that pockmark the muddy lot. A little hodgepodge game of tag and hopscotch is developing. The bigger kids slap backs and hop off, one explosive sploosh to the next.

"Family?" I ask the women.

They look at me, but don't say anything. Mothers and daughters possibly, dressed in string-shouldered tank tops and long pleated skirts, fanning themselves and shielding their eyes from a blinding sun that's decided to join us again. I stand there with my hands folded in front of me in a way I hope is respectful.

It's the riding gear. I look totally weird. Cinderella in a submarine.

I slip out of my bulky riding jacket, narrowing my frame like some sloppy doppelgänger refining its ill-fitting human suit. It's hushed tones up there in the truck. I can't see much of the patient. I'm able to make out feet dangling weathered slippers in a lazy 'V' but nothing more.

I wander back to the church where a little boy squats on his heels and plays with something on the muddy ground. I circle wide and approach slow so I won't startle him. One of the women back at the truck eyes me, her fingertips curled delicately under her chin. I smile at her. After a careful moment, she smiles a little as well.

"Hi there," I say softly. "Whatcha' doing?"

I kneel next to the boy. He looks up at me with both hands shielding his eyes in the fresh glare. I kind of expect him to hustle over to mom, but he smiles at me and points at a little toy car waiting for him in the mud.

Just another pale invader.

There are cracks in the church's foundation, damage I hadn't noticed before that I clearly see here kneeling on the ground. The downpour must have masked the broken stone and brick half-buried in the mud here.

How far is this from the epicenter?

A rather ornate brick in the slop catches my eye and I fetch it free. The elaborate carvings are packed full of mud, but even so it feels really heavy for its size. I squeegee off some of the muck and push the rest through with my finger.

I scan the walls above for a mate, for any hint this piece even belongs here. It was hand crafted by someone who clearly enjoyed their work and viewed each of them the same, not just for the cohesive beauty of the assembled hundreds, but for each individual brick. I don't see another like it in the walls above.

The little boy stops his tooty engine noises behind me. I turn back to find him gazing at me, puzzled.

"Brik!" he says in a soft gleeful voice, pointing at the thing with a dismissive shrug.

I laugh and kneel again. He watches me with a happy grin as I plop the brick back into one of the larger puddles. I point at the car and he motors it across the new bridge, safe and dry.

"Hey!" Beth yells from the truck. "Come over here!"

I jog back to her. She stands on the open tailgate, little hands on little hips.

"What's up?"

She takes a deep breath, like she's about to confess something truly awful.

"You any good with that thing?"

"What? The bike?"

She nods.

"Well, I still have all my limbs!"

She doesn't smile.

"Sorry. Good how?"

"I mean, are you safe? You're not some kind of crazy daredevil showoff? Or serial killer?"

"I— huh?"

"Never mind. Are you heading north? Or," she tilts her head, "do you even know where you're going?"

"Well, I'm heading south. But it's too late to make the coast tonight."

"Coast?"

"Yeah. There's a town there. I think it's called Margot, or—"

"Marigot. We're based in Jacmel, a little farther down."

"That's where I'm headed!" I blurt. "I mean, that's my next big stop. I'm heading all the way down the coast."

"Okay, good," she chews her lower lip. "Hold on a second."

She turns back to the others. I can see the patient better now. A young man, maybe a bit younger than me, reaching up with a pale, IV-tethered hand to gently touch their wrists when they tend to him. Beth speaks animatedly to the scruffy one who nods almost constantly. She grabs something and heads back.

"Move it," she barks and hops down. The something in question appears to be a satellite phone, nearly the size and shape of that old brick. She talks rapidly into the thing, pacing quickly and trying to hide her conversation. I don't want to stare. I try not to. But she's unmetered energy. A five-foot supernova.

She really means to be here.

She hangs up after just a few seconds and turns to me.

"Look. You can say no if you want to."

"Okay…?"

"I'm sending them back tonight," she thumbs over her shoulder. "He won't make it long without better treatment. But—"

She eyes the nearby women and tugs my arm to follow her a few feet away.

"But I need to go back north. There's a village a few minutes up the road. You probably passed right through and didn't even realize it."

"I think so, yeah."

"There's something there I need to take care of and I have no idea when I'll be back this way. So, you can say no, okay? But if you could give me a ride up there in the morni—"

"Totally fine. I'm not on any kind of schedule."

"Really?" She looks relieved, like she'd expected me to refuse. "Great! I'll call back and let him know. That was my CO. Have to get his approval. Anyhow, yeah, I'll call him back…"

She curls her lips again.

"No schedule?"

"Nope."

"Sooo…what are you doing here?"

"That's a very good question."

She waits for a better answer.

"It's weird."

"Uh-huh."

"I mean it's not *weird*-weird. It's just weird to most people. I think."

"Hmmm. No schedule. Nice bike. You're a journalist."

"Nope."

"Photographer."

"Nope."

"So, you're a hobo."

I laugh. I kind of fit the bill.

She shakes her head. "Well, hobo—" she extends her hand.

"Greg."

She fixes my grasp to a gentleman's shake, not the girly one I'd gone in with.

"Well, hobo Greg, we'll be crashing here in the church tonight. The missionaries will be back soon. They have some cots in there we can use. They're still up there making their rounds or whatever," she rolls her eyes, "but they have better food than me though, so, you know."

I giggle like an idiot.

"Okaaay. Why don't you go get your stuff there or whatever you need to do. I gotta' finish up here, so," she claps her hands as she talks. Her eyes are wide like I've completely freaked her out.

She spins about and jogs to the truck while I just stare.

"So, let me get this straight."

"Oh Christ," I sigh.

One of the missionaries looks at me sternly from across the echoing church.

"You have a little girl back home. And a wife."

"Sort of," I correct.

"Whatever. And you're here alone. Without a schedule." She raises one finger, Exhibit-A fashion. "On a motorcycle that probably cost more than this church did."

"Well, I wouldn't put it that way."

"Fine. Then put it the way you would."

I pause to collect my thoughts, but it's tornadic in there at the moment.

"See?"

"But it sounds so terrible when you say it that way."

"Why? You're here doing *something*. I don't know exactly what that something is, but when you figure out how to put it into words, well, I guess you'll tell me."

We're in the far corner of the church, far away from the pews and faux statues, chatting a dozen feet apart on flimsy blue fold-out cots. The missionaries are busy cleaning up the paper plate buffet they set up earlier. It was pretty amazing of them, really.

They welcomed us right in with a nice meal and a place to sleep. They're Americans, most of them middle-aged, all soft in the tummy and every one friendly beyond comprehension. They whisper to one another as they work with sheepish little grins and barely averted peeks cast our way.

"Well, what's really weird is that I'm usually the one who never shuts up."

"Beg pardon?"

She props up on one elbow.

"No! I didn't mean, no. What I'm trying to say is that I talk a lot. On and on. Chatty Cathy, I guess."

"Hmmm," she hums. She's done this a few times tonight. It's a tic. A cute one. A sort of audible smirk.

"Fine," I sigh. "I'll tell you what I'm doing here. But you have to promise you won't laugh. At least not right away."

She laughs.

"I can promise not to try."

"Right," I lie back and stare up to a dark ceiling I can't see. "I'm here to fix motorcycles."

She doesn't laugh.

"I wanted to help. Just like everyone else. But I didn't want to write another check and I didn't have anything else I could do. I know, I know. It's not a very good plan."

I look over. She's still propped up, studying me.

"What?"

"You're wrong," she flatly states.

"How's that?" I ask.

"Not everyone wanted to help."

"Come on. You're here. And those other people on your team?"

"Sure. But sometimes I think it's almost expected of us. How many regular people drop everything to lend a hand?"

She continues before I can correct her.

"Yeah, yeah. Regular people *can't*, right?"

"Well, you seem pretty regular. You might be a doctor and all, but you seem pretty normal."

"Awww. Poor delusional hobo."

I roll over and close my eyes.

"Now *you*, on the other hand," she mumbles.

"Hey now."

"What? I mean it in a good way."

"Mean what?"

"I mean you're not what I expected. I lost money on you."

"Huh?"

"We saw you ride in. I pegged you for some douchebag world traveler type. Nothing personal."

"Gee, thanks."

"I bet the guys you were one of those types who posts to Facebook every few minutes whenever you see a new kind of bug or have what you feel is a truly original thought."

"Screw that. You're talking to a proper relic here."

"Oh? Sore subject?"

One of the missionaries clears his throat a little too loudly before speaking. "We're about finished here for the night. You guys need anything else?"

We look back and see all four craning their necks to see us.

"Nope, we're good. Thanks guys! That was truly awesome. Mucho appreciato!" Beth says with a big wave.

They say quiet things to each other and shuffle off through closing doors.

"I think that was code for 'Hey heathens! Shut up and go the fuck to sleep!'" I whisper.

She snickers into her pillow. For a moment, we're the kids they think we are.

"I only have the one helmet," I blurt.

"Um."

"But I don't think it will fit you."

"Um."

"You can try it out and see. Over there. Try it on."

She rolls off her cot and pads over to where I've stacked my gear. The helmet rests atop the pile like the tombstone of some liquefied spaceman.

She picks it up and tries to put it on without flipping the face open first.

"It's a modular helmet."

"A whosit?"

It doesn't matter. It's too big and she's able to slip it right on.

"Dang! It's heavy!"

"Yeah, they can be if you're not used to them."

"I don't think I'd ever get used to this."

She shakes her head side to side. The helmet sways a step behind.

I laugh. "See?"

"Hmmm." She slumps. "Well, just go extra slow, I guess."

"Right."

"How do I get it off?"

"That red tab on the front. Feel around for it."

She taps around the side of the helmet, zeroes in on the top vent, and fiddles with that instead.

"Nope, no. Here. I'll help."

I hop up, click the tab, and flip the face of the helmet open. It's so ill-fitting that her face is cockeyed in the thing. One eye hides behind the liner.

"It's really damp in here. Like, *wet*." She wrinkles her nose. "Do you sweat that much?"

"Shit no! That's from the rain."

"Ahh. I was gonna' say."

She pushes it off and hands it to me.

"I don't know how you deal with that."

"Eh, beats blunt force trauma. You'd build up a tolerance. Besides, being a little uncomfortable on a bike isn't always a bad thing. Keeps you awake."

"Great. Can't wait."

"Don't worry. Tomorrow's easy. I meant uncomfortable on really long days. Like five, six hundred miles or more."

"You're dumb." Her face lights up. "Oh! Speaking of. Come with me. I have to show you something."

She jogs to the front door. She's wearing a baggy sweatshirt, very short jogging shorts, and shush-shushes across the stone floor in little fluffy running socks. I follow her at a somewhat ulterior pace.

She leads me out into the big dirt lot, away from the church. The ground is still damp and she strips her socks off after a few wet steps.

"C'mon, look."

She turns around with her hands clasped to her chest.

"Okay. Look up!"

And I do.

"Have you ever seen anything like that before in your whole life?"

"Nope, can't say that I have," I lie.

She digs through her pockets.

"Want half?"

"Half what?"

"Tictac?"

I cup a hand to my mouth.

"No, dummy. Sleeping pill."

"Trust me, I would. I totally would. But it's probably not a good idea tonight. You know, right before my riding skills will be put to the test and all."

"Ah, good point. Clever boy. See? You're not all useless."

"That reminds me," I point at Sissy.

"You're not going to kill me or anything are you?"

I stop in my tracks and turn, but she cuts me off before I can say a word.

"Relax. I just watch a lot of Law & Order. You seem fine. Go on?"

I raise an eyebrow at her.

"Hush it."

"Climb up," I instruct her at the bike.

"Why are we doing this again?"

"I need to show you something. Humor me."

She frowns at Sissy, looking for the best way to hop on.

"There's really no graceful way."

"Is it going to fall over?"

"Not a chance. Here," I reach out and grab the grips to steady it. "Now it's super safe."

"Wouldn't it be easier if the bike was, I don't know, normal? Like, standing up?"

It's not at a severe angle on the side stand, but she has a point. I throw a leg over and swing it upright.

"Okay. Climb up."

She sighs. "Fine. But if this thing falls over, I'm totally punching you."

"Noted."

"In the face."

"Fine. Stop whining already."

She doesn't get on. I look over my shoulder. She's standing there, arms firmly folded and hips now cocked as well.

"Really?"

"I'm kidding!" I laugh.

"Hmmm."

She looks just like someone. That stance. That...*purposefulness.*

She plants a foot on the peg, tip-toes the other up high, and sort of clambers aboard in a fashion I've never seen before.

"Alright. This is what I wanted to show you. Look down at your left foot. See that?"

"I think so. The shiny thing?"

"Yup. That's the muffler. See how close it is to your ankle? You'll need to wear pants tomorrow. And real shoes."

"You could have just told me that."

I feel her leaning and looking around.

"Where am I supposed to hold on?"

"See those handles there? They look like bars. There on the sides?"

"I'm not supposed to hold onto you?"

"You can if you want to. But just be very careful if you do. Don't lean away from me. What I mean is, don't—"

Her hands slip around my waist.

"J-just don't—"

Breathe...

"—just don't lean against me. Away from me, I mean. Lean how I lean."

"You're not leaning at all."

Her cheek is pressed against my back.

"I mean when we're riding tomorrow. Lean as I do. Lean *into* the turns. Stay with me. Your instinct will be to pull away from me and lean the other way. You're going to feel like the bike is falling over. Which it kind of is. But that's a good thing. That's how it turns. If we lean together, everything just works. But if you lean the other way too much, then—"

"Then?"

"Well, then the bike could straighten up and we could run off the road."

She leaps to the ground like a gymnast.

"You know, maybe this isn't such a good idea after all."

"It's okay! Trust me. It's going to be fine. You don't even weigh enough to worry about changing the preload..." I trail off.

Pointless detail. Dumb.

"Preload?"

"Sorry, yeah. You adjust the rear suspension for luggage. Or another rider. Two up, they call that. You adjust the preload on the rear shock to compensate for the extra weight, but in your case that's just not necessary."

I can't see her expression in the dark.

"That just might be the nicest thing anyone's said to me all week."

Beth's struggling to find a comfy position on her cot. Every little squeak echoes sharply off the stone walls.

"Hey," she says quietly. Her voice is syrupy, like she's fighting her dose.

"Yeah?"

"What did you do?"

"Hmm?"

"What did you do before? You a trust fund baby? Bank robber?"

"I used to make video games."

"You made video games? So, you played games all day?"

"Yes, I played games all day because that's how games are actually made."

"I'll slap you right in your damn face. I swear I'll do it."

"Geez, grouch."

She frowns at me with a drifting finger pointed squarely at my nose.

"Anyhow," I sigh. "A long time ago, I started a company with a few other guys and we made games. The end."

"Wow. Exciting."

"Can I ask you something?"

"Nope. Tomorrow," she slurs. "Ask me anything tomorrow. Right now I'm asking stuff and you're answering stuff so you just hush and stuff."

She hums and falls silent. I wonder if she's drifted off.

"Did you like it?" she whispers.

"I did. For many years"

"So, why'd you stop?"

"I missed my little girl."

She clicks her tongue. Slowly. Over and over.

"I didn't want to see her grow up in pictures."

"Buuut—"

"But I'm not there now?" I finish.

"Yeah."

"I know. It's a problem. A real matter of consequence."

"Hmmm."

I turn over to look at her. She's lying on her side just a dozen feet away, tucked snuggly under her one blanket. Her eyes are barely open.

"I was right about you," she mumbles.

"How's that?"

"You talk weird."

She's fast asleep a few seconds later, her hands tucked sweetly under her cheek, looking more and more like someone I cannot recall.

Beth's up and moving before I've even opened my eyes.

"Rise and shine! We gotta' get moving!" she barks and walks outside. She's all business again. I roll off the cot, slip into my gear, and stumble outside. She's unpacking her medical satchel on the front step, laying things out in neat rows.

"You probably don't have a lot of spare room in those cases, do you?"

"No, not a lot," I chew it over. "We're coming back this way, right?"

"Yup. Provided you don't kill us on that thing."

"How much room do you need?"

She sweeps her hand over the cache.

I pop the release on the top case and carry it back inside. One of the missionaries freezes mid-scribble to watch me.

"Oh, I'm sorry. We were under the impression you two weren't staying."

"Nope, not staying. Just leaving some stuff here for a few hours. I mean, as long as that's okay."

"Well…" he trails off quietly. "I just need you to understand that we're not here all day. People come and go, you see, and I won't be able to vouch for the security of your things."

"That's okay. It'll be fine."

I'd probably share his concern back in the States, but I feel less vulnerable here for some reason. I remove half the items from the top case and stack the pile against the back wall. It's mostly clothing, various electrical chargers, and some of the smaller tool kits. I unfold my blue tarp widthwise and cover the stash.

The missionary stands behind me with his hands folded politely. I nod to him as I walk towards the door.

"Do you know that young woman?" he asks.

"I think I do, yeah. Do you?"

"Oh, we've seen her team in town before. They seem helpful, but it's almost impossible to keep track of all the various organizations these days. We've seen so many new groups lately that it's difficult to believe they're all legitimate."

"You don't believe?" I ask.

"I beg your pardon?"

"You don't believe she might be here with only the best of intentions?"

"Why of course I do. That's not what I'm saying at all."

"Oh. It kind of sounded that way."

He hesitates.

"No, I'm pretty sure that's not what I said."

"Alright," I sigh. "We'll be back in a few hours. Thanks again."

I find Beth checking her cell phone on the front steps.

"Signal?"

"Nope. The guys have the sat-phone in the truck. Was just gonna' let them know we're heading out. No biggie. How'd you sleep?"

"Like the dead. Had weird dreams, though."

"Like you suddenly felt the urge to repent?"

"Hell no. Cold dreams. Like I couldn't warm up."

She nods at the front door of the church. "That thing kept blowing open all night. I'm surprised it didn't wake you up."

She packs the culled out top case with field-scale IV drips, individually wrapped things I can't identify, an honest-to-goodness stethoscope, a box of latex gloves, the biggest bottle of Purel I've ever seen, water bottles, fruit snacks, granola bars and little boxes of Nerds I reflexively reach for.

"Shoo! Not for you. The kids love 'em. I'm not above bribery for a temp check."

"Who are we going to see?"

"You wouldn't know her."

"You never know. Maybe I fixed her scooter."

"Right," she looks up at me. "Have you actually fixed anything yet?"

"I have. I'll have you know I've fixed *two* different motorcycles."

"And you've been here how long?"

"A week."

"Mmmhmm."

"One of them wasn't technically a motorcycle."

"Really."

"And the other one was technically my own."

She slumps her head.

"Pitiful."

I lock the top case and reposition it on the bike. I close up the helmet and place it near the front door of the church.

"Why'd you do that?" she asks.

"I'm not wearing one if you're not. I'll have to slow down this way. If something happened to you, but not me? Sorry. Can't have that."

"Well, you're the expert."

"Hardly."

She furrows her brow at this.

"Relax. I'm a good rider. I've never had an accident."

I just drop 'em like it's my job.

"Besides, you wouldn't want my helmet slapping all around and banging your forehead the whole time."

She peers over her sunglasses.

"You sure got a purty' way of putting things."

"Wif' mah purty' hobo mouf'?" I twang and slide into the saddle.

"Okay, eww. Don't ever use that voice again," she sneers and hops on the bike like a seasoned pro.

We amble down the long gravel drive back towards the main road. It's dry this morning, but it might as well be raining. The humidity is insane. It cloaks the distant trees and cobwebs them all together.

"At least it's not dusty!" she yells. "It's the one thing that really bothers me here!"

"Good point! Hey?"

"Yeah?"

"Remember to lean with me when we get up here. Don't tense up! Don't put your feet down!"

I've always hated yelling back to a passenger. Half the time they don't hear and you end up compromising your focus for nothing.

"Okay!" she says. "But I think you just want me to hang onto you!"

I laugh, but she's not entirely wrong.

"I have a lot of questions for you! For later!" I bark.

She pats my side.

"Why? So you can update your bliggity-blog?"

"Exactly!"

We're approaching people now, people who stop and stare and wonder why in the hell we're yelling at each other. Beth must notice, too. A gaggle of kids spots us as we merge north. All of them ten or younger, all of them shirtless. They freeze for a second before giving chase and whoop wildly behind us. I feel her turn to wave at them.

"Wanna stop?" I tap her leg.

"Shit no!"

The bike does handle a little differently with her on the back. I'm not too surprised. It's the first time I've done any off-road riding with a passenger.

Slack, slack, slack. Loose and relaxed.

Beth tenses up on some of the slower curves when we lean over more than she'd probably like, but she acclimates fast. She leans with me.

The biggest issue with the road is it really just isn't one. The uneven and craggy ruts trenched in by the tap-taps and large trucks traveling this route everyday makes it a nervous ride. I'm a little surprised we haven't seen one of those colorful taxis this morning.

Maybe later. On the way to the coast.

I'll be taking her there later today. To her place. The mere realization of it unspools bundles of anxious nerves in one rapid snap.

Does that mean anything?

Are we friends?

Will we hang out?

Does she have a spare room?

A roommate?

Is she married?

Have I even looked at her finger?

What if he's the coolest, most handsomest fella' ever?

What if I drop the bike in front of her?

Am I saying this shit out loud again??

She leans around me and points ahead.

"Slow down!"

"Where should I stop?" I holler.

"Anywhere!" she yells back. "Anywhere is fine!"

I slow and look for space along the shoulder. They must call those tin shacks something.

"What do they call those little things, anyhow?" I point to one as we wheel to a stop.

"What? Homes?"

Right. Idiot...

"Okay, hop down. It's easier if I'm still on her."

"Her?" she teases. "And does *she* have a name?"

Beth pulls one knee up, swings it behind my back, and stumbles to the ground. She immediately squats and stretches like some idiot ballerina.

"You alright there?"

"Yeah, fine. Just kinda' hard on my knees."

"Jesus, ya' old lady!"

"Watch it. I'm sure you're waaay older than me."

"Says you."

"When were you born?"

"March. '73."

"See? Told you so."

"Sissy."

"Excuse me?"

"That's her name. The bike. My little girl named her."

She looks around. There's maybe half a dozen little homes here.

"I'm gonna run back there and ask around. I know she's here, but I'm not exactly sure where."

"Can I help?"

She thinks it over. "Maybe. It probably won't take very long. I'll be back for my stuff in a second."

She jogtrots down the road, skipping over the bigger pits and mud-cast tracks with a strong and measured stride. She looks like a runner.

I strip my jacket and gloves off and lay them out across the seats. I eyeball the tires for unusual wear, check the headlight and running lamps, and clean the little windshield. Part of me was hoping there'd be something to fix.

I wander to a patch of tall grass at the edge of the road, flatten it some with my boot, and plop down to look at Sissy a while. I've done this before with Gerty, my other bike. She's in storage now. Alone there back in Portland, not with everything else in Texas. For whatever reason, Texas is still very much my idea of home. It takes a while to etch new stone, I suppose. Or maybe home isn't a place. Maybe it's why I've always been comfortable on the move like this, kicked back in the grass.

I stare at the tall blades swaying in the morning breeze and let my focus blur. The sun peeks out now and then through low, fast clouds to warm my exposed skin and I feel something I haven't felt in a long while.

I hear children somewhere down the road and peer through Sissy's front wheel spokes. Two little girls chase something too small for me to see. There's a hierarchical feel to them, the way sisters play. I lean over on my side to see them better and they spot me peeking. They huddle together, frozen, like they might bolt up the road, but giggle and push each other my way.

I tuck back and watch them through the wheel as they cross the road. The younger girl limps along with a tiny cane in a practiced fashion that suggests it isn't new.

I surrender my hands to the air when they clear the front tire.

"Hi ther— um, bonjour? How are you girls today?"

They stare at me with bashful smiles and giggle.

"No French?" I shrug.

They whisper to each other.

"Are you sisters?" I ask, pointing to each of them. "Sisters?"

"Se'?" one says.

"Se'? Sister?"

They giggle.

I point at the bike. "Sissy! She's se'!"

The older one scrunches up her face and points at the bike. "Seessy?"

"Yup! Sissy!"

"Making friends?"

Beth squats down next to the girls and engages them in what sounds like perfectly fluent Creole. I gather from her gestures that she's asking about the cane. The little one whispers in short bursts while her sister confirms what sounds like a rather complex story.

Beth nods patiently as she listens. She points back to me.

"Listen up. I've asked her to tell you what she just told me."

I sit up and give the little girl my full attention.

"She was playing here with her sister," Beth translates, "here on the road. We, I mean *they*, play like that all day. Sometimes the nice people coming here wave or sometimes have nice things to give. One morning, some nice men came and played with us. Them. Sorry. They had big smiles and they said pretty things. Her siste— her mother. Her *mother* came out to say hello and picked her up, but the men wanted to take her someplace new and they pull on her, pulled her away from her momma, but her momma didn't let go and the men yelled mean things and my mother turned with me in her arms to walk down the hill and the men made a pop."

My eyes dart to Beth's.

"That hot metal broke. It came through her mother. It came into her. In her knee."

The younger girl becomes animated and her sister leans close, somewhat protectively, as if she means to shield her sister from the very words she speaks.

Beth smiles. "She keeps calling them 'scrap nails'. Anyhow, she says those scrap nails are still in her knee, but she's glad they are. They're from her momma. When she walks and it hurts it's okay because it's just her momma not letting go. She's still here."

There's no sadness in their eyes. I don't see the hurt I feel right now. I struggle to my knees in the bulky riding pants and awkwardly try and hug each of them. They are dirty and unwashed and it is the best smell in the world.

They pull back, more than a little alarmed.

"Way to go," Beth scolds. "Scare the locals."

She asks the girls something with a stern little finger and they both nod excitedly.

"Open that case. They're gonna' help carry stuff."

"You found her?" I ask.

"Yup. She's not as bad as they'd said."

The older sister carries a stack of Beth's gear balanced across her arms while the little one clutches crinkly plastic packages in her free hand. I wonder how many canes she'll grow into.

The girls take a shallow angle across the road and I have to physically bite my tongue and fight the parental impulse to herd them quickly straight across. We weave between homes and stumble down a little rain gulley doubtless carved in by the frequent showers. It's craggy and slippery and both girls navigate it far better than we do.

"You should be going first," Beth smirks over her shoulder.

"Whatever. You just want to see me fall on my ass."

"Better you than me. You're padded!"

Back on the road it looked like maybe three or four families might live here, but many rows of homes extend down the hillside, the tin giving way to thatched huts that appear well-built and cozy. There are few adults but many children, naked and potbellied. They chase each other with leathery, bare feet and smile at us. The adults do not smile. They are guarded and watch us with slow eyes when we pass.

"Stay here," Beth instructs, stepping carefully past colorfully dressed women surrounding a small hut. "I'll call for you if I need anything."

"Got it."

She leans close and whispers. "She's not dressed in there, so, you know."

"Really. It's fine."

She gathers the packages from the little girls and selects only the things she knows she'll need.

So purposeful. She truly means to be here.

She steps through the open doorway and vanishes in the darkness of the small home.

I ignore her request and shuffle off to have a look around. The huts are close together, just like the tin homes on the road, but this feels somehow more communal. I cross grass intersections, squeeze between huts, and smile at the friendly faces I see inside.

Swiiiish Swaaaaaaaaaaaash

Swiiiiiiiish Swaaaaaaaaaaaaaaaaaash

A narrow figure fifty yards away swings a makeshift scythe. He's an older man, twiglike and grey with tired skin stretched over sharp points. He skives the reedy grass with strong strokes, pruning right up to the tree line bordering his village. His stance is surefooted and stout for his age, and the cast of his powerful sweep reveals cordlike muscle torn and rebuilt by the task.

I jam my thumbs in my waistband and watch him a while. He stops every few swings to slap wet clumps from the blade, and when he does, an odd critter perched at the very edge of a swaying branch a few feet overhead scolds him unmercifully, chittering directly at him, its tail switching and slapping at the air.

The old man spots me and smiles.

"Uhh..bonsoir?" I venture.

"Bonjou!" he corrects, grinning.

"Bonjou, yes. Um, oui. Mes-mesi?"

"Oue, mesi. Trè bèl," he curls a gnarled finger at me. "En-engaleesh?"

"American, oui."

"Dokte?"

"I..."

"Dok-dok?" he tries again.

"Oh! No. No doctor. Fixer," I mime a wrench. "Fixer."

"Oui?"

"Vrooom," I twist an imaginary grip. "Fix vroom."

He claps his hand to his chest. "Oh! Oui!" he laughs.

I point at the scythe in his hands. "s—s'il vous plaît? Oui?"

He looks down at it.

"Oui," I nod, extending my open hands.

He shrugs and holds it out for me to take. It's been cobbled together with what appears to be materials readily at hand There's a knot as a brace for the supporting hand, and a filthy scrap of cloth wrapped around the wooden middle for grip. I try to hold it as he had.

"Oui," he nods.

I turn it over in my hands, testing its weight. It's heavy, but nicely balanced. It's not incidental, his grasp or the geometry of this blade. It's the result of trial and error by someone well versed in the work. I spread my legs and take my first swing. The grass bends to the blow and springs right back.

The old man barks and gestures, holding his palm flat in demonstration while the critter laughs overhead. I swing again and this time the blade bites in with a slushy reverb.

"Oui!" the old man claps his approval behind me.

I shake a fist at the chatterbox above and the old man cackles, grasping the crown of his bald head with long, spindly fingers. I stagger my stance and swing again. My left hand burns against the knot, but it's not wholly unpleasant. Blister work. The old guy's palms must be weathered to thick rawhide.

I peek over my shoulder every so often for approval he grants time and time again. After several minutes, he checks out and sits down against the nearest hut with a long lit weed in his mouth. A tendril of unbroken smoke wanders high above him while a mangy Tom figure-eights the crook of his shins. He scratches its perked ears while the cat gnaws openly at nothing.

"You lose a bet or something?"

Beth's watching me. I don't know how long she's been there.

"She okay?" I ask.

"Yeah, it's fine. She's good."

"Anything serious?"

"Nah," she thumbs at the blade in my hand. "So?"

"What? I like it!"

I wave to the old man. He waves back with both hands, the smoldering root still clenched in a few brown teeth.

"Well, I'm ready whenever you are," she sighs and plops down next to him like they're old friends. I turn to finish my patch of grass and listen to them speak in soft whispers.

We leave the village just before noon. Many of the children follow us to the bike, running ahead then back between us, suddenly very shy then very much not. Beth stops from time to time to snap pictures of them. The older boys flex and pose, so serious for the lens and her attention, but fall right back to playful and silly whenever the shutter clicks.

So different, yet so very much the same.

She keeps her promise and hands out the little boxes of candy. She forms a single line and each child is invoiced a high five in return for his or her treat. The little girl with the cane stands last. She takes hers, slips it into a pocket on the front of her sweatshirt, and turns like she's about to follow the others.

But she doesn't. She walks up to me and offers me her cane. I kneel to take it, unsure of what she's asking me to do. She shuffles around before I can even stutter a question and takes a single hop-step forward to wrap her arms around Beth's leg. Beth bends down, kisses the top of her head, and whispers something through the girl's uncombed hair.

"Orevwa!" she chirps, taking her cane and hustling across the road. "Orevwa!"

I can't tell if Beth's affected by this at all. Her shades haven't been off all morning.

"You left your stuff here?" she points at my jacket on the bike.

"So?"

"Yeah, well," she taps at her bottom lip, "remind me to tell you about the Icelander sometime."

"Right. Were you okay on the ride up?"

"Sure. It wasn't that bad. I thought it'd be way scarier. That your little girl?"

She points at the picture of Maggie on the tach.

"Yeah."

"Wow. She's really cute. Who's the father?"

"*Thanks.* What do you mean scarier?"

"I thought you'd go crazy and show off or something. You know, doing jumps or whatever. She's blonde."

"Yup. That'd be my mom's side. You got a little dirt bike back home or something?"

She laughs. "Nah. I think my dad had a Harley at one point."

"*Potato-potato-potato-potato,*" I blubber.

"What the hell?"

"What? That's what they sound like!"

"Soooo weird…"

"Oh!" I realize. "Let me get something. Just a sec."

I rummage through the left sidecase. Beth watches.

"What is that?"

"A splitter," I reply. "For music."

"I don't have headphones."

I've traveled so often in this riding jacket that the numerous pocket's have slowly become individual 'drawers' of specific goods. I unzip the left front and fish out a coil of packaged earbuds.

"Spares!" I beam.

"Wow. What a Boy Scout," she smirks. "No cooties?"

"Brand spankin'."

I snap both sets of earbuds into the splitter and click it into my phone.

"We need to work out some shorthand. We won't be able to really hear each other at speed."

"*Huh?*" she bellows.

"Exactly. How about this. Tap my right side for a right turn. Left for left. But if you need me to stop for any reason? Pee break or whatever? Tap the top of my head. Cool?"

"Sure. Should I tap your shoulder or your arm? Or does that mess you up?"

I'm pretty sure you've already messed me up.

"Either one. Whatever works. But do it early enough so I can merge over if I need to. Is it pretty straightforward? The road to the coast?"

"Yeah, it's not bad. It smoothes out when we get closer. There's a little river crossing down south, but that usually goes pretty quick. I'm sure we'll run into some traffic after that. Oh! Watch out for chickens. And goats. They seriously don't care if they're in the way."

"Got it. How long to Jacmel?"

"Depends. Few hours. But that's in the truck with lots of stops. It's gotta' be better on this thing."

I hold my earbuds up and mime the process. Her eyebrows rise and fall reflexively as she rolls the foam between her fingertips and slips them in.

"Is that right?" she yells, turning her head side to side.

Diamond studs. Hadn't noticed those before.

"They're in. Can you hear?"

"Unfortunately!" she smirks.

"F u c k. O f f," I mouth.

She gasps and snaps a jab to my ribs.

"The nerve!"

I kick up the side stand and swing southbound. Energized, sun-warmed, and unexpectedly happy.

My stuff is right where I left it in the church. The missionaries aren't around and it's disappointing I won't get to thank them once more for their generosity. The awkward conversation this morning doesn't change this. I don't share his outlook, but I can at least try to see things from his perspective. Maybe I'm just frustrated that this place has obviously affected us so differently. Or maybe I've barely scratched the surface here and I may yet see what he does. I scribble a quick thank you note and leave it on the pulpit.

"That's awfully thoughtful of you," Beth muses. "You're much nicer than me. I just eat their food and leave."

"I don't believe that for a second," I sniff as we mount the bike. "I bet you'd do the same thing if I wasn't here."

"*Ha.* Show's what you know."

The road down the south side of the mountain is in markedly better shape and just twisty enough to introduce her to the more pleasurable aspects of riding. I reach back and tap her knee after a few miles.

"Having fun?"

"Sure!"

She's not nearly as tense now. From time to time, her knee brushes my thigh as she taps her foot to the music. I think she's having a good time. I hope she is.

She wasn't wrong about the wildlife. More than once, I'm forced to stop for stubborn goats who've just parked themselves squarely in the middle of road. They're not oblivious to our approach. Merely indifferent. They stand there staring at us with a sort of practiced and thoughtless regard; 'This is our place. Go find your own.'

The sky remains clear and I'm greeted with my first glimpse of the southern coastline before long. Blinding, late-afternoon refractions shimmer wildly along the blue, deeper shades bleeding at the horizon like the waves stretch on forever. At Marigot, we pass through the first real intersection I've seen since Port-au-Prince. It's a different vibe here and cars blend in and out of the fray like ants. I find myself slowing down to create safer gaps ahead, gaps other motorists are all too happy to immediately fill back in. I find it mildly terrifying, but Beth seems blissfully oblivious behind me. Maybe she's looking around and isn't reading the traffic the way I am. Or maybe she's just used to it.

It's strange to sail through like this, wondering if I might've talked to that person there or taken a look at the bike on the sidewalk, the one balanced on milk crates with its rear wheel missing and broken drive chain spilled out on the ground. It's a little town and we're soon spat out the other side in a flurry of decrepit trucks and stinking cars chasing coastal route 208 west.

The beach to our left is often just twenty yards away. The smells of the sea refuse to blend, salt and rot so individually strong they repulse and fight one another for a supremacy the wind never permits. I want to stop here for a moment, but there simply isn't anywhere safe enough to try.

Traffic thins as we wind west, but we soon catch another long queue and cars quickly begin stacking up behind us. While I may not enjoy being throttled back, I prefer that to having anyone behind me whatsoever. With a quick downshift and a fistful of go, you can often use slower traffic to your advantage, putting the dawdlers between you and the distracted lollygagger there just inches from your precariously exposed rear tire. But such a maneuver isn't wise right now. I accept the sluggish pace and nervously ride my mirrors.

I spy a crooked little sign and lean back to Beth.

"This us?"

"Huh?"

"Turn?" I holler.

"Nope!"

She leans forward after several moments. "Stop worrying so much! I'll tell you when!"

The cars ahead turn off one by one and we're soon sailing this westbound ribbon all alone.

Beth's really moving now. The occasional foot tap has grown to a full body throb.

"Who is this?" she yells.

"It's good, isn't it?" I yell back.

"I think I kind of love it!"

I look out far beyond the surf, way out to where the waves crest and the blues blur.

"Isn't this amazing?" I yell.

But she doesn't answer. She wraps her arms around me and things crest in me. She holds me tight and everything blurs.

I need no sign or shoulder tap to know we've reached Jacmel. She yells something I miss as a hulking heap diesels past. I yank the earbuds free.

"What?"

"I *said* just take it easy up here! This place gets pretty crazy!"

I'm not sure how Jacmel's population compares with Port-au-Prince's. The mirrors are a blur of activity and vehicles of all description dive-bomb as we thread our way deeper in. In spite of the chaos, I still don't feel anything resembling animosity or frustration from the other drivers.

I need to spend more time in this country. It can't be like this all the time.

But when I smile at someone, they smile back. When I wave, they wave. This exists all around the world, but it feels unrehearsed here. There's a certain truthiness to it, not simply the nth performance of some tired script.

Beth slaps my side a mile in.

"Left! At the green building!"

I time traffic to avoid a full stop at the turn.

"Just head straight! We're close!"

The smell of the sea channels freely here. Run-down cars are parked everywhere, most with two wheels up on the cracked concrete that passes for sidewalk. Dry vines scale every exterior wall, two and three stories up to thinly latticed balconies where curious faces peer down and watch us from rocking wicker chairs.

"Right there!" she taps. "The Lemon!"

Bright yellow and two-stories tall, it really is a big brick Lemon. Faded white pillars frame it top to bottom, bracketing the balcony's iron latticework that's stamped every few feet with decorative metal birds. I'm not sure what I was expecting. She'd called it an 'apartment' a few times, so I'd pictured something smaller. Something cramped. I didn't expect this and the surprise of it prompts a grin that Beth notices and leans around me to confirm. I roll to a stop at the crumbling curb out front.

"Try the alley. Somebody parks their bicycle in there sometimes, but it should be empty this time of day."

It's a five-foot canyon between the Lemon and neighboring building. I plant my feet and tip-toe the bike in. She climbs down gingerly this time, much slower than this morning.

"Oh. My. God. *Really!*"

"Yeah, it can suck," I say, hopping off. "It helps to move. You know, shift around and stretch a lot."

"Go all ants in the pants?"

"Yeah. Kind of like you were back there." I level her with a wry smile. "So?"

"So what?"

"Was it fun?"

"Sure. It was fine."

"It was *fine?*"

"What? I thought I'd be more stressed out. I didn't freak, did I? You want a medal or something?"

"Eh. No helmets? No rush. You'd feel differently with a helmet."

"That sounds totally backwards."

"Twisty roads. You know? I like to play."

"And that sounds dumb."

"I think we made good time," I change the subject. "It can't be very late."

She checks her watch. "Nope. In fact, I'd say that's a record."

We spend the rest of the afternoon unpacking and separating our stuff. Beth throws in the towel after a while and curls up in a large bowl-shaped chair lined with what must be a dozen pillows.

The place is really nice. Everything's incredibly clean and awash in white, like someone fell asleep on the undo button. The floors, the walls, the stairs. Everything but a few turquoise stools that offset the blank.

"Is that your bed?" I call from the kitchen.

"Sometimes. I'll pass out here if I don't head up right after my pill. It's comfy, but it kills my neck."

"Ambien queen. I forgot."

"Whatever. It's not like I want to."

"Hey, not judging. I have to drink to sleep."

She sits straight up.

"What do you drink?"

"Whatcha' got?"

"Rum. Lots of rum." She wrinkles her nose at me. "But I figured you for a cheap wine, paper bag kind of hobo."

"Hell, I'd drink it. Hobo wine, box wine, moonshine…"

"A proper lush, are we?"

"Almost. But I think you gottta' carry one of those little flasks around to qualify."

"You don't have one?"

"Nope. Well, not a flask. But I do have a big booze tank on the bike."

"Really?"

"Yup. Well, an empty booze tank. Some kids got to it."

"*What?*" She leans forward, incredulous.

"No! No. It's okay. They didn't drink it. I think they tried to start the bike with it."

She looks totally confused.

"It's just a theory," I sigh wistfully at the floor. "But it's all gone now. No booze, no booze."

"Well, they put rum in everything here. Order a milkshake and it'll be spiked."

"You can get a milkshake here?"

"Ha!" she scoffs. "As if."

She stands to stretch, dressed now in yoga pants and a t-shirt.

"Do you run?" I ask.

"Used to. Can't really run here."

"Too busy?"

"Well, yeah. Between work and the sheer lack of anywhere decent to run, there's also a curfew here from midnight to five AM."

"I see."

"Do you now," she teases.

"You hungry?" I ask. "I'm kind of digesting my own stomach here."

"The maid cooks," she explains. "She usually comes in the morning before Philippe and I get up and again around now to make dinner. Even if we're not hungry. She'll cook and put it in the fridge. It's non-negotiable. She came with the house."

"That's pretty dang cool."

"I guess. I think it's pretty weird. I don't really do maids. I'm a slob, don't get me wrong. If anyone needs one, it's me. But I don't typically eat what most people consider real meals, so

I just feel like she's wasting her time on me. But that's how it is here. I just try and fit in."

"Who's Phil?"

"Phil*ippe*. Don't ever call him Phil. He's my roomie."

"Ah, cool. Was he with you guys yesterday?"

"Yup. Beard? French Canadian. He's our logistics guy. He doesn't talk much. Unless he's been drinking. Then he won't shut the hell up."

I peer upstairs. "Is he here?"

"Nope. He's still at the Box," she arches her back and all sorts of pops and crackles echo off the thin walls.

"How can you stand riding that goddamn thing all day?"

"That was just a few hours!"

"I know! And it was *plenty*. Anyways, I hope you like lobster. Or crab. Nearly everything she makes is lobster this or crab that."

"Oops."

"Oops what?"

"I'm allergic to shellfish."

"Seriously?" She slumps. "You came to the Caribbean and you're allergic to fish?"

"Not fish. Shellfish. Shrimp, crab, lobster. All that seabug stuff."

"Huh. Good to know," she looks at the floor a long while. "I'm sure she can make something else. But hey, if not? I've got EpiPens galore!"

"It's fine. I have some food in the cases."

"What? Hobo chow? Some old leather belts and rusty nails?"

"That *would* explain a few things."

She laughs.

"Go shower. I didn't want to say anything, but you actually do smell homeless."

"That I do." I point up the stairs. "There?"

"Yeah. Let me show you."

She shuffles up the stairs, her knees cracking loudly with every step. The stairs do feel steeper than most.

"It goes without saying that you're sleeping here tonight, right?" she asks over her shoulder. "Consider it payback for the ride."

"Fine by me. I don't know that I'd find someplace else this late anyhow."

"Nah. There's a nice hotel right down the street. Right on the beach. Like a resort or something."

"Really?"

"Yup. This city is a little strange. You've got the locals, the tourists, and everyone else like us. It's really pretty if you ignore certain spots. Like the trash tide. You can see it from the roof sometimes."

"Trash tide?" I ask.

"Well, that's what we call it. It's like the Trash Heap took a big dump right on the beach."

"Wow, a Fraggle reference. Well played."

"What? We're like the same friggin' age to the week or whatever."

"Oh?"

She hadn't admitted this before.

"Yeah. But you're still older than me."

"Maybe. But my knees don't pop like that."

The upstairs is just as cozy, with two bedrooms sharing a little bathroom between them. The rooms are small, just large enough for a simple bed and tall mirrored-dresser apiece. A narrow glass door in her room opens out onto the balcony.

"The shower sucks. It's way too short, even for me. But don't move that showerhead or it leaks like crazy. The hot water is super hot so be careful. Oh, and it's backwards to what you'd expect. Right for hot, left for cold."

She taps her chin and looks around her room.

"Towels. Let me get you one."

She bounds down the hall and into what I presume is Philippe's room. I sneak out to the balcony. A pair of grizzled old men slouch on their own balcony across the street. They peer left and right around me, as if looking for Beth.

She comes back with the towel and a tiny box of soap.

"You ever put on a little show for those guys?" I ask.

"Every night. It's this little arrangement we have. I slowly undress in here with all the lights on, and then I get to triple-C when they arrest. Keeps me fresh."

"Pretty confident there," I tease.

"Well, I'm not a *troll*."

She's wrong. The shower doesn't suck. It's quite possibly the best shower I've had in years and I stretch it out until the hottest water runs cool.

The sidecases are by the bedroom door. They're not exactly easy to carry and I feel bad that she's lugged the heavy suckers up those steep steps. I slip into a t-shirt and shorts and for the first time in nearly a week, I'm barefoot.

I find Beth in her big chair with a laptop across her knees. She's let her hair down. It's much longer than I thought.

"You'll go blind doing that," I scold.

She doesn't say a word. Her face is just a few inches from the bright screen. One hand hovers over the touchpad and she nibbles at the fingernails of her other.

"Mmmm. Hungry?" she mumbles.

"I'm pretty sure we've covered that."

She lifts her head, but not her eyes which remain trained on the screen. She calls out to the maid in what once again sounds like fluent Creole. I hadn't even noticed her in the kitchen.

"Impressive!" I say.

"What's that."

"You speak Creole. I'm impressed."

"Don't be. It's not that good. I just brute force it. On any given day we're speaking three or four languages at work. It's all sorts of dumb."

"Wow. Okay, then *that's* impressive."

"Trust me, it doesn't mean a thing. It just moved my name up the list."

I fall down on the chair opposite her with a thud. It's not as fluffy as hers. It's not fluffy at all.

"That reminds me. I still have a million questions for you."

"Great. I can hardly wait," she groans.

"Oh, we don't have to—"

"No, it's fine. Sorry. That came out wrong. I just don't like talking about myself. Unlike some people..."

"Hey now."

She looks up at me finally. I can't see her mouth, but I can tell from her eyes that she's smirking.

"I'll only ask important stuff. Fair enough?"

"Sure."

She snaps her laptop shut and asks the maid something.

"Come on." She hops up and drops the laptop in the comforters behind her. "We've got twenty minutes."

If she's still stiff from the ride, I'd never know it. She bounces up the steps, rounds the corner, and jogs down the upstairs hall. I follow at a slightly more age appropriate pace.

"Jesus, old man. Come *on*." She's standing at what looks like a small closet door. "This you gotta' see."

She slides it open and reveals spiral steps. The staircase is narrow, barely wide enough to stand between the center column and delicate handrail circling up and around. The few slatted steps are spaced far apart and force long, stretching lunges before ending in a little wooden stall atop the building, also whitewashed like seemingly everything else here. I duck through the open doorway and find myself on a roof Beth's already crossed. I crunch across the loose gravel to join her.

"It's still a bit early."

"For what?"

"You'll see."

She nods out to sea before falling onto a cheap lounge chair already mostly reclined.

"Ugh," she grunts.

"Tired?"

"I'm always tired. Dreading the Box tomorrow. I'm pretty sure this was my first day off in a month."

"Are you serious?"

"Yeah. Everything backs up whenever I take time off so it's never really a break. I'm just making some other day ahead of me that much longer." She lets this hang in the air, tilting her head to look up at me. "So really, I should be blaming you. You could have said no."

"Well, I'm not going to feel bad."

I fall into another the other chair and find my legs adopting the same gangly angles as hers.

"Where ya' headed next?" she asks.

"West. Far as I can."

"I can't remember what's over there."

"Some villages. Another coast. More water."

"So you're telling me you've really got this all planned out."

"Well, I had the first day mapped out. The shoving off bit. I figured I'd wander around after that."

"What exactly are you hoping to find out there?"

"More bikes. Anyone I can help. And if it's a bust? Hey, it'll still be a good ride."

She chews her thumbnail.

"Greg, you know they came around a few weeks ago and bought up a lot of that crap. Don't you?"

"I— no. I was not aware."

I wait for her to continue, but she just nibbles at her nail.

"Who's they?"

"UN reps. From the capital. They came around and offered anyone with a car or truck or bike or whatever they had cash. Right there on the spot. Provided it was running."

"Well, that's good then," I sigh.

"Huh?"

"I'm not here to fix *running* bikes."

She rolls over to look at me like I've just said the dumbest thing she's ever heard. Maybe I have.

"How in the heck are you going to find them if they're not running?"

"Haven't figured that part out yet. Maybe I'll find a place to stay a while. You know, spread the word some. Hope that people hear I'm there. I can make house calls. Like you."

Her eyes cloud over with barbed reactions. She rolls back with a huff.

"You should be in Port-au-Prince. You could do a lot more there."

"Maybe," I should probably just stop. I don't. "But there's already so many people there. It's crowded. They have a small army of people already helping. You know? I'd just be in the way."

I pause to look at her. She continues staring skyward.

"Beth, trust me. That was the initial idea. But over the past month, more and more people have been showing up there so it fel—"

"Where did you hear *that?*" she snaps.

"The news, I guess. More than one place. Some of those relief camps set up outside of town? The folks running them said—"

"Okay, look. A lot of that stuff is promotional. They come in, set up, and shuffle on home. Not everyone. I'm not lumping everyone together. What's-his-face? He's been here from the very beginning, which is pretty goddamn awesome. But for a lot of people and a lot of companies it's not real compassion. It's a *show* of compassion. They get things started, sure. Then they leave it to people who don't know what the fuck to do. The intentions might look good, but sometimes they hurt more than anything."

She flips her hair like she's sunning at the beach, one leg stretched, the other folded up underneath her.

"All those cars and stuff? They hauled that crap back there. They probably have a huge parking lot full of things for you to work on."

"But why? What was the point?"

"They said it was to build up a fleet of workable vehicles for distribution or something."

"But they had to be running. Right? So there's nothing to fix."

"Have you seen the vehicles around here, Greg? Running is kinda' relative."

"But what about all those truc—"

She cuts me off. "It really pissed me off, you know? You can't just wave cash around and expect people here *not* to take it. And they fucking knew it," she snorts. "They even tried to buy our truck! And we have goddamn logos on them! They just went door to door and asked if the car outside was whomever's." She's frustrated. "I don't know. You should ask Jon. He's got his own conspiracy theory."

"Jon?"

"Yeah, our driver."

"How many people work for you?"

"Well, nobody works for me. We have five teams here. Our team is just the three of us right now," she sighs. "They keep telling us we'll get another RN, but they haven't even extended our contracts yet so who knows. From time to time, we'll get some help from the locals. Usually when they've called us.

"Four," she corrects before I can ask anything else. "Sorry. Forgot Virgil. He's our CO, but he doesn't really count."

I raise an eyebrow.

"He works the office," she shrugs. "He's our line back home. He doesn't 'Do the Field' as he puts it. He doesn't do boots or whatever. Some stupid joke of his."

"I think I've heard it before."

We hear a truck approach in the street below. It idles a second before cutting out. One door opens and shuts.

"And that would be Philippe," she says, one foot tapping at the air. "Oh! Damnit! Damn, damn, damn. Look," she sighs and points west.

The sun has slipped beneath a western range framing the bay a few miles off. Rays of orange and violet spill out in blended cottony strokes against the deep, dusk blue.

"Something else, huh?" she murmurs.

"Yeah. How do you top *that?*"

She thinks a moment. "Why would you need to? You're here right now."

Footsteps shuffle up the spiral staircase behind us and crunch across the roof.

"Hey Philippe," Beth welcomes him without looking up.

"Hello," Philippe says softly behind us.

He's thin, bearded, with a curly crop of dark chestnut hair. His gold-rimmed glasses glimmer in the sunset rays.

"She loves this time of day. She makes everyone watch this."

"Hush," Beth growls.

"I can see why," I offer.

"Yes, it is quite something," he says and stares with us. "Our food is ready. No rush, of course. Whenever you guys want to come down."

Beth breaks her trance without a word and tip-toe-runs to the stairwell. Philippe and I fall in behind.

"Does she always have this much energy?"

"Yes," he sighs. "I cannot say that I've seen her otherwise."

The kitchen smells of warm spicy things, and my jaw drops when I see what awaits us. The plates are enormous. They must be to accommodate the sheer amount of food heaped upon them. It's not lobster in the way I've seen it served before. It's the whole damn thing, mutant large, with creamy flesh mushrooming up from their monstrous tails.

Beth makes funny drooling sounds. "See?"

"It certainly looks impressive. I'll have to take your word for it."

Philippe's puzzled. "Not hungry?"

"He *can't*," Beth waves her fork at me. "Allergic."

Philippe rolls his head back. "Oh, I am very sorry for you," he teases. "And yet, somehow, this isn't all bad news…"

He eyes the extra lobster on my plate, arching his brow to Beth who's already nodding 'YES'.

The maid cleans the kitchen as we eat a few feet away at the small counter. I feel very uncomfortable about doing so and spend most of the meal thanking her.

"Really, thank you so much. Merci magne…mange matin," I struggle, forcing my brain through the haze of a language I don't speak. She smiles shyly, but says nothing. Beth and Philippe snicker, however, and this seems to embarrass her further.

In exchange for donating my crustacean they've both given me their 'Goodness Cakes', as Philippe calls them, little corn fritter things, like deep-fried pancakes that are salty, sweet and ever so tasty. A small mountain of roasted vegetables and a glass bottle of bright yellow banana-flavored soda finish off the most welcome meal.

"Well?" Beth asks when I take my first neon swill.

"It's like liquid candy."

"*Alcoholic* candy!" Beth beams. "Told you so," she plays with her food a bit, twirling her fork as she talks. "I'm normally a wine girl, but it took me, what?"

"Less than one day," Philippe offers without hesitation.

"Right. About a day to adapt. And let me tell you, they like their drinks capital S strong here," she finishes. "Oh! Tell him about your bootlegging gig!"

"Huh?"

She smacks my shoulder with the back of her hand.

"The booze tank, dummy!"

I sheepishly tell Philippe my tale of sober woe.

"Well, that must be disappointing," he offers.

"Sir, you've no idea."

The maid shucks her apron and dons a colorful knitted sweater. As with so many of the beautiful Haitian people, I'm unable to tell if she's eighteen or forty.

"Merci mange matin!" I offer one last time.

She bites her lip and bolts out the front door. Philippe laughs loudly, which is bad enough. But Beth flat out chokes on her food.

"*What?*" I beg. "What the hell did I say?"

They try to swallow between snorts.

"You kept saying 'Thanks morning'!"

"'Thanks for eat morning'!" Beth says, tearing up. She leans back to smile at Philippe, but he doesn't notice. He can't. He's palming his own tears away.

"Well that's just fucking awesome. *Mange matin! Merci mange matin!*" I sneer and the choking fits start all over again.

"I bet," she can hardly speak, "I bet she thought you were making your smooth American move!"

She elbows me gently as I search the ceiling for excuses.

The three of us retire to the balcony as night falls. It's not cold, but Beth hops up after a few moments and returns with several large blankets. Philippe and I each get one, but she keeps most of them for herself.

"We do this most every night," Beth says.

The old men are back across the street. We raise rum-filled coffee mugs to them and they return the gesture.

Cheers to weirdos.

Beth asks me to tell Philippe about my travels thus far.

"Oh, wait! Tell him what you used to do first!" she continues before I can defer. "He used to make video games."

I glare at her.

"What?" she mocks surprise. "I looked you up. You didn't tell me you made *those* games. My brothers play that stuff. They freaked when I texted them."

I nearly choke on my booze. "Game developers are like Countach posters. Or ninjas. They're only cool to twelve-year-old boys."

"Huh?"

"Lamborghini," Philippe sighs quietly.

"Jesus Christ," Beth shakes her head. "Dumb. You're both dumb."

"Hey, you brought it up!"

Beth gives me a snarly look.

"Go on. Tell him what you did."

"A long time ago I started a company with four other—"

"No, dummy. Tell him what you did *in* the games."

"I was an animator. And not a very good one, either."

"So you moved all those thingies around?" she gestures wildly with her fingers.

"Yes," I mime it back. "I moved those thingies around all silly like."

"I will beat you. Don't think I won't just because you're homeless."

"Is that so?"

"Fact," she says firmly.

I lean close to Philippe. "It wasn't nearly as exciting as she seems to think."

"Long hours with computers," he sighs. "This too is my life. I understand."

I raise my mug and we toast to nothing in particular.

"Wow, should I leave you two alone?" Beth moans.

Philippe and I feign dreamy looks at each other.

"Oh, *do* fuck off," she scoffs.

The old men across the street stand and stretch, appearing ready to call it an early night.

"*That* is a very good idea," Philippe says, eyeing them. "It was a rather long day."

"Oh shit. Was it?" Beth winces.

I don't get the impression that Philippe's commenting on her absence, but she's apparently taking it that way.

"Yes, very busy. And the AC isn't working again," he sighs. "Nothing terrible. Just long."

"Sorry I wasn't there."

"It's fine."

She stares at her mug.

"Shall I sleep downstairs?" he asks.

"Nope. I'm sleeping in the big chair. Greg's taking my bed."

This is news to me.

"Beth, you don't have to do that. I have my sleeping bag. I can lay that out just about anywhere."

"Nope. I insist."

"But—"

"Shut it. I sleep in that chair several times a week. I'm used to it."

"Usually not on purpose, but yes, this is true," Philippe confirms with a yawn and walks back inside.

The sounds of the city fill the quiet moments Beth and I allow. I try to pick one discernable track from the many.

"It actually gets louder. It's only really quiet right before dawn. It's pretty lame."

"Crazy night life?"

"It's been a little strange lately. They cancelled Carnaval this year. That never happens, so people really didn't know what to do."

"How does one cancel Carnaval?"

"Well, I should say they tried to. They changed it up. It was supposed to be this three-days-of-mourning thing instead, but a lot of people tried to celebrate anyhow. I think not having that outlet made things worse. It's still a fresh wound. People can't just switch it all off. But it was loud before the quake too, so who knows."

"I didn't know you were here before the quake."

"You never asked. I have pictures. You can see what it looked like before. You should see them sometime before you leave."

"I'd like that. I've taken zero pictures since I got here."

"And why doesn't that surprise me."

"I used to take pictures," I defend, "but I just sort of stopped a few years ago. I know that's selfish. We take pictures for other people. Right? To share them?"

"I guess. I take them for me. I have a horrible memory so I kinda' have to. Why'd you stop?"

"I found I remembered things...no, not better, more *vividly* if I was just seeing things up here and not through a viewfinder. It sounds strange, I know. But the entire memory is preserved this way for me somehow instead of just appearing in some old album or folder on my laptop. It's not earmarked, I guess, so the whole memory sort of flows as one big scene in my head. I think the act of taking a picture always condensed the moment into this singular, flat thing I could never really get back."

"I think," Beth says, fumbling over the edge of her chair for the rum bottle, "for one, I think you think too much."

"It's a problem, yes."

"And second? It sounds like you need to take a photography class. Maybe you're just doing it wrong."

She pours a bit more into her coffee mug and hands me the bottle. I do the same, only more so.

"Easy there," she says, eyeing me suspiciously.

"Never fear, I'm a responsible drunk."

"Is that so."

"Really. I will have you know that I almost always wash my Prilosec and Zantac down with the first double."

I want to tell her about my careful little studies, but I can't seem to remember the details.

"Spoken like a true addict," she smirks.

"Spoken like one recovering."

"No such animal. Cheers," she toasts. "You having any withdrawal issues yet?"

"Not yet. Figured the DTs would be hitting pretty hard, but that was only, what, two days ago? I've had this Candida thing for a while now, too, bu—"

"Nose?"

"Yeah, but it seems to be, well, gone."

"Just so you know, I don't do free check-ups."

"Oh, I know. It's just weird. Isn't it? That stuff usually doesn't clear up on its own."

"It can. If you stop drinking and eating anything yummy."

"You know what I mean."

"Yes, I know what you mean. And you're correct. It doesn't just go away."

We sit and listen to the evening beyond. Smells of the sea and things best left unimagined drift in and out on the breeze. The air is sticky with it. Beth has snuggled deep into her blanket pile in the dark. A lazy old street lamp tries unsuccessfully to switch itself on half a block down, clicking dead for a minute before buzzing back to a dim half-light that never increases.

"What was that missionary saying to you this morning?"

"You heard that?"

"I saw you guys talking, but I couldn't hear anything. Probably something about me."

"Yeah, kind of."

"Oh?"

"Well, it wasn't about *you*. Not specifically. Or anyone in your team for that matter. It was more like this general observation of anyone here who isn't god-fearing or spreading the good word. He seemed to have a huge amount of distrust for, well, the rest of us."

I study her face in the dark.

"So? Are you? God-fearing?" I venture.

She's struggling to get the comforter over her bare feet. She finally just whips it in a way that sends the thing billowing out and over the whole chair.

"God fearing? No. God phoning? Sure. But he never answers my calls."

I think she's peeking over at me, but I can't see her eyes.

"That's probably the lamest thing I've ever heard."

"*Whatever!*" she squeals. "So I presume you're not?"

"No. As a kid, yes, but I wasn't given a choice. I was raised in all of that. But something bad happened and we got out. Free will for me, thanks."

She leans her head heavily on one palm, gently curling her fingers along her cheek.

"You know?" Her lips pop a little and I know she's smiling there in the dark. "It's all kind of making sense to me now. The bike? All the deep thinking and wanderlust crap? Who's that guy? The guy who—"

"Nope. Off limits."

"Hmmm," she purrs.

"You're kind of a brat."

"*Me?*"

"A little. Maybe just the right amount."

"Well, I've been called worse. My husband calls me a moody bitch all the time."

She doesn't hesitate. She doesn't backtrack.

"He hasn't said that in a long time, but we haven't talked in two weeks, so, you know. Whatever."

I'm not sure what to say. She doesn't notice my shock. At least, I don't think she does. I muster something resembling nerve.

"How long have you been married?"

"Three years? Our anniversary was in October, so I guess it's a little longer."

"Is he here? Working?"

"Oh hell no. He's an ophthalmologist back in Portland."

"What?" I sit up. "I was living in Portland before I came here!"

"Maine?"

"Oh. No, the other one."

"I thought you lived in Texas."

"I did. That's a longer story."

"Huh. Anyhow, no. I'm the thrill seeker. He's the normal one. Someone has to be or the kids would be in therapy."

"Wow."

"What? Surprised I have kids?"

"No, not at all. Just surprised you're so...private, I guess. I didn't know any of this."

"Well, considering you've known me, what? All of twenty-some hours? I haven't even had *time* to hide anything. Besides, I'm lucky to even get a word in edge wise with you."

She's teasing, but my gut tumbles.

"So, kids? As in a small army?"

"Feels like it. Just three. Ten, six, and baby boy. He just turned two." She takes a big sip from her mug and notices my raised eyebrow. "Second marriage."

"Oh."

"Oh?"

"Yeah, I just, wow. I don't know what to say!" I really don't. "How do you do it? I mean, being over here?"

"Hell, how does anyone do it? It just sucks and you deal the best you can. I fly home every two months. It's sort of forced, so even if I didn't want to go back it wouldn't matter. But it's not like it's forever. This? Here in Haiti? This is pretty much what I've always wanted to do. Even as a little girl. I always wanted to see more than my backyard, so it is what it is. The first week away from them is always the toughest, but it get easier."

"It does?"

"Oh yeah, that's right," she realizes. "You're in week one right now, aren't you?"

I haven't told her enough. All she knows is that I'm here and somewhere back in the States I have a wife and a little girl. She thinks I'm married. She thinks I'm here like she is.

"Kind of."

"Kind of what?"

"It's kind of not really week one."

"I thought you got here last weekend?"

"I did."

"You're losing me."

"There's a bit more to it all."

"Do I need more rum for this?"

"Probably not. But I sure as hell do."

I pour another and tell her the whole story. I try to paint the picture in the right way. Not a good way, but the correct way. I don't skip gleefully over the dark cracks in the reality. I call it by its real name.

She listens quietly. She doesn't tease. She doesn't judge. In fact, she doesn't say anything at all. At one point I stop, half expecting to hear her snoring away all snug in her down-filled nest.

"I'm listening," she says softly.

"That's all there is."

"I don't believe that. What happened at your company? Why'd you quit?"

"I already told you."

"You told me about your daughter, but there has to be more to it."

"I don't know. I felt gluttonous. I can't think of any other way to put it. At some point, I started taking stock of the life I'd lived and found I pretty much had all I wanted. Like after Thanksgiving dinner. You gorge, you stop, you rest. You don't keep shoveling food in your mouth when you're stuffed."

"Speak for yourself, buddy. I loves me some gravy. And pie. Wait, so you quit before *pie?*"

"You know what I mean." I take a deep swill. "I wouldn't change things, though."

"Not even with your little girl? You left your company to be with her, but now—"

"Yeah, okay. I know. Maybe I'm not all-seeing just yet. But I know what lies ahead for her. All parents do, I guess, or we think we do. But I've been on both sides of that gun. I've been dirt poor and I've also seen the super shiny side. I don't know. How it feels and how it sounds? It doesn't add up. The math gets wonky somewhere."

I take a large gulp.

"I guess I can imagine the same thing happening to Maggie."

"Maggie? That's her name?"

"Yeah, my wee lass. I can just see people driving her towards that shiny side her entire life. School. Career. Strive. Don't look around. Don't look inside. Don't travel or figure out who you are. Just keep on that straight and narrow and lock it down before someone else steals your shot. I feel obligated to prepare her for that or redirect her in some way so she won't have to deal with it like I did. But you can't, right? You just can't do that. She's got to get there on her own. In my case, it happened so late that—"

I pause.

"You know," I tangent, "I heard that a lot as a kid. My dreams were all regarded as these flights of fancy. I always wanted to make games, even when I was really young. Like eight or nine years old. But that wasn't even a real thing back in those days. That was something most people did by sharing code, line by line, page by page, in magazines so other people could sit down and copy their stuff, line by line, page by page, and hopefully recreate what they'd developed. So it was frustrating to answer that question honestly. They'd ask, 'What do you want to do when you grow up?' And I'd tell them. Honestly. Then they'd say, 'Oh, that's nice, dear. But just make sure you focus on a real job first so you can do that other stuff for fun. As a hobby.'"

I shake my head.

"They were the grownups, right? It wasn't just my parents. Teachers, friend's parents, bosses. They had knowledge and experience to pass on. 'Focus on a career. The other stuff is fluffy. Get that solid foundation underfoot and then do all that other stuff. But only if it doesn't interfere with The Career.' So I began to think and feel and plan in that way. I'm kinda' sad for that younger me, believing that was the only way."

I stretch out in the chair and sigh.

"I had that same spark. Like you. For something beyond everything I knew or was told to expect. The backyard thing?"

"Yeah?"

"I get that. Totally get that."

"But," she begins, confused, "you ended up making games, right? And it sounds like you did quite well for yourself. I mean, you ended up doing what most people thought was a total fantasy and look at you! You're here right now. You like being here, right?"

"And that's where shit gets tangled. If you go back and start tugging at knots way back there? What happens here and now? So, sure. You're right. That shiny life got me here. It's allowed me to meet you."

She looks down.

Ooops.

Her black hair falls all around her face and I can't see her expression. I've said something I probably shouldn't have and I quickly continue.

"After I left, I started redefining what happy actually meant to me in these silly little ways. For instance, happy was an empty aisle at the grocery store. Happy was finding I had a bit more Scotch than I thought or a spare twenty in my wallet."

She peeks at me through dark tangles. "Those aren't bad yardsticks."

"They're cute and all, sure. But I've redefined happy this past year all over again. Hell, it's even morphed in the few days I've been here. Now I'm thinking happy is a pair of dry socks. You know? I'm starting to believe the definition is always changing."

"Travel can do that to you," she muses.

"Maybe a satisfied mind needs newness."

"Hmm."

"What?"

"I think a satisfied mind needs nothing."

"....wow."

"What?"

"That's well said, Beth."

"You sound shocked."

"Not at all."

"The rest of us don't have to redefine everything or run away just to have a deep thought, you know."

"I wasn't doing it consciously," I sigh. "It was this, I don't know, like this evolving collection of coping metrics. A change. A midlife chrysalis."

"Okay, now *that's* the lamest thing I've ever heard," she groans.

"So? What do you think? World's greatest dad?"

"Well," she starts. "I think you're being too hard on yourself."

"Ha! I'd say not nearly enough."

"No, I mean it. I went through a nasty divorce. Like there are any good ones. But mine was real bad. Like, cops involved bad. And whenever kids are at stake? It's always flat-out warfare," she stops. "I wanted to run away. And I would have. I think. If I could have."

"But?"

"But he went batshit and tried to kill himself in front of our kids. My six-year-old called me at the hospital and said 'daddy's sleeping on the floor.' So, *that* happened. He went to jail, then he went someplace where they try to fix that kind of crazy. I couldn't run. I didn't have that option. I had my babies and they had me."

I slump back in my chair.

"I'm surprised you can even talk to me right now. He just ran away a little differently."

I'm actually shocked she hasn't walked away.

"I don't see it that way. Did you want to give up? Did you want a divorce? "

"I didn't. I liked being a husband. I liked being a dad. They were the two jobs I had a modicum of control over doing well."

"See? I think that's a big difference. It sounds like she gave up. Not you." She chews her lip. "I'm not defending it, mind you. But I get it. I just don't know how someone knows. You know? How do you really know when you're done in any relationship?"

"I have a theory."

"Oh Christ."

"What? I don't have to share it if you don't want me to."

"Please. I insist. I could use the laugh."

I draw long on my mug.

"I think you're done in any relationship when you no longer care if someone else is making your wife or husband or boyfriend or whatever the hell they are, when it never crosses your mind at all, not during the day or when you can't fall asleep, when you just flat out don't even *care* if someone else is making them come."

She chokes.

"What? I think it's pretty accurate. If *that* doesn't phase you? It's curtains! Right?"

"I'm starting to see why she wanted that divorce," she kids. It's playful, but in that half-drunk fashion that harbors a little more truth than jest.

"Nice."

"How long ago was this?"

"Was *what?*"

"How long ago did that all happen? When did she file?"

"Oh. Last September. Thereabouts."

"So, six months?"

"Something like that."

"And that was the last time you saw your little girl?"

I nod.

"When's the last time you talked to your wife?"

"Same time. I mailed Maggie Christmas and Valentines cards, but I haven't talked to Janet since I left."

"Janet," she articulates. "That's the first time you've said her name."

"Huh."

I just want to drink. Can I just drink now?

"What's she like?"

"Maggie?"

"No, Janet."

"Oh, she's cool. She's probably the nicest, most decent person I know. She'll respond to a jury summons the same day she gets it, you know?"

"So you're saying she's dull."

"Not a bit. She's..."

"Yes?"

"She respects the rules. She's decent, not like me. I don't know how else to put it."

Beth closes one eye and regards me long enough to realize I won't bite.

"What does she do?"

"Besides call me very bad names?"

"I'm guessing that doesn't pay very well."

"She's a librarian."

The eye remains closed.

"And you guys end up together because...?"

"Because we met in high school."

"Aww. How sweet."

"Not really. I dated her best friend for years."

"Wow."

"Yeah, yeah, I know. Ancient history."

"No such thing for a woman. If you've known her as long as you say you have, you'd already know this."

I start to argue a point before realizing I haven't one to posit.

"Well, my husband isn't like me at all either, so maybe the whole opposites attract thing actually holds water."

She's quiet and rocks in her stationary chair. She chews on her thumbnail when she finally speaks again.

"Look, nobody can really tell you what you did was right or wrong. Relationships are complex. Even when things are good. Hell, look at me. I'm here away from my kids and will be most of this year. They get me back for a few weekends, but that's it. That's all they get. Most people would say that's pretty fucked up. Most *do* tell me that, in fact. I guess what I'm saying is I'm not judging you."

"You probably should."

"Aww, someone's having a wittle pity party."

"Boohoo."

"Wah." She kicks the blankets to the balcony floor. "Stay here."

She pads softly into the bedroom. Before I can even reach for a refill, she's back with a little pill bottle that she waves over my head like a magic wand.

"Tada!"

"Gonna' make me disappear?"

"In a manner of speaking? Yes. Yes, I am."

"Well, it's as good a time as any. You sure that's not the acid you were really popping the other night?"

"Cute. Here."

She drops a tiny pill in my palm.

"A whole one?"

"You're normal size. I have to take midget doses or bad things happen."

"I think they prefer the term little people."

"Little people, midgets, dwarves. I *am* one so I can call myself whatever the hell I want to."

I roll the little pill between my fingers.

"What do you mean bad things?"

"If I take a whole pill I tend to say too much. Or hallucinate. Sometimes both. It kind of feels like truth serum. Apparently I've sat there in Philippe's room talking all night, just chatting away without a care in the world. It's not that I say stuff I wouldn't ever say. It just nukes the filter."

"What's wrong with that?"

"Nothing," she shrugs. "But when you wake up and your roommate tells you some of the horrifying things you don't remember ever sharing with him? It's time for midget doses."

I shrug, pop the pill, and wash it down with my last bit of rum.

"I kind of want to watch you and see what happens," she stares at me like some entirely new breed of creep. "I'm trying to picture you unfiltered."

"Do you really think I'm capable of talking even more?"

She feigns a full body shudder.

"Come on. Let's go in."

I doubt I'll have any trouble crashing. I don't feel anything yet, but she's insistent that I will soon enough.

"This bed isn't the comfiest," she warns, "but it beats a sleeping bag. You want the Wi-Fi key?"

"Nah, I'm fine. I'm gonna' read a little."

"Oh yeah? What's on the ol' portable nightstand?"

"My Dearest Friend. It's a collection of letters Abigail and John Adams wrote to each other."

She looks absolutely dumbfounded.

"Christ, what are you? Seventy? Shall I get you a nice tall glass of Metamucil?"

"Trust me, you'd like it. Read it someday and tell me Abigail wasn't our first Mrs. President. She was something else."

"Something else?" she pushes. "Was she a swell dame? A real special gal?"

"I'm sure she was!"

She shakes her head and flips the bed sheets down to peek underneath them.

"Lose something?" I ask.

"No. Just making sure it's maggot free tonight."

"*What?*"

"I'll tell you tomorrow. You probably won't sleep if I tell you now."

"Gee, thanks. You do realize it's a little too late."

"Oh relax. It only happened once. I'm just easily paranoid."

"Hmmm."

"Okay," she clasps her hands together under her chin.

Married!

"I have to finish a few emails. Get some sleep. You can come with us to the Box tomorrow if you'd like. See how this whole shindig works."

"Knock-knock."

"Oh god," she rolls her eyes. "Who's there."

"Mange matin," I mumble. I doubt I'll be reading much tonight.

"Pitiful."

She cracks that crooked little smile and something else melts. *Fuck.*

"Alright gramps. Go to sleep. If you get up, the light switch by the stairs is on the right side. But be careful on those steps. First night on Ambien and all. I've fallen down those fuckers and once was enough for me."

"You're like my little, midget drug dealer," I say. At least, I think I say this. It sounds like someone else may have.

"And you're my mental hobo drunk. Power couple."

"Hippocampal boxcar hopping alcoholic, if you please."

"Good lord. Goodnight, goof."

She slips from the room with raspy little shushes as the comforter drags behind her. I fall into a shallow sleep the moment my head hits the pillow, but find myself sitting up every so often to see if she's come back. To watch over me. She's left a table lamp on in the corner of the room, but I can't imagine switching it off right now.

I look under the sheets for maggots. I look for her.
She isn't here.

My arm is dead asleep under her pillow. Morning sunlight floods the room with an intensity that renders perception pointless, so I lie there a while, pretending I can't smell her on the sheets, wondering if she's already left for the day. I listen for hints of them downstairs, but all I hear is the city din beyond the balcony glass.

After a while, I swing my stiff legs out of bed and tiptoe into the bathroom to cup cold water over my face. My nose seems fine. Completely fine. No blood, no congestion.

Did they try to wake me?

I still don't hear them. I pad to the stairs and peek over the thin iron railing. Philippe's sitting shirtless at the kitchen bar with a tall mug of steaming something glued to his bottom lip and reading what's probably the local newspaper. Beth's wrapped up in her nest like some quilted python's low-calorie breakfast. She's peering very closely at the laptop again, her face bright blue in the glow. She nibbles on twirled strands of her hair.

"Morning."

They both grunt something resembling greetings. The scents of buttered toast, fresh coffee, and something citrusy I can't readily identify swirl about in the fan spun air.

"Stuff's in the kitchen there," Beth mumbles.

Philippe's eyes track me, but the steaming mug never leaves his lips. "How did you sleep?"

"Hard."

"First ever Ambien," Beth says. "He was goofy."

"I was not. Was I?"

"A little. But you didn't tell me where you buried the bodies or anything."

"There's toast, coffee, some mango," Philippe offers gently. "Typically we have quite a large lunch catered at the office, so we try not to eat too much in the morning."

I wonder if they have more rum in the kitchen here. I wonder if they'd notice.

"Sounds good to me," I say. "Work perk?"

"Wait 'til you see it," Beth calls from her nest. "It's totally bananas."

"What time do you guys like to get there?"

"Oh," Philippe sighs, "anytime before nine is okay. It really depends on traffic around here as it tends to be rather—"

"Fucked up," Beth finishes.

"We saw some of that coming in last night," I nod. "You just have to sort of assume everything's going to be okay and go with it."

"That's what it feels like to me as well," Philippe agrees. "It operates much like a herd, or school of fish. But it works, which is truly interesting to me as there isn't any real order or sense of control to it."

"It does *not* work," Beth interjects. "Everyone just lucks out. Until they don't. That's all."

I butter my toast and sneak some mango slices before I notice the oven clock. It's already past ten.

"Shit! Are you guys late?"

Philippe closes his eyes and shrugs. "Eh. It is not the end of the world."

"I didn't want to wake you up," Beth says. "And yes, you're welcome."

"I'm sorry. I didn't—"

"Really, it's okay."

"I'll eat fast. You guys need to shower or anything?"

"I like to shower in the evening," Philippe explains. "Beth doesn't like to shower at all."

"Whatever! I shower. Just not every single day."

"Well," he says with a smirk, "in this place it is pretty much one and the same."

"*Ass,*" Beth growls under her breath, but I know she's grinning.

We're packed into their company truck thirty minutes later. Sissy was exactly as I'd left her. I asked if we should move her somewhere else before leaving for the day and Philippe seemed to think this was a good idea. Even if Beth was all too happy to inform us we were both out of our damn minds.

"You can't even see it from the street! One of the neighborhood cats might rub on it or use the seat as a litter box. Big whoop."

He drives, Beth's popped a satellite dongle into her laptop to continue working in the passenger seat, and I straddle the two rear seats and watch the world through a windshield for the first time in months.

"Philippe, Beth tells me you're a logistician."

"That is correct, yes," he says politely.

"What does one do as a logistician?"

"Well..." He pauses a bit too long and Beth snorts. He looks genuinely surprised. "What?"

She just smirks and shakes her head.

"I'm responsible for procuring supplies. Medical components and so forth. Sometimes I do inventory, sometimes cost analysis," he tilts his head a little. "Pretty much everything unrelated to fieldwork or transportation."

"Except today," Beth corrects without looking up. "God*damn* this connection." She peeks out at the dense cloud cover.

"If that thing's anything like my GPS it's having trouble finding satellites," I explain.

"Yes, today excluded," Philippe continues and turns to look at me. "Normally Jon has the truck, but he was driving the other one last night."

"I'm surprised you guys even got home in that bucket," she jokes.

"It was rather a bit touch and go, admittedly."

"I meant to ask about him. Did he make it?"

"Unfortunately, no. He seized halfway."

A cell phone rings somewhere in the cluttered center console between them.

"Ack," Philippe fumbles for it in the mess. "I must have forgotten it here overnight."

"Well, well!" Beth giggles. "That might be your first time."

"It's Jon," he says, peering at the little screen. He answers and immediately yanks it from his ear.

"Yes, Jon. Okay. Stop yelling. It was in the truck. Okay, Jon, I unders— yes! Jon. Jon. Hold a moment, alright? I'm handing you to Beth."

Her face wrinkles up as she takes the phone. "I'm here, Jon."

She listens. She's quiet. She closes several emails on the laptop and opens a map in their place, but it's very slow to load, painfully so, and she tic-tic-picks at the edge of the keyboard with her chewed down thumbnail.

"Okay. I think I know where that is. How long did it take you? Got it. Is it pas— okay, right. Hang tight, we're on our way."

She hands the dead cell back and zooms into still-loading topography with rapid little taps. Neither of them speaks. Philippe takes a quick left and ups the pace.

"Careful near the gallery. There's always a million fucking people there."

"I know."

Even here, the collapsed remains of buildings line the streets. I didn't realize the quake had leveled structures this far south. Some buildings stand, inexplicably untouched, alongside massive piles of unlucky neighbors. In some places the buildup blocks most of the road and traffic's forced to pass single-file.

"What's going on?" I ask cautiously. They aren't panicked, but I sense it's not far off.

Philippe looks to Beth to explain but she's checked out, trying to plot a route on a map that refuses to load. She chews her thumbnail now.

"This fucking connection!"

"I thought you already had those maps saved locally."

"I *did*," she stresses through clenched teeth. "I thought I did." She glances up. "Not this left but the next one. Then right. That road just goes straight."

"I thought he sai—"

"No. It's that big cliff there. Past the hotel," she snaps.

Philippe follows her directions. He's nervous and gripping the wheel far too tightly.

"We don't know," Beth finally sighs over her shoulder. "He didn't say much, but it's probably too late."

"I think he was crying," Philippe says quietly. "It sounded like he was crying."

Beth exhales and closes the laptop. "I know."

The road Beth's navigated us onto ends at a berm a half mile up ahead. Several ATVs, just discernable at this distance, streak off the pavement and onto what must be some sort of trail beyond the road's end. They fly over the shallow dune single file, each one kicking up huge blooms of wet earth and steam before vanishing altogether.

"That's not good," Beth says flatly.

"What?"

"That would be the UN Police. They got those fancy new four wheelers to use during Carnav— well, what was *supposed* to be Carnaval. If they're here?" She sighs. "Follow them."

"Yeah," Philippe whispers.

It's a rough stretch, carved in by off-road vehicles like those ahead. I brace my knees against the seatbacks.

"Wider tracks. There. In the mud," I point ahead. "Another truck's been this way."

"Okay, good. Hold on."

The trail seesaws over uneven knolls that threaten to high center the long wheelbased truck. More than once, Philippe slows far too much and we roll back over muddy rises, bracing to repeat it over and over again. It must have rained recently. The deepest tracks are full of water.

"This can't go much farther," he growls in disbelief. "The coast must be right here!"

Beth rolls her window down to listen and a surprisingly chill wind whistles through the cabin.

"Yelling," Beth says. "We're close."

The trail dips and turns once more before ending in a bluff at the coastline. Light bars on numerous rescue vehicles splash useless yellow over the bleak sunless surroundings in weakly expanding streaks. Every door's been left open. Too many people stand at the cliff's edge.

"I don't see Jon," Beth mumbles, shucking her seatbelt with a force that cracks the metal tongue against the door.

"I don't see *anything*," I say.

"You won't. They're down the cliff."

"Who?"

She turns to look back at me.

"Greg, you should probably stay here."

"What? Why?"

"You might not want to see this."

"Can I at least help somehow? Can I do anything?"

"I don't think anyone can. I just don't know if you want to see this."

"See *what?*"

Beth leaps from her still opening door before Philippe's even brought the truck to a sliding stop in the muck.

"*Damnit!*" Philippe hisses under his breath. "She's going to get hurt!"

I scan the crowd for anything at all. Beth's already grabbed the elbow of someone who's yelling in her ear over the howl. She's nodding anxiously and looking over the edge. The passenger door suddenly slams shut.

"Come on. Come with me," Philippe snaps.

I hop out. Freak gusts whip our clothes and challenge balance. Philippe runs to the back of the truck and opens a utility box built into the quarter panel.

"Here!" he shouts, tossing me bundles of neatly coiled rope. "And these!"

He throws a wad of heavy gloves, but the wind sends them kiting high above us, five fingered gliders we'll never see again. He curses and runs to the crowd, slipping in the mud like everyone else. I'm underdressed for this. We all are. I rip my sandals off and chase barefoot after him.

Beth's pale and gasping for breath. She grabs Philippe's forearms and yells something before noticing me.

"GREG! *STOP!*"

"What?" I yell back. "Why?"

She runs past me without a word.

"Beth! It won't work!" Philippe screams through cupped hands. He looks ill. "*BETH!*"

I lean to the wind and push past him. Everyone's throwing life preservers and cushions and anything even remotely buoyant into the surf some seventy feet below. But it's pointless. It's all caught in the squall, every piece, and everything sails back far overhead.

I fight to stand. I'm knocked back by unpredictably violent geysers arcing twenty feet overhead, spiraling high and white to cascade down in cold heavy thwacks. The gale rips at the edge and I kneel for support, unready for the chaotic soup of grotesquely compromised shape and color in the rollicking white below. It is a hopeless and terrifying scene so utterly unexpected that comprehension outright fails, clearing slates for rushed and random guesswork that does little more than fall far short of the mark. The coils of rope are comically useless and fall from my hands.

It's only wood!

But it's not wood. The souls reaching up to me are not wood.

A lone chunk of fractured ship swings in the torrent, distinguishable only for the mast reaching bizarrely skyward to swirl and tip and somehow remain attached to some other unseen percentage of fractured ship. The mast whips down through board and bone to snap clean in half with a terrific *craaack!* Everything's splintering to fractions.

The few who've managed to grab hold of anything are unable to cling fast for long. They scramble and claw to string seconds together in their final minute. Some are simply frozen. But they all look to us with eyes shocked saucer large, eyes we ape in paralyzed agony.

They know.

We're helpless. Those not yet frozen continue to struggle, blind to lifeless bodies twisting and smashing past everything around them. Some bob at the perimeter of the nightmare wrapped in bright orange life vests while others cling to these luckier few. Far too many of them clutch children.

"Hey!" I yell and point, but another curl crashes and they too vanish, broken to the will of the sea.

I stumble back into Philippe. His face isn't right.

"What the hell is she doing?" I gasp.

"I don't know. I don't know." He's blank, unable to process or revolt.

Beth's leaned half-in, half-out of the truck. The wind slams the door into her legs, but she kicks it open time and time again.

I stumble and run to her.

"BETH!"

She's prying at the seats. She's trying to fit a crescent wrench to bolts that don't exist.

"Drive the truck closer! These will float!" she yells.

"Beth!"

"Drive the fucking truck, Greg!"

"Those seats won't come out like that! You'll never get them out!"

I grab her shoulders.

"Let me go!"

I wrap my arms around her and she flails. The door slams the backs of my thighs.

"Beth! *Stop!*"

She turns around and batters my chest with clenched fists. She shakes and struggles against me. She pulls an arm free to swing again and I pull her closer.

"Babies, Greg!"

"I know."

She buries her face in her hands and she cries. I hold her. I don't move. She sobs and shakes in the cold wind and I hold her.

"I don't want to go back. I can't go."

"I can't either. We don't have to."

"Don't go over there."

"I won't."

"Please."

"I'm staying right here."

"Okay."

I lean into the cab to block the wind.

"*I'm not here for this!*" she shrieks but I hold her.

"I know."

"I'm not!"

She is defiant and she is a doctor and she is helpless. Her heart breaks mine and I console her with empty whispers.

Philippe walks back to the truck with pocketed hands. He doesn't look at us. He stares at the ground below.

We drive in silence, the uneasy stillness punctuated only by the shrill squeegee of old wipers across the drying windshield. Jon and Virgil ride back with us and I'm introduced to them both along the way. Jon is young, probably in his early twenties, and incredibly lean. Virgil's older, bearded, with shades of salt peppered here and there. It's impossible to know much more about them under the circumstances.

The Box, I learn, is named simply for its shape; a laterally expanding semi-trailer built for office duty, expandable by merging it with other such cubes. Once inside, it looks like any other small office space. The epic lunch Beth described is here and waiting for us, but we don't partake. Few do.

Philippe's hidden himself behind a large monitor. Beth left an hour ago. I have no idea where she is. Virgil lounges on a little couch shoved up against the wall. It's brightly colored, adorned with cartoon flowers and little smiling suns. More like a child's bed than sofa.

The silence has followed us here.

A small TV in the corner flickers soundlessly as a local station revels in the coverage. We've learned it was a refugee ship, an apparently common thing in Haiti these past two months. Entire families in many of the rural communities are bundling up what little they still possess to board these flimsy vessels bound for larger municipalities. Some of them come here, to Jacmel. Some head to the capital. The hope is things are better in these larger cities. Migratory optimism.

This morning's disaster is difficult to even comprehend. These boats are about as seaworthy as chocolate canoes and often piloted by hapless, saltless short-strawers. But perhaps the most painful aspect of this morning's tragedy is their luck, or distinct lack thereof. The quick storm trapped them against the single stretch of rock along that coastline. The only one. Had they been a hundred yards out to sea, they would have skirted it. Had they been just a few yards closer to shore, they would have beached in harmless sand. It's astounding odds to have been right there, right then. Of the fifty plus aboard just three survived. There's been no mention of their conditions.

The video from the cliff is shaky and low-quality cell phone footage that's unfortunately clear enough to see it all unravel in sickening slow-motion. At first it doesn't even appear they're in imminent danger. The boat tips a bit in the quickening surf, knocking gently against the cliff to harmlessly retreat once more with the tide. But the surges intensify and repeat and the boat splinters. People leap.

Beth barges into the room and snaps it off. "Leave it," she scolds as she rushes back out. She's dealing with this in a way that works for her while the rest of us seem unable to. I want to follow her. Her purposeful stride is back.

"Well?" Virgil sighs. "You want the nickel tour?"

Virgil spends the next thirty minutes showing me their operation. He refers to these office quads as MCCs, or Mobile Command Centers. He tells me that their primary mission here is CEP, or Cholera Education and Prevention. They hope to reduce the number of cases by helping the Haitian people understand how to best expect, plan, and cope with the inevitable outbreak this coming spring. This, he states more than once with an extended, stubby digit, is the primary goal.

"We'll never eliminate it," he tells me, "but if we make a dent in the numbers, then it's mission accomplished. Anything else is absolutely secondary. *If* there's time. *If* we have spare resources to allocate. Only then will we take anything else into consideration. No exceptions."

He's a very professional man. He never deviates from his well-polished script. He uses acronyms with strong pronunciation before breaking each one down in granular detail.

I realize now why Beth asked me for a ride back to that village. She didn't call Virgil for approval, like she'd said. She fake dialed him for my sake. Helping that woman in the village was her idea. Something she did alone. Because she could. Because it was right to do.

When we finish the tour, I'm left with the sense that theirs is like any management-heavy operation and more a bureaucratic circle jerk than anything truly helpful.

"How often do you hold clinics or classes?" I ask.

"I don't follow your meaning," Virgil frowns and hitches up his slacks. He wears a broad leather belt, ill-fitting with age and failed diets from which not one but two phone holsters dangle.

"I mean, how are you educating people?"

"Well, we're working our MD-LS pretty heavy. Or Message-Delivery, Large-Scale. At the moment, we are visiting and meeting with the local health providers. That sort of thing. When we get them up to speed, we'll have a better conduit for the product to reach as many people as possible."

"The product?"

"The MD-LS."

"Hmmm."

"*Hmmm* what?" he snorts.

"Oh, sorry. Just thinking about your process."

"Look. It's the only avenue we have. Is it perfect? No. But did I say it was? Could we improve on it? Absolutely. Even if we did our job to 100% perfection. We can always improve."

A few years ago I would've simply nodded along with this sort of banal rhetoric. Not to agree. Just to get on with the rest of my day.

"Perfect is improvable?"

He plants his chunky hands on his hips. "Of course it is! Everything can *always* be improved! And let me tell you, I've been doing this a mighty long time. I just might know what I'm talking about. Beth told me a little about you, you know,

and if you think *you* can do a better job? Than all this?" He
waves his arm. "Then please. Be my guest. Show us how it's
done. At the end of the day, it's real simple, bud. We don't
know what we know until we know it."

"But..."

"But *what?*"

"But that would imply that you don't know very much at
all."

He scowls at me. "What she *failed* to tell me is that you're
quite the wiseass."

I close my eyes and sigh.

"Damnit, Beth. I told her not to forget that part."

"We're done here," he grunts and storms off, pulling one of
his two cells free.

Well, Virgil. PMFY. Pardon Me and Fuck You.

I spend the rest of the afternoon in the Box with Philippe. Beth
sneaks in from time to time, but I can't read her. Her jaw's
clenched and she moves at a pace that would've left me wasted
hours ago. Philippe's a little over-polite in his replies to her and
maybe a little smaller in his office chair whenever she's near.

"Come on," she pops her head through the doorway a little
after four o'clock. "Let's go."

"Well, I suppose that's fine," Philippe shrugs and switches
his monitor off. "It's enough on a day like today."

We find her and Jon waiting for us at the truck. She has an
elbow propped on the hood and palms her sagging chin for
support.

"Hey guys," Jon greets us.

"Is Virgil coming?" I ask as we hop in.

"I haven't seen him in a few hours," Jon shrugs. "But he stays
late most days so who knows."

"I heard," Beth turns slowly in the passenger seat to face me.
"I heard someone pissed him off."

"Shit. I'm sorr—"

"Puh-*lease!* Seriously," she sniffs. "I don't know what you said to him, but he was all sorts of red."

She smiles. "High five."

I don't leave her hanging.

"My work here is done!"

We all spare appropriately sized laughs. It's not much. But he's right. It's enough on a day like today.

"Mate, you might be drinking here alone this evening. Care to join us?"

Jon and Philippe tell us they're going out to eat as we pull up in front of the Lemon. I can't quite tell where Jon's from. He's a mix of Italian and something else I can't place. He eyes Beth as he speaks. I look at her, but she just shrugs.

"Nah," I say. "I've still got some bike stuff to take care of. Appreciate the offer though."

Beth and I hop out and watch them drive off under the broken glow of that scatterbrained street lamp. I sneak into the alley to check on the bike while Beth digs for her keys. The sun hasn't fully set, but it's already pitch black in the brick canyon. I lean down and plant a quick kiss on Sissy's mirror.

"Tomorrow," I whisper. "Tomorrow, we boogie."

I hustle back around the corner and right into Beth.

"Who ya' talking to back there?"

"Nobody."

"Were you," she curls a droopy finger. "Were you just talking to your motorcycle?"

Her tapping foot casts a long, bizarre shadow down the fractured sidewalk.

"What? People talk to their cats and dogs and birds and all sorts of stuff. People talk to plants for crying in the sink!"

"Okay. First? Cats and dogs are real."

"Sissy's real."

"I mean real as in *alive*, douche. Second? Crazy people talk to plants."

We head into the house which smells of another new meal. It's nothing if not pungent and I'm not entirely sure I like it.

"Calalou," Beth sniffs. "Ehh."

"Icky?"

"It's fine. It's like this spinach and lamb thing. Like a big messy stew. Looks like puke."

"Wow."

"It's good enough. I'm not cooking, so it's that or microwave pizza."

"I'll try it."

"Just don't look directly at it. I usually eat it after dark."

"Jesus, I bet the maid just loves you."

"What? She *adores* me."

"Well, you can wait if you want to, but I'm pretty hungry," I say. "Is that cool?"

"Sure. Knock yourself out."

"You're not going to join me?"

She sighs and chucks her big shoulder bag on the cozy chair. "Fine."

We dish up big bowls of the stuff. It does in fact resemble vomit, and we head to the relative dusk of the balcony. Our chairs are right where we left them last night, as are the empty coffee mugs and the forgotten bottle of rum.

"Oops," she shrugs dismissively.

We say very little as we devour the ugly, tasty goop. We lift mugs to the old men across the street who return the gesture a few more times than necessary.

"They're playful tonight," Beth muses. "They must be drinking."

They do seem a bit mischievous. Every fresh toast elicits waves of laughter from them. Our returned gestures become increasingly grandiose in kind as well, each of us bowing a little deeper with every encore. It's no mere coincidence that the flourishes coincide neatly with our own emptying bottle.

"So, why are *you* here?" I ask.

"I thought that was pretty obvious."

"No, I mean why are you here now? For so long? With kids and a husband back home waiting for you?"

"Yeah," she chuckles and rolls her eyes. "I get that a lot. Usually what people are really asking is 'what the fuck's wrong with you?'"

She peers at me in the dusk.

"We're not so different, hobo."

"Whatever. You're actually helping people here."

"*Please!* You saw what our daily routine is like. Oh!" she perks. "That reminds me. What in the hell did you say to Virg today?!"

"Nothing!"

"Spill it."

"I mean it! I just asked a few questions."

"Well, what did you ask him?"

"Christ, I don't even remember now. I admit I was a little surprised he got so hot. But, c'mon. Let's be fair here. It was a pretty shitty day for everyone."

She looks like she doesn't really believe me.

"Look. Alls I know is the man gots *two* phone holsters on that belt." I hold both palms up in mock surrender.

"He wears 'em like guns!" she laughs. "He's not a bad guy. He means well. He's just from a different school of thought than most of us. He's not in the trenches."

"Yeah, that's tough for anyone. Like this morning. He probably knew he was way out of his element at that cliff. What's he gonna' do? Manage things? Hell, what could anyone do? I still can't fucking believe that happened. I mean, at one point I saw thi—"

"Stop. Just stop. I don't want to talk about it."

"What? I was just saying that I could actually see—"

"What the hell *happened* to you?" she snaps.

I look at her and wait until she does the same.

"What is that supposed to mean?"

"I mean what terrible tragic thing happened that fucked you up so badly? I think there's more to it. I think something bad happened a few years ago and you can't or won't admit whatever it is. Normal people don't just walk away from that kind of life."

I don't respond right away and listen to the hammering thrash of the city.

"I realized I was far more interested in the expansion of concentric rings than the geometry of perfect circles."

"Huh?"

"I also became somewhat fascinated with time. In really weird ways. Like, in the middle of the night I'd wonder what I'd been doing at that precise second, say, three years earlier. And sometimes I could even verify it. You know? I'd look up old emails or texts or whatnot and sometimes it would actually *be* right to that exact minute. So I'd sit there and contrast present thoughts and ideals to way back then. And then, for whatever reason, it always seemed to be that exact moment from there on out. I'd wake up and look at the clock and...yup! It'd be that exact time. To the minute. But then I started to really freak out about time as this generally accepted mental construct. Think about it. We split days into hours, hours into minutes, minutes into seconds. Right? But you can continue to split it further, on and on. It's not an absolute measurement. It never will be. You can't have zero time, so you can reduce, split, halve it, for...what? Forever? That freaked me out. Watch the clock and *you* unwind? Ever wonder why they call it a wristwatch?"

I wait for a response she seems unable to muster.

"So I had to stop thinking about time pretty much altogether. But then really strange things began to happen. Well, not really strange things. Perfectly ordinary things that I began having really strange reactions to. For instance, I would read about some abstract scientific fact somewhere and see it come up in my daily life over and over again in the days and weeks to come. And not because I'd just read about it. I mean coming up for the first time ever. Stuff I had only just learned even *existed*. It was suddenly all around me. Like some part of me had invented it. Or I'd hear about some old band and without fail, songs I'd not heard in years, their songs, would pop up in the grocery store. Or an article or interview with them would show up in some magazine in some random place I'd never even been before, like an airport in some city I'd never even been to before that point. It was like this really creepy sense of déjà vu that had me wondering if I was even alive. Wondering if I even existed at all. Like I'd caught the ol' great and powerful drunk behind the curtain."

She looks utterly stupefied. I think. It's really dark.

"Yeah, yeah. I know. You know that saying 'He's cracked'? Gone crazy and cracked? Do you know why they say that?"

"I have a funny feeling you're about to tell me."

"You run out of sandbags and the whole wide world leaks in."

"Greg, I'm trying to be serious here."

I match her little half-shrug in the dark. She's waiting for the same thing every other sane person wants to hear.

Fine.

"I gave up."

"What do you mean?"

"I mean I gave a lot of thought to things like properly sized tarps, barrel length, an—"

"What the *hell* are you talking about?"

"—*and* case, primer, powder charge, wad and shot. All the instrumental bits in scattering those trickier memories against the wall."

She freezes. She's expecting the filtered version.

"Look, when I left the working world I began to regress. In a good way, I mean. Into someone I used to be. I started *thinking* about things again. I started caring about things I'd forgotten about. Like in your late teen years, when the world is just opening up. When it's all new and interesting? For some people that lasts. They find some arcane way to carry it through. But I think most of us lose that. We start working day in and day out and it's really hard to balance those two. Some careers, sure, maybe it works out. But mos—"

"Just wait a goddamn second. You wanted to fucking kill yourself?"

"Not directly. It was always more of a passive thing. I—"

"With a little girl depending on you?!"

"I just stopped caring if I ever woke up," I stress. "And yes, please. Underscore the obvious. She never crossed my mind, Beth."

I'm really not drunk enough to be this sarcastic.

"Goddamnit. I was so right about you."

"I tried new things! Believe it or not, I'm sitting right here? Aren't I? Just because I felt that way doesn't mean I actually did it! I tried to toe the line. I tried the whole 'Now what do I want to be when I grow up?' thing."

"Fine. Tell me. What things."

"I tried a few things."

"Such as?"

"There were a few things that didn't really wor—"

"Such. *As?*"

"More rum?" I ask, topping her up before she can decline.

"Wait. Wait. Let me guess. You quit those, too."

"Yup."

"What was it? Dental school?"

"YES!" I mock.

"Ass. What else?"

"It doesn't matter."

"You said a few things. Why can't you talk about it? What does it matte—"

"I asked my old partners if they'd take me back."

"Oh my," she whistles. "And how did that go?"

I roll my head and fix her with a lazy gaze.

"It. Went. *Great.*"

"I bet. What'd they say?"

"They said no. Kind of."

"They said maybe?"

"No. They just ignored me. I felt like the fat kid asking the cutest girl in school to prom. Only she was far too nice to say no. I think that's when I really started to crash. Not because they said no. They didn't. They did what the cutest girl does. They did the merciful thing. They didn't say a word."

"Geez," she says quietly. "Listen, I'm trying to understand and all. Really, I am. But I still don't understand how you could walk away from all that in the first place."

"I had to pull my own rug out from underneath me to do so. I just didn't know that was happening for a few yea—"

"No, I don't mean *how.* Why? Why did you just walk away from all that money?"

"Christ, Beth. That's a helluva' thing to say."

"You want honest, right? I don't get a real big 'Please lie to me' vibe off you. What I'm trying to say here is that most people work their whole lives for half of what you probably had."

"I think I'm missing your point."

"My *point* is you can be a good dad and still work. Plenty of guys do it. My husband isn't the best dad either, but he's doing it! What I'm saying here is that most people would never even consider walking away from that kind of life in the first place. That's like ripping up a winning lottery ticket. Am I way off here?"

She's not, but it's the 'either' that really stings.

"Beth, money wasn't all that important to me. I really don't give a shit what most people do. It wasn't why I started making games."

"But you guys made a ton of money, didn't you?"

"Sure, but that was never my goal."

"Right. Because most kids say 'When I grow up, I wanna' be poor.'"

"Listen, I really don't like thinking about money! Okay? In a fucked up way of looking at things, the only way I could ignore money was to make far more than I needed. I've never liked budgeting or balancing or saving or any of that crap. I just wanted to be happy. Satisfied. That's all. And when we started making big money? That all changed! It all got really blurry for me. It became this, this big paper chase. Nobody tells you that shit happens! Everyone's more than happy to tell you to run towards it your whole fucking life, but they never tell you what it costs. And when my little girl was born? It all changed again. I just wanted to be a dad."

It felt like she knew me! Why the interrogation now?

"I wanted to be a little more concerned with real values. Human values. You know?"

"No, I guess I don't."

"Okay, look. All of my future goals and all my happy thoughts, all of that stuff was line of credited against these big royalty checks that didn't even *exist* yet. Cash band-aids, we used to call them."

"I—" she tries.

"Nearly imperceptibly I became someone I'd always feared. It took years. And I mean real, full-length other-awesome-happy-shit-is-happening-at-the-same-exact-fucking-time years, so there weren't any clear warning signs for me to miss. No hints. No fucking rat dreams when they might've actually mattered. In fact, I ended up doing some really bad things that should've snapped the trance, but even that shit didn't do it. I was like any old fucked-up soda machine at every fast-food place out there. It takes a really long time for them to go bad. Years. Imagine tasting Cherry Pepsi one day when all you wanted was water."

She stares at her lap.

"*This is water?*" I plead a little too loudly, feigning an upheld imaginary cup of unwanted carbonation. She's silent. Which is more than fair considering there's nothing very useful to say to philosophical drunks.

She's about had it. I can't see her, but I really don't need to. "Let's...okay. Let me ask you this," she begins.

"Sure."

"You got there. You got to be what you always wanted to be. Dream come true. *Blah, blah, blah.* Was it the life you always wanted? Before Maggie?"

Variations of a dream, striations on the theme...

"Yes and no. I guess I'm lucky I even got to wonder at the tippy-top of my mountain if the climb was worth it."

"You're lucky you even *had* a mountain. Look around!" she snorts.

I turn and lie sideways in the chair to see her better. That twinge flutters, oddly warm and suffocating. I'm drowning here just a few feet from her. I know she sees it. I lie there silent and mildly terrified of this erstwhile emotion scavenging the empty air between us.

"So, a tangent. *Again,*" she scolds.

"But you asked!"

My mouth is numb.

"C'mon. So?"

"So I talked to them about coming back and nothing happened. Radio silence. And I crashed. The end."

"In other words, you gave up on purpose."

"No. But not grabbing a ledge on the way down might as well be the same thing."

"C'mon."

"What?"

"All of these things you're talking about? Those are first-world *dreams,* Greg!"

"Oh, trust me. I know. I hated myself. How could I feel anything *but* fortunate? I think it was the timing of it all. It's a tough spot for any dad. For any husband. You're expected to make everything okay. To provide, right? Forever and ever. And up to that point I had that shit pretty much covered, but when the fire academy gig didn't work out and the movie thing unraveled? It all just hit so fast. Then those guys ignoring me? Don't get me wrong. I'm glad they did what they did. I wasn't in my right mind. They just knew it before I did. I don't know. I think the timing of it all just really stung. This all happened in the span of one month. It was too much. I never really came up for air after that."

"Fire academy?"

"I was too old to apply after graduation."

"Movie thing?"

"Doesn't matter."

"Do you have some aversion to anything, I don't know, *normal?*"

"Apparently so."

"Do you feel better now?"

"What, do I feel better here?"

"Sure."

"I do. I'm not sure what I'm doing here yet. I'm not sure how I can be truly useful, but I've felt better since I got here. Since I met you."

She looks down at her lap again. She's doing that a lot tonight. Like she's got a crib sheet buried there in the blankets on how to best deal with overemotional fuckups.

"When's the last time you talked to Janet?" she asks quietly.

"You already asked me that. Not since I left," I groan. "Months."

"I really think you should call her."

"I wouldn't even know what to say."

"Seriously? How about 'Hi. Sorry it's been so long. How's my daughter?'"

She's upset. I'm getting there. I drink.

"I think that's a littl—"

"What, you think it's a little rude of me? After this morning? After watching those kids drown, Greg? How can you not want to call her?"

"I—"

"All I wanted to do was run home to my babies," her voice is mostly controlled.

"I know."

"Do you?"

"Yes, Beth. I do. I realize I'm not going to win any father of the year awards, so, yes. Hooray for me. Hooray for the loser who's abandoned his little girl and ripped up his fucking lottery ticket."

"I'm not saying what you think I'm saying. I bet you're a good dad."

"Good dads don't abandon their kids."

"That's not fair."

"Fuck it ain't! It's what happened!"

"But you said she was leaving you!"

I drink more.

"It was going to happen anyhow, right?"

"But there's no difference to Maggie! Any defense here is academic and manipulative! How many dads get custody? Even joint custody?"

Her feet twitch madly under the comforter.

"Plenty. Plenty do. I told you last night that I might have done the same damn thing. Maybe I'm wrong, but you didn't want a big fucking battle so you made it easier for them. Maybe not emotionally, but how does a big custody battle help anyone?"

"I appreciate you saying that, but you really don't have to."

"I'm not trying to make you feel better, Greg! That's not me! I don't do that. I'm actually *thinking* about things here."

"Whilst all rummed up," I interject.

"Whatever. Seriously, would I have done it any differently? I really don't know. Christ, some people say I'm already doing that right now. The only ace up my sleeve back then was how fucked up my ex-husband was. I've seen friends go through it. It's messy. Always. And custody battles are just fucking ugly. I honestly don't think any kid survives that fully intact. Yeah, so they grow older and life goes on. But some part of them vacates. Something gets robbed."

She takes a deep breath.

"It *never* comes back," she looks over, somewhat apologetically. She fidgets with her mug. Her feet vibrate at the edge of the chair.

"I care about what she thinks, Beth. I do. I wrote her a letter before I left. In case things went badly here or whatever."

"Her who?"

"Maggie."

"And you sent that to a five-year old. Really."

"No. I gave it to a friend. He's gonna' hang onto it."

"For how long?

"Until I get back. Then I'll collect it in person."

"And how long do you think that will be?"

"I don't know."

"And what if you don't?"

"That's why I wrote it."

"You're fucking weird."

"What?"

"That's really weird. Like some melodramatic message in a bottle bullshit."

"I suppose I shouldn't have explained a few things? Why I came here, or what happened back there?"

She glares.

"Yeah, yeah. I know. I shouldn't have to explain things I shouldn't have even done in the first fucking place. I know. *Thanks.*"

She stands up quickly and marches inside.

"You need to call Janet," she yells as she walks downstairs. "And you should be in Port-au-Prince. You can actually help somebody there."

She hasn't just broken some silly unspoken pinky promise. She's broken the damn thing off.

The old men are still sitting there on their balcony. They see me here alone and raise one more toast. I return the gesture with my mug, wondering what they've heard. I polish off my rum and close my eyes. That stupid light down the street buzzes on and off every thirty seconds. Midnight swings in and everything's far too loud again. Beth returns and throws herself back in the chair.

"You okay?" I ask cautiously.

"What if you had OCD, and the world ended? I mean like full-on Apocalypse ended. And you have OCD. Really bad OCD."

"You confessing something here?"

"Shit, you've seen my apartment. Seriously. Think about it for a second. How long would you last? You can't wash your hands fifty times a day when you're rationing drinking water. Hell, you couldn't wash your hands at *all.*"

"Did you already take your Ambien?"

She glares.

A horrible screeching erupts from her little nest. She rolls her eyes, slides her finger across the cell she digs out, and tosses it back in the heap of blankets.

"What the hell was that?"

"My husband."

"Do you need to call him back?"

"Nope. We've talked three times today. I think he's just keeping tabs on me. Do you miss home?"

"Sure. Sometimes. I mean, some things. But when I think of home back there though, I dunno. It feels flat and empty, like there's real elevation here. Do you?"

"Of course I do. My babies are there. The hubby. It's what I dream of every single night."

There's more but she lets it evaporate.

"I didn't mean what you're thinking," she offers softly.

"Yeah, you did. It's fine. What I feel is a different matter."

"And what that might be?"

"It's of no consequence."

"Sure it is."

"How can it be?"

She starts a few times before finally getting it out.

"I don't believe that. And I don't think you believe it, either."

"But you can't prove that, can you?"

"Hmmm."

"Yeah, *hmmmm.*"

"You leave tomorrow then?"

"I do."

"I really wish you'd listen to me, Greg. You're not going to find anything out there. You need to be in Port-au-Prince."

I groan.

"Just listen to me! Alright? That guy who came through here buying everything up, Benjamin something? He was doing all the talking. You should find him. I mean it. You'll have a shitload of motorcycles and cars and all sorts of stuff to work on."

"Don't you think they probably have people already doing that?"

"Ha!" she grunts. "You didn't spend much time up there, did you?"

"No, not really."

"Trust me. I bet they brought back more crap than they know what to do with. Even if they do have people, you can still help. But out here? Out west? You'll just be that douchebag-hobo tourist I lost money on. Trust me."

"I used to trust people, I'll have you know. Repeatedly. What did you mean 'tabs'?"

"Huh?"

"You said 'keeping tabs on me' or whatever."

"I might've mentioned you. Greg, look at me. I know what I'm talking about."

"Okay."

"Don't sound so surprised. I *am* pretty awesome, you know."

"Is that a fact."

She's quiet and rocking in her stationary chair again.

"You know I'm just kidding."

"Oh, I know you're not awesome."

"Ass."

We trade awkward goodnights before she heads downstairs. I pull out my laptop and open the ongoing letter to Logan. It's been several days since I've written anything.

```
And so, a metric fuckload has transpired in the
last...Christ, it's only been 48 hours??    I
refuse to believe that.  I'm in Jacmel. I made
it  here.    And  this  morning  I  witnessed
something I will refrain from even attempting
to describe. If it's on the news there, you'll
know.  Oh, and I met a girl and fell in love.

What the holy hell am I on about?    I'm glad
you're intrigued!   Because I, good sir, find
myself in rusty territory.   I don't know what's
going  on  precisely,  but  I  must  admit  the
seemingly improbable, if not impossible: I am
in  the  courtship  throes  of  love.    Or  not.
Perhaps it's merely a crush.  Or whatever that
```

puppy love shit actually is. But one thing's
clear. I'm unable to describe how I feel in a
way that would eliminate all doubt from your
mind as to its authenticity. I feel like I
know her. Like I always have. There's
something in our connection that feels natural,
like we weren't just cut from the same swatch
of odd cloth, but with the same fucked-up pair
of shears. Perhaps most amazing of all? It
feels like she knows -me-. Whatever this
mystery 'malady' is, it has rendered me alive
beyond belief.

Which means I'm utterly and completely doomed.
Ugggh. I leave in the morning for parts
unknown. I should be excited, but I'm not. At
all. I'm staying with her and her roommate,
Philippe. They're part of a cholera
awareness/prevention team here teaching the
locals how best to prevent, or at least
curtail, widespread outbreaks. It's a noble
mission, and a tricky one to pull off in the
way they want to. Still, in the short time
I've been with them I've seen them help two
different people, both cholera-free. In other
words, they're not just sitting around glued to
keyboards. They are doing Good Things here. I
met them in the mountains a few days ago, and
Beth, the 'her' of whom I speak, sent the rest
of the team back to Jacmel when she saw the
bike. We took Sissy up to this tiny village so
she could do her doctorly duties. Yes, she
rode with me. It's a primal, manly feeling and
don't pretend you're not jealous just 'cause
Shelly rides her own bike and all.

So, yeah. It's been quite a whirlwind. I'm
admittedly having trouble keeping my feet on
the ground with this newfound lease on things.
She's triggered something. Maybe she's
verified a pulse. She's a good doctor like
that.

That shit this morning, though. Goddamn. I
realize I said I wouldn't discuss it, but it's
painted on the backs of my eyelids. I mean,
the dumb luck to hit -that- cliff at -that-
point in a storm. The fact that such a storm
even HIT this time of year! It's absurd. It's
unbecoming of any atheist to go imagining some
savage deity playing with His toys in the
bathtub, but that's exactly what it looked like
to me. I'll certainly have very bad dreams for
a very long time. Hopefully I can surf the
shock of it a little while longer. Because
it's all about my needs, don't you know. I
think it picked at scabs that aren't healing
very well. I miss Maggie something terrible.
Beth just might have something to do with that,
too. And yes, there's a problem. Or four.
She's married. With kids. Just a minor speed
bump. Sigh. I'm not sure if most hearts
operate in such a selfish and infantile manner,
but right now mine's saying: 'It ain't like
this happens everyday, bub!' Apparently my
heart is a scruffy looking bum. Come to think
of it...

Too much here today. Time to call it. Gotta'
pack up in the morning and find the emotional
fortitude to somehow wheel away.

"Move."

It's dark. I don't know where I am. I twist around,
disoriented, looking for anything to anchor me. There. The
balcony doors. Okay. Okay.

"Move over."

Her blurry silhouette hovers in the dark. She's wrapped up in
a comforter. I think. I can't see much. I scoot backwards,
trying to unsheet my tangled feet.

"It's not what you think," she says, dropping the comforter to
the floor and quickly slipping into bed next to me.

I remain frozen at the far edge.

"Everything okay?" I whisper.

"No."

I place my hand on her shoulder and squeeze reassuringly. She grabs my wrist and wraps it around her, folding her body neatly into mine. Something warm trickles over my fingers.

"I miss my babies."

"I know," I whisper.

I hold her close. I stroke her hair. She sobs and I hold her close. For a few hours, we sleep like this. Dreamless. But together.

My cell vibrates and skitters across the thin wood floor. She's not here. I lie back awhile and wonder if I've experienced my first epic Ambien hallucination.

"Owid yuseeep?"

She tiptoes around the corner, not so much brushing her teeth as scraping them with outmatched bristles.

"Huh?"

She says it slower, no clearer for trying.

"....*huh?*"

She gives up and shakes her head, casting billows of long black hair over her shoulder when she spins. I wish desperately for a much larger bedroom as she pads back into the bathroom.

"You just gonna' sleep all morning?" she calls out from the bathroom.

"Maybe."

"Cold dreams again? You were moaning all night."

"Nope. Just comfy. Like I was weightless."

"I tend to have that effect on men," she kids, walking back and dressed now, to my dismay.

"You sure you have to leave for work? I actually wouldn't mind a bit more sleep."

"Hey, do whatever you want. You'll have to lock up and bring the key by before you leave. You still going west?"

I don't reply.

"Jesus. You are, aren't you?"

"I think so."

"Well, don't call me up in a few days just to tell me I was right."

"But see, now you've piqued my curiosity. That's the problem. How can I not go and see for myself?"

She's truly frustrated by this rationale. She sits down hard on the corner of the bed to tie her shoes. I try to sit up, but I'm incredibly sore. I struggle to budge at all.

"Wait a second. You don't want me to leave."

"That's *not* it," she snaps.

"I don't believe you."

"Greg—" her eyes swing to mine. She wants to say something, maybe yell it, but she just exhales and blows the hair from her face.

"You're an absolute mess." She hops up to check the balcony for anything we've left out.

"Did he come back?" I ask. "I didn't hear anything."

"Yeah, he was home before I came up last night," she says, clicking the balcony door shut behind her. The morning sun cuts ribbons through the glass that burn up the white walls.

"So, is this, like…" I trail off. "Will he be *weird* about this?"

"Why? We didn't do anything."

"No, but you know. It looks like—"

"Whatever. He saw me in the chair when he staggered in. You worry too much."

"I worry precisely the right amount, thank you very much."

We rush through a quick breakfast. Philippe shuffles down the steps eventually, looking absolutely deathly.

"Florita?" Beth asks through hasty bites the moment she sees him.

"No," he says gently. "Jon's friend. You know. What's-her-name."

"Ayida? *Seriously?*"

Philippe nods gingerly, like his head's about to fall off.

"You do realize that woman is out of her shitting mind."

"I do now, yes, thank you," he offers meekly.

"You knew that last month! What did you guys do?"

"We drank."

"What? Embalming fluid?"

"Absinthe," he whispers.

She scowls like a tsk'ing mother.

"Really, Mr. Heavyweight? For you that might as well be the same goddamn thing."

She's genuinely mothering him. But he just stands there and this alone appears to drain him before our very eyes.

"Tell me you realize that."

"I do now, yes."

He eases onto the blue stool next to me and lays his cheek on the cool counter.

"How many?" I ask softly.

"Several."

"One," I hold up a single finger. "Two, with patience."

He groans and switches cheeks.

"She cuts them with gin."

"What? Instead of water?"

"Yes."

"Wow. Then Beth's totally right. That woman is directly out of her shitting mind."

We finish our scrambled eggs and toast while Philippe sips cautiously at water. He informs us that he's decided to stay home and tells Beth he'll call in around noon for a ride.

"Fat chance, pal," Beth scolds. "You're gonna have to take a cab like the rest of us."

He heads for the stairs, towards the comfort of his bed, scaling each step one at a time with both feet. Left. Right. Stop. Left. Right. Groan. He makes it halfway up before turning back.

"It was a pleasure to meet you, Greg. I'm sorry that I am unable to see you off under the current circumstances," he says very politely over the course of what must be one whole minute.

"Current fucking circumstances? Go to sleep. I'll bring dinner home tonight."

He peers at her, uncomprehending.

"It's Sunday. *Hello?*"

He closes his eyes and continues the labored climb back to his sarcophagus.

"He rarely drinks," Beth says in a low voice. "And even then, he's a quick ninny."

"That could have gone bad," I whistle.

"It *did* go bad!"

She helps me with my stuff and carries one of the heavy sidecases out to Sissy. I snap them in place, lock the lids, and walk the bike from the alley.

"That seems like such a hassle," she says eyeing the riding gear I've piled on the sidewalk. "All this stuff."

"It's not so bad once you get used to it."

"Yeah, but still. Why not just drive a car?"

My shoulders droop.

"Okay, okay," she mutters apologetically, scuffing at the curb with one shoe.

I should check the tire pressures and give the bike a once over. But I don't. My heart isn't into leaving at all and the enormity of it is finally settling in. Everything's slow motion in her gravity. The white pickup turns the corner and hustles closer.

"Come here," she sighs.

She wraps her arms around me and tip-toes up to rest her forehead against my lips.

"You have my number. Call if you need to."

"What if I want to?"

"I guess you can do that, too."

I kiss the top of her head.

"*Don't,*" she whispers. "Please."

The truck is already idling behind us.

She inhales deeply. "Ride's here. Be safe, okay?"

"Okay."

She steps around me, refusing to meet my gaze. She hops in the back seat. Virgil's up front, staring stoically ahead and also refusing to meet my gaze, though for vastly different reasons. Jon's driving, likely worse for last night's wear as well but apparently functional.

Look at me. Please. I'm still here.

She doesn't. She looks straight down. At her phone. At her laptop. At crib sheets. Something. But she doesn't look at me. She doesn't look back when the truck pulls away and drives under that broken street lamp, gone still and quiet in the daylight gloom.

The ride out of town proves a bit of a puzzle. She'd warned me over breakfast it would be a bit tricky. It is. Two-way roads suddenly aren't anymore and if you don't branch off before it happens, you spawn up a downstream. I make this mistake more than once.

Jacmel is far busier than its size would seem to indicate. Some of the intricate and often horrifying masks crafted for that aborted Carnaval rest on balconies and up against walls here and there. I try to imagine that sad week in these narrow streets. It really must have been an astonishing thing in person. Beth said they gave up trying to leave the apartment after the first day and just watched the somber parades from the balcony.

Pictures!

She'd offered to show me pictures, but we never got around to it. My childish heart rallies at the realization and kicks up a million instant reasons to return right now, ferociously negotiating in a completely unfair assault to re-route the day or the week or maybe even the rest of my life.

I'm more or less prepared for the river just west of town. Nothing seemed to indicate, including Beth, that it would be all that exciting and when I reach it I have to laugh at the reality. Everyone here calls it a river, though it hasn't been one for some time. It's a wide riverbed with a trickle of its former self snaking the center. Still, she'd said, the water is often fast-moving and tricky to navigate for nothing other than its complete and utter opaqueness. It resembles milky tea and gauging either current or depth is simply impossible.

I arrive at the back of a short queue lined up and waiting to cross. Each approach is a little different. Some drivers simply head straight across. Others are more guarded and hustle upstream a little to offset a southerly drift they appear to anticipate. But no one approach works better than another as everyone makes it safely across, whooping and hollering to celebrate at the far side.

Watching this reminds me a curious trend I'd noticed at Maggie's elementary school last year. Younger children aren't allowed to walk home after school these days like I did at her age. Someone designated must collect them when the final bell rings each day and there were two ways to do this at her school; you either drove up and waited in a carpool lane, or you walked.

This alone wasn't interesting. What was, however, was the binary cut of the decision. When someone committed to doing it one way, that was it. It never changed. You were a 'driver' or a 'walker'. Day after day, year after year.

It made me wonder if it was possible to reach accurate or consistent conclusions about those who chose one option over the other. Was this mundane facet of everyday life a social knife? Would I discover shared opinions with those who drove versus those of us who'd always walked? I lived less than a mile from the school, so for me it was actually just easier to walk, never mind that my hyperactive sense of mechanical sympathy outright prevented the mere consideration of such a short drive. Sure, I'd drive and park down the street if I'd gone out for lunch beforehand, but even on those days I never used the car-pool lane which often stretched circuitously out and back down a side street, sometimes forty vehicles long. I'd study them as I walked up, wondering how they managed to sit there locked up for the better part of an hour every single day. Was it worth it? The time sink? The abuse to the vehicle? What about the mood-altering nature of such a thing? Hell, what about the idling emissions emitted at this and every other school operating this way around the country? Did they think about these things while sitting there three hundred hours a year?

It was a silly thing to dwell on, but a dividing line I couldn't ignore. What else could be drawn from this simple observation? Were drivers more prone to vote one way or another? What about the walker's religious beliefs? Was one group happier? Did we share favorite colors? Music? Books?

The observation was simple and clearly right there for anyone at all to ponder, but it was the *expansion* of the equation that really intrigued me. It was a sort of bread-crumb trail. Fresh batteries in the old flashlight. I was looking at the world in a very different way. I was fascinated with things like this, things I'd never noticed before. Patterns that may or may not have meant anything, but patterns I was suddenly noticing. Patterns I was taking stock of. I was waking up again. Perhaps it connected things. Perhaps it was the fine-tuning of some broader understanding. Maybe it was possible, I thought, to collect bread crumbs right to the very core of me.

I wasn't anticipating some major discovery. I was just thrilled to be thinking in fresh ways again. I'd worked in a very creative and high pressure environment for years. It'd been the perfect place for someone like me, but even that became routine. Somewhere along the way, grooves became ruts. I'd stopped thinking beyond the scope of a project and the work became my solitary focus. I simply didn't think about anything else.

But the after-school observations reset something in me and I feared that going back to the work-a-day environment would snuff it out. Not because it had to, or because I'd no longer want to broaden the equation, but anything routine has a sneaky way of stealing our oxygen. Our focus narrows in, day after day, and we stop lifting our heads for a look around. We stop thinking beyond our boxes and the hours left in them. Even the most exciting, dangerous, and unpredictable jobs in life end up routine. Formula 1 drivers get bored. Astronauts daydream.

It's my turn to cross. I paid close attention to where the waterline rose on the cars ahead, indexing them by scale. Small economy cars with perhaps fourteen or fifteen-inch wheels had submerged all four tires just shy of the top shoulder. The pickups, also small, were about the same. Only the lone cargo truck with its makeshift flatbed gave me any comparative delta to work with.

I slip the clutch and ease into the murk. Right away, I'm moving too slowly for the pace of a slight and hidden current. The bike sways quickly left with it, but with a bit more throttle I manage a balance that scoots me safely across. It's only when the tires are drying half a mile down the road that I remember to whoop and holler.

The morning passes. And while the road and bike are pleasant enough, it's a very different story inside. The momentary distraction of escaping Jacmel is gone and no longer protects me from the emotional storm I've been dreading all morning. It's palpable, an actual physical ache in my chest that only grows more painful with each passing tick. Minutes crash together, every single one another missed opportunity. There isn't a single moment where my focus is complete, where I trust my faculties. Part of me wishes I'd dropped the bike in the river.

The road is twisty and entertaining in spots. But where I'd normally fetch a lower gear to blast past slower cars, I just fall into formation and try to ignore the dust and exhaust cascading over me in waves. I should care. I know. She's probably right, after all. I don't have to head this way.

Why can't I help out there? In Jacmel?

My mind races with the possibility and I find myself gradually reinventing her reality. I imagine for a moment that she feels the same way. I tell myself this doesn't happen very often.

Certainly the passing of miles will help.

I try bartering with it, assuring the last shreds of optimism that we'll find new surrogacy in fresh terrain. But it doesn't work. I know it won't be okay on some other coast. The sticky tendrils of it all refuse to release their grasp around what little logic remains. They're pulling me back there. Back to her. I glance at the clock. It's been seven minutes since the river.

I look for a place to stop.

It's barely noon. I've covered less than twenty miles, a pathetic travel day by any measure. I'm near nothing. I slow and let a parade of frustrated drivers pass by. I want to hit the killswitch. A mile passes. I watch trucks approach in the mirrors and I trace the road's edge to allow them by. Some go around with a wave. Some of them wait until the last possible second to merge over and it's these drivers I hear laughing through glassless windows.

A trail of white-washed rock branches steeply up and away from the road.

It might be another driveway. I don't care. It's away.

I arc in and both tires immediately sink in the quagmire stone. After a slow climb, the path curves left, then right again before I spy the slightest hint of an ill-cambered shoulder. I pull in and clumsily walk the bike back and forth until I'm facing out the way I came. I can see the main road from here. A short distance out, the sea stretches endlessly away. I had no idea I'd been so close to it. I couldn't see it behind the growth along the road. Hell, I hadn't even smelled it.

I heel the stand down, slip from the saddle, and sit on the ground. I peel my gloves off. I remove my helmet and pluck the earbuds free. They dangle from my fingertips, synchronized for a moment as they swing side by side in the gentle breeze before shifting gradually out of phase.

The last few days were good. There's still thread here, with enough fight in the fiber to stay together. But it's already starting to fray. I wish I'd thought to bring some of the rum.

I unzip my jacket pocket and remove my phone. Part of me is convinced I have no choice but to say it. Full disclosure. But I also want to just hurl the fucker out to sea.

Come on. Fish or cut bait.

I cave, write it out, and immediately hate it. I do this many times. I start to wonder if I'm even capable.

Every mile I ride is a thousand revolutionary mistakes. I miss you. I'm thinking about coming back.
Sent: 12:21PM

I start to delete it.

Fuck it.

SEND

I give in and look through the various emails and texts from the past week. I listen to a missed call from an old friend telling me he was in Dallas for a few days, then a follow-up voicemail and text telling me he was there four days ago.

The phone buzzes in my hand.

busy. will txt in few. not ignoring u.
Received: 12:29PM

I keep checking the phone. Ten minutes go by. Twenty. I try to maintain a rational perspective, but the ability slips away like the tide.

In few. I'd assumed minutes.

Did she mean hours? Days?

I put my face on my forearms. This is ridiculous.

Sparse traffic passes down below, most of it Jacmel bound. There's nothing out west, she'd said. She's not out west.

Is that what she meant?

My heart's taken full control of the situation and seeks no further approval from the computer upstairs.

A husband! And kids!

These are what other people refer to as important details, but somehow they're mere trinkets to my ticker. I know they matter, but I can't seem to make myself care.

And what of my trinkets?

Another smokescreen. This is absurd. Entirely absurd! And yet this chaos resonates with such fervor that every other doorway's been bricked in, patched over, and completely forgotten already.

How does that happen in two days?

There's a clacking on the road below. Just a faint report before the rickety contraption hobbles into view. I have nothing in my recollection to relate it to and several seconds pass before I even process the image. It's a cart built for beasts of burden obviously absent. It's loaded much too heavily for the man to be pulling it the way he is.

"What are you doing?" I whisper. "Where are you going?"

He seems perfectly capable, however, and pulls the thing at a slow and measured pace. The spindly wheels roll *clicklack-clicklack*, weathered wood over warm pavement.

His hat turns. He's looking at me. I should wave.

At least he has his hands full. I'm just a mess. Just like she said.

I lie back on the ground. I haven't removed my heavy riding jacket and I don't bother. I rest the cell phone on my chest and stack my gloves in the dirt for a pillow. I can see the phone this way, just out of focus on my chest, pulsing every so slightly with my heartbeat. There's a pathetic kind of parallel between the cold, plastic conduit beating in time with the conflicted one beneath.

Pitiful. That's what she'd say.

The sun is wildly displaced. My eyelids are hot. My legs tingle. I cover my face with my forearm and feel for the phone, but it isn't there. I lift my head and scan my chest with eyes that refuse to function. I slap the dirt at my sides. It's not here. I am beyond stiff. Something's wet.

I'm not alone. There's a man next to me in the dirt with his knees up and his arms draped over them. He stares out to sea like I had.

"It's here," he says in perfectly clear English. He rotates his wrist and there it is, gently grasped in his long fingers.

I struggle to sit up a little. My thighs are damp. I don't think he notices.

"It fell down. I held it for you," he says.

He doesn't sound Haitian.

"O— oh, okay," I stutter. "Thank you."

"My pleasure. I saw you from the road."

His voice is not what my brain expects. He's a muscle-packed man dressed in purple, yellow, and green. His shirt purposefully sleeveless, his shorts ending just past the knee. His sandals are well worn but well made, though the brimmed straw hat on his head appears just as ready to come apart as I am.

"I see you up here. I see you and I wonder if he is really fine," he speaks in a bright voice, like a teacher to children.

I must look perplexed.

"You fell down! One second you sit, then you don't! But when I find you? And you're fine? I think, yes, I understand. I too would nap here."

"You had the cart?"

"Yes! You see me?" he beams.

"I did. I asked you where you were going."

"Did you?"

"Yes."

His smile is astonishingly bright.

"Most people on this road? Much too rushed. But you seem very content up here. You not going anywhere?"

"I am. West."

"But?"

"I'm thinking about going back."

"You come from there?" he points east.

"I did."

"You forgot something?" he asks.

"I think so."

"You don't know?"

"I'm not sure."

He wrinkles his sweaty nose at me.

"Not something. Someone. I think I forgot someone."

He closes his eyes and that smile somehow grows even wider. He pulls his hands over his chin in a manner of great discovery.

"You forgot a woman!"

I shrug.

"And you wait for her to call?" he gestures at the phone.

I shrug again.

"You in love?"

He whispers something I don't understand, wagging a finger at the sky with a giggle.

"You cursed!" he slaps me on the shoulder and shakes me with his large hand.

"Yeah, I suppose so."

"Why you here?" he eyes Sissy. "What you doing here?"

"I thought I knew."

He tilts his head a bit. He doesn't ask anything else right away. He seems to be thinking it over.

"What about you?" I ask. "You don't sound like you're from here."

"Me?" he covers his chest with his entire hand.

"Yeah, your accent is…different."

"I was born here, but I live in Miami for many years. Go there with my uncle, oh, ten years ago? You know Miami?"

"I do."

"Ah! Such greatness! I want to go back, you know? I love the women! The food, the music. Everything! The place has a real spirit."

"Why'd you come back?"

"Yes, well, I do not want to. But my uncle and me, we, ah, not legal they say. Overstayed? So," he shrugs, "we come home."

"Where's home?"

"Probably not where you're going. My home that way a little bit. Cotes-de-fer. More here than west," he gestures towards the ground around us in a big circle.

"I see."

"I born there. My uncle, my sister. All my family."

"Where are you going with that cart?" I look for it down below.

"It's there," he says. "My uncle and me, we build them. Sometime we must take them and this is okay. It's not far."

"You build carts?"

"Carts? No! You blind? Sèkèy!"

"Sek...?" I struggle.

"Yes, mmmm," he mulls the translation, "you know, cercueil? Uh, coffeen? Yes?" He measures the air this deep by this wide. "For the mouri? We build them for a hundred years, my family."

"Oh. Caskets."

"Kaskets?" he says, tapping his hat.

"Coffin?"

He waves me off. "Come. I show."

He stands up, dusts himself off, and offers his hand. I take it and he damn near yanks my arm off.

I fall in behind him in that unsteady downhill-walk that's all but impossible to pull off with any sense of grace.

Why are my fucking pants wet?

I check my phone between clumsy steps. There's a text. I stop in my tracks and quickly thumb it open.

have u called Janet yet?
Received: 4:27PM

I shove the cell in my pocket and stumble to catch up. The cart's there, pulled several yards off the road in the soft gravel I'd wheeled through myself. It's even bigger up close, clearly built for ox or horse or mastodon.

He folds his massive arms and leans back on rocking heels with a proud sort of glow.

"You see?" he waves his arm, presenting his craftsmanship.

I wish I didn't. Coffins. Just like he said. Stacked neatly. Four tall, five deep. Packed carefully to use every available inch of the cart's considerable real estate. But these coffins are little.

"We build each one, my uncle and me. We use a," he searches the sky for the word, "a quality, yes?"

"There's too many," I manage.

He looks down at me.

"Too many? Too heavy?"

"There are so many."

He bows his head some. He hasn't been jovial or joyful in a way that's inappropriate.

"I see how you mean," he says quietly.

"Where are you taking them?"

"I take these where you come from. I take these for the aksidan. The boat."

"That many?" I ask with some trouble. "I was there, but that many?"

"Oh, *no!* Not all of them for Jacmel. Lots of them though, yes." He shuts his eyes tight. "You say you there?" The pitch of his voice swings high in disbelief.

"I was."

"You seen?"

"Yeah."

"Bondye mwen an— you see them small bodies."

Yes. I see them small bodies.

He looks uncomfortable, like he's struggling for a way to take it all back. I'm sure building these caskets is a faceless craft most days, but it's children's faces right now. Four high, five deep.

"You come. Sit," he ushers me to the front of the cart where he plants unceremoniously in the grass. I sit next to him and pull at weeds that snap between my fingers to bleed darker green.

"You come here to see us? See us now?"

"I came to help," I point up the hill where Sissy waits unseen. "I came to fix motorcycles. Like that one. I can fix them."

"Why?"

"Well," I say after a moment. "I wanted to do something. I wanted to help."

"I see."

"But I'm not helping very much."

He waits until I look up.

"But you come. No matter how you do. You come."

He pulls at his chin with one eye closed, the other leveled straight at me.

"Maybe you running."

"From Jacmel?"

"From ghosts!" he says. "I run from my home. My ghosts," he illustrates broadly with his hands. "I run to there. You run *from*." He beams at me. "Same wood. Not so different."

"Nope, not so much."

"Who you run from?" he jabs.

"All of them."

"Oh?"

"All of it," I look at the cart. "Too many caskets."

"I see," he lowers his voice some. "You run from your family?"

I don't answer.

"You no love them?"

"I love them very much."

"But you run from them."

"Yes, but it's…that's complicated."

"Eh?"

"It's—" I slump. "It's just caskets."

"Okay, okay." He folds his arms.

"I miss my little girl."

"Oh, you papa?"

I nod.

"I see."

He can judge me. He has every right to judge me.

"Me too," he offers. "My son? Big, strong boy." He flexes his immense arms. "He never like work. I never get him to help. I try to teach him. My uncle teach me, so I teach him, yeah? But he love to play. He dream to be a footballer."

"Oh yeah?"

"Yes! He love it! He play, he have posters. He train. Every day. All the time. Learning? No good. He only train. Always play."

"Is he any good?"

He looks down the road at a lone truck approaching from the east.

"He still good. He died eleven years ago. But he always good."

I remain very still for a very long time.

"When you were in Miami?" I finally ask, somewhat hesitantly.

"No, no. Before," he nods deeply. His lips pull back over that splay of gleaming teeth, and then they don't. He forces that smile now.

"I miss him, you know? I just don't see him. I still his papa. I'm always his papa. Pou tout tan."

I have nothing to offer and stare at the dirt. He probably built his boy's casket.

"That motorbike?" he asks. "You like it?"

"I do. That's Sissy."

"Thisy?"

"Sissy. Sis-*e*. Like sister."

"She have a *name?*" he asks with a little half shriek.

"Yup. She's my buddy."

He smiles. "I like the name. Thissy. A good motorbike?"

"Yeah, she's not too shabby. She's more bike than I am rider."

I'm not sure he understands, but he smiles all the same.

"It is a nice machine. A real sparkwheel!"

I chuckle. "Yeah, she's pretty good."

We chat some more. About good stuff and nothing at all while the sun dips behind us.

"I must go," he stands abruptly, stretching his large frame.

"Yeah, I need to start looking for a place to camp."

"You sleep outside?" he asks.

He thinks I'm kidding.

"I have been, yeah. I may just sleep up there tonight. I haven't seen any trucks or anything on this hill, so it should be safe."

He eyes me warily.

"Right?"

"You brave, blanc."

"Calculated stupidity."

"Eh?"

"Nothing. Just stupid."

"But you have heart. Even if you stupid."

He turns suddenly. He's close. Too close. He grabs my hands.

"You not right to come."

His eyes are suddenly very serious. They trap mine.

"The world collapse and you come here. To help. Who? People in this world. There? Always looking for darker smoke. They look ahead to find when it lights, but it has already burned. It been dying some long time. A bird dies in flight. Its body not suddenly here on the ground. It fall, but it hit the ground and it bounce. It not alive. It just look so. Then it still. So they pretend. They pretend not to know."

My hands are numb in his vice-like grip. It sounds like he's a million miles away.

"If the bird is too big, it may bounce many, many times. It think it still flying! It not *know*!"

His face goes stormy and that bright smile flashes ghastly. I look down at my hands. I can't see them in his.

"Birds die. A little one falls? No one hear it. But you heard. It has no magic to trick itself. It no trick anyone. Only when it still. That's when."

I don't understand what he's saying at all.

"You are not wrong," he says.

His hands relax. Mine fall free. I don't know what the hell just happened.

"I want to believe that."

"You will."

"My—I'm Greg, by the way," I stammer.

"I know."

"I—"

He winks.

"I see your name on the phone!" he points at my face with a silent, open-mouth laugh.

I shake my head and sigh a nervous laugh.

"I will see you soon, Papa Greg."

He flashes that big smile and we clasp hands once more, gentlemanly this time. He slaps the straw hat back on his head and swivels to his cart.

"You want some help with that?" I ask.

"Oh no. It not too heavy."

I watch him for a second.

"Wait," I stop him. "I have something for you."

I run back up the hill.

It's dark when the bus finally creaks into Jacmel. I have both pannier liner bags stacked in the seat next to me, shoved full of the things I've kept. The air is thick and sticky in the metal beast and I'm eager to step outside for a bit. I'm just not sure when this thing is going to leave again. Could be five minutes. Could be an hour. The driver hopped off the moment we stopped and I haven't seen him since.

Beth hasn't replied to my last text.

Something happened. Can I see you? Coming back on tap-tap. I'll call when I get in. Please answer if you can. Need to tell you something.
Sent: 7:48PM

I fetch the cell, take a deep breath, and dial.

"Hello?"

"Knock-knock."

"Hey!"

"Hey. Sorry about the text. I know it was a little vague."

"It's fine," she sighs. She sounds uneasy.

"So, I'm back. In Jacmel."

"Yeah, that's what you said. Everything okay?"

"Noth—I mean yeah, I'm fine."

"Where's your bike?"

"I gave it to someone."

"   "

"You there?"

"Yeah, I just, you did *what?*"

"I met someone who needed her more than me."

"Okaaay."

"I know it sounds crazy."

"Because it is, Greg."

"No, it's a good thing! I feel good about it. He'll be able to use Sissy to tow this cart. I mean this really big cart. He needs her. In a way that matters more. More than me. Look, if you'd been there I think you might've agreed."

"Yeah, well, it sounds *nuts,*" she chews her thumbnail. I can hear it. "So, that's it? You're just done?"

"No, nothing like that."

"But?"

"But what?"

"Greg, it's just—" she sighs. "This is really strange."

"Why?"

"*Really?* Who does that?"

"Nobody? Me? But who comes here like I did anyhow?"

"Plenty of people. Lots of people come here to help because that's what we do."

"Listen. This isn't what I wanted to tell you. I didn't mean to upset you."

"I'm not upset. I just don't understand what's going on."

"I'm not real clear on that myself."

She exhales heavily, like she's been holding her breath all day.

"Did you call Janet?"

"Yes," I lie.

"And?"

"And it went about like you'd expect."

"Did you get to talk to Maggie?"

"No. She had a playdate or whatever," I grit my teeth.

"Hmmm."

"I'm going to call her back. Don't worry."

"I'm not worried. You keep saying that."

My tongue clicks.

"What the heck happened, Greg?"

"You know what happened."

"I do?"

"Yes. Don't pretend like you don't know what I'm talking about."

She's silent.

I stand up and walk to the back of the bus, pacing where there's really no room for it. I slump down in the back seat and look through the rear glass at the masses of people everywhere. Some of the other passengers smoke on the nearby corner. Some of them sit on the curb. The streets are already loud. The traffic hasn't thinned at all in this late hour and cars careen by, obeying their organic and herd-like laws.

There's a car parked across the street with the headlights on. I wipe at the grubby windows with my fingers and peer through the streaked clean spot. It's not a car. It's a truck. It has logos on the doors.

"Where are you?" I ask carefully.

"Home."

"Oh?"

My heart pounds.

"How's Philippe feeling? Did you guys ever pick him up?"

"Nope. He slept all day. I dropped the other guys off and got home a little bit ago."

It could be another truck. Surely there are others like it.

I spit in my palm and try to broaden the clean spot, but all I do is make a bigger mess.

"Are you okay?" I ask.

"Yes, I'm fine," she sighs.

I chuckle.

"What?"

"You don't sound fine."

"Yeah, well," she pauses, "the last few days haven't been the best."

"Really? I thought they were pretty good."

"That's not what I meant."

"I know." I clench my jaw. "Can I see you?"

She doesn't reply. I hear her crooked little grin.

"I don't know."

"You don't want to see me?"

"You know that's not it."

"Then what?"

"I just don't know. It's just, I can't do…this."

"I know. But I want to see you."

She sighs. It takes a really long time.

"I want to see you," she whispers.

"Then see me."

"Greg—"

I hop from the seat and hurry to the front of the bus.

Street. Truck. Her.

"You should be in Port-au-Prince," she scolds.

"I know, Beth. I think you've mentioned it a few times."

I plunge down the steps.

"I'm taking your advice. That's where this bus is headed."

I dodge cars. I walk to her.

"But I'm here now."

"Greg. Stop."

"No."

I walk the twenty strides.

"Beth," I sigh. "Listen to me."

I place my palm on the window. She brushes her hair from her face. Her eyes aren't the bright happy eyes I left this morning.

The words form, ethereal vapor in my lungs. Three simple syllables, innocent and evil as light on the stillborn dead.

"*Beth—*"

I don't say them. I try. But the words bind in my throat, my tongue their tombstone.

She slips her hand free to meet mine against the glass, stretching smaller fingers to fit.

"Greg, I can't be who you want me to be right now."

She tries to flash that crooked grin. She tries. But her hand falls from the window. The cell drops in her lap. She rubs her eyes with the back of her hand and looks at me one last time through dark tangles. She mouths something I don't catch.

"*What?*" I plead.

She doesn't hear me. She checks her mirror and eases into the street. I stand in the road and beg for brake lights.

Please. I'm still here. I'm still here.

I still have the damn phone to my ear. Cars swerve, but I'm paralyzed. She slows. But doesn't stop. She turns right and vanishes in the dark.

The trip to the capital takes most of the night in the lumbering bus. The swell and heave of the uneven mountain road and frequent honks of vehicles passing ever closer around a million blind corners prevent anything resembling rest. I can't believe I'm back here in one of the behemoths I'd dodged countless times, now a mere passenger back to the one place I tried to avoid. Halfway up the south side of the grade, I begin to recognize some of the places I passed just a few days ago. All too soon we're passing through the village where I met her. I convince myself there's no good reason to look long before we approach, but I peek out through the dark windows anyway. It's a vacuum out there. Empty to everyone but me. It's sweltering in the bus, even this time of night.

Just as well. It tastes the same.

The bus creaks and rolls into the city and that overpowering stench greets us, a most unwelcome welcoming party. Port-au-Prince is in the throes of a tantrum. She's tired. She's filthy. She stinks. The broken buildings and wrinkled roads plead for attention. She just wants to feel better, but nothing soothes. Just about the time I wonder how far we'll be shuttled in, the bus grinds to a sudden halt. There's nothing here. No depot or signs of life. It's just as far as the driver will thread this needle. I wait for the families and strangers and travel-worn foreigners to leave first. Nobody talks. They shuffle off, just another disembarkment, and the bus rolls and sways with each departure on worn out leaf springs. I grab my overstuffed bags and stumble off as well. The driver stands nearby, smoking furiously.

"Thanks for the ride," I offer. "Listen, do you happen to know the city?"

"Hmmm?" he puffs.

"Do you know where the UN is? United Nations?"

He looks like he doesn't really understand what I'm asking, but nods all the same. He turns to trace a map in the air with his lit cigarette. He pauses, takes a deep draw, and cocks his head to one side.

"Eh. I take," he shrugs.

I don't resist the offer. My bags are heavy and I don't particularly want to hump them clear across town. We hop back on and he starts the poor bus with a great, clattering racket.

"Gun?" he shouts over his shoulder.

"How's that?" I yell back.

"Gun? You have gun?" he turns his head to yell this time.

"No! No gun!"

"No UN? No Army?"

"No, not Army."

He adjusts the broken mirror until I fill it. He navigates the city with trepidation, scanning each side street we cross. He scans the sidewalks. He scans my face in the mirror. I want to say something to calm him, but I'm nervous, too.

"At airport!" he yells. "Airport!" he repeats, miming a plane with his hand. "UN," he doesn't finish. He shakes his head and whistles.

The tantrum rages. This is the hurt I've seen in pictures and video, the clenched fists of the still proud city I ignored nearly one week ago. This is the reality I'd wished away. The topography of destruction is arrhythmic. Some buildings stand, old and worn but somehow intact in a constant dare to anyone desperate enough to enter. Others are anthills, pushed out and away into big messy mounds.

Where will this stuff go? What do you do with it?

The rampant crush of televised hopelessness hasn't been mere fodder for the talking heads and fear mongers. It's far uglier than that. It's the simple realization of what's humanly possible. The cold sum of ghastly math.

I try to absorb what I can beyond the smeared windows, but somewhere in the city my focus simply collapses. I turn and stare straight back through my clean spot on the glass.

The vibe shifts with distance and the necrosis fades some. The walking dead are slowly replaced with faces not yet deplete of all earnestness.

"No closer," the driver declares and abruptly stops. I pitch forward violently and only just brace myself from leaving the seat. The airport sprawls before us a few blocks away.

"Where is it?" I ask.

He points at the airport.

"Do I walk around the side, or—?"

"No, through!" he barks. "*In!*"

I have other questions, but I shut my mouth and gather my stuff. I thank him and he nods precisely once. He doesn't smile or shake my hand. He watches the mirrors.

I hitch the heavy sacks over my shoulder and set off across a busy intersection, then another, skirting cars and Jeeps and official-looking trucks in the airport lanes out front and step through the yawning sliding doors of the terminal.

It's hot. It's airless, and nobody smiles. I immediately want to turn around. I look for the familiar UN logo, but I don't see it. The vehicles in the departure lanes out front were stenciled with it and armed officers stationed along the walls seem to indicate their presence. I stand on my toes and peer at the extreme ends of the long terminal for anything useful, a kiosk or a help desk, but it's just a sea of anxious people stuck mid-escape. Lines are formed, but I can't tell where they begin or end.

The heavy liner bags over my shoulders smack into already pissed-off people as I struggle through gaps I repeatedly overestimate. I give up after a great deal of swearing and approach one of the uniformed soldiers. His eyes flick over me for a moment, drift left, then back to lock on. His grip tightens on the slung rifle. I pretend not to notice.

"I was wondering if you could help me."

He takes a strong step forward.

"Sir, I'm going to have to ask you to drop those bags."

"Of course, yes," I swing them off my shoulders and drop them at my feet.

"Please release them."

I untangle my fingers from the long tie strings and let them coil upon the heaps.

"I— I'm looking for someone. With the UN," I stammer. "I was told to look here."

"Who told you that?"

"Doctors. In Jacmel. They said I'd find him here."

"Are you with a group?"

"No. I'm here alone."

One brow dips.

"American?"

"I'm not sure if he is or not, actually."

"You. I'm asking you."

"Oh! Yes."

"What's the nature of your business?"

"My business with the UN? Or here in Haiti?"

The other brow dips.

Shit! My passport!

"I guess they're one and the same." I'm not breathing at all and my words jam together. "I'm here helping and I was told to speak to someone named Ben or Benjamin-something with the UN."

"I can direct you to someone who will take your information."

"Yes, please. That'd be great!"

"First thing you need to do is walk straight back out. This is a departure terminal. If you're not trying to get out of here, you need to leave. When you exit the building, you will head west. Around the airport. Follow the service road and look for the structures. Both are marked. They might be able to help you there, but do *not* approach them with those bags like you did me."

"Got it."

I hoist my stuff and start to walk off.

"Thanks!" I offer over my shoulder. He starts to nod back, but sternly stops midway.

I trudge outside, following his directions and hoping I've heard him right. I walk for some time along a shallow concrete wall. There are whole groups of people just standing around and not one of them fails to notice me. I smile or nod when I pass, but it's never returned.

I don't see any structures. I see large tents, like the canopy deals found at air shows or outdoor festivals. I jog across the access road and finally spy the twin, stenciled letters I've been hoping for.

"Name?"

"Ben? Or Benjamin maybe?"

I've leapfrogged a chain of armed and important-looking people who've each pointed me to another. Soldiers upended the contents of the bags and patted me down at the first big tent, and after repacking and another short wait in line, I'm being quizzed by a no-bullshit woman in a starched uniform seated at a flimsy fold-out table who's somehow mercifully forgotten to ask me for a passport I no longer possess. The corners of a dozen stacks of forms flutter in sudden gusts and she tries to stifle their restlessness with her forearm.

"No. *Your* name."

Her pen has frozen an inch above blank boxes.

"Oh, sorry. Greg."

"Alright, Greg. Do you happen to have a last name?"

"Maurus."

"And a phone number?"

"I do." And I give her the number.

"Look. I'm not going to lie to you. Lines of communication here aren't real reliable yet. We're improving, but I can't promise we'll find this guy. We have a lot of people here and trying to narrow down one person with a first name only? Honey, it ain't likely."

"He deals with vehicles or transportation. Stuff like that. I'm not sure if that helps or—."

She's shaking her head 'no way' before I've even finished.

"Not one bit. It's not how we're structured."

"Karen, what was that name again?" a voice calls out behind me.

"Greg."

"He's looking for Greg?"

"No, he's looking for Ben."

"Or Benjamin." I turn to him. "Or Benjamin."

"Well, I know a Ben," he says. His attire is far more casual than most here. I can't tell if he's military or press or what. "Might not be the same Ben, but it's worth a shot, right? He's the only Ben here I know of."

"Can't hurt!" I concur.

He fishes a phone from his pocket, peers at the screen for a moment, and pops it to his ear.

"Ben? Hey! It's Collin," he turns away and plugs his other ear, pacing from the line. I can't hear what he's saying. He turns back to me a minute later.

"Yeah, I've got him right here. You wan—sure, you bet."

He hands me the phone.

"To whom might I be speaking?" the voice drawls.

Tennessee or Kentucky. I can't tell.

"Greg, sir. My name's Greg. Sorry to bother you this morning, but I was told I should get in touch with you."

"That so? Who mighta' said that?"

"Beth, down south?"

Jesus. I never got her last name.

"She told me to talk to you about the cars. And the bikes. The stuff you've been buying up."

"Hmm. I don't recall no Beth, but we meet a lot of people these days."

"I bet. She's one of the volunteer doctors down there in Jacmel."

"Hell, Jacmel was a month back! But yeah, that woulda' been us. You got a donation for me?"

"Uh, no. Nothing like that. I—"

What do I say?

"—I think I can help you."

"That right?"

"I think so, yeah."

"What kinda' help we talking 'bout?"

"I think I can help repair some of that stuff. The motorcycles."

"That so? You some kinda' wrench?"

"Sort of. Not by trade, I mean. I'm not certified or anything."

"Don't matter. Ya'ny good?"

"I think so."

"Well, don't go selling yourself now!" he hacks.

"I usually don't break more than I fix. How's that."

"Ha! That I can appreciate, sure. Listen Greg, I'm not big on yankin' chains. It's just me and a coupla' guys. That's it. There ain't no budget and most what we did have been spent already. There ain't no pay is what I'm sayin'."

"That's fine."

"I'm not sure how that's fine, but okay. Sure. It's a start." He clicks his tongue through bleats of labored breath. "Now, it ain't none my business here bud, but I don't like getting screwed around. I like knowing who I'm dealing with."

"I just want to help. I came here to fix motorcycles and just sort of wander around and help. I saw a way I might be able to do that. I met Beth in Jacmel. She told me about your gig and..." I trail off. "And yeah. Here I am."

"Huh," he says.

But it's not the usual 'huh' I've grown accustomed to these past few months. There's an honest smack to it.

"Well, that's a bit nice to hear."

"I wish I had more repairs to back it up."

"You ain't fixed nuthin'?"

"Yeah, two. But one of them was mine."

There's a sturdy pause before he laughs hard enough to cough.

"Well hell! You ain't useful when ya' stuck!"

"Not so much, no."

"Tell ya' what. You at them tents behind the terminal?"

"I am."

"Alright. I'm cross town right now, but if ya' want to see what we got here, you're more than welcome. What say I pick ya' up in an hour?"

"Works for me. Want me to just hang out here?"

"Sure. There or the mess hall. Gitchya' something to eat. It's not the best chow, but it's a damn sight better'n none."

"I could eat, yeah. I'll look for it."

"Alright Greg. This here a good number to reach ya'?"

"Yup. No, wait. Sorry, not my phone," I realize, turning to Collin who's been listening. I give Ben my phone number and tell him I'll see him soon.

"Well what do you know about a thing like that," I whistle.

"I call that damn lucky. That's what," Karen mutters, never lifting her hard stare from pages of inked-on protocol.

I wander the little camp and look for the kitchen. The entire outfit is actually on the tarmac. From the looks of things, cargo planes are able to land and unload right at the tents. Curiously empty warehouses line the far end of the strip.

I'm asked often enough to display a badge I don't possess that I begin to wonder if I should just wait outside, but I finally find the makeshift mess hall and buy a pre-wrapped sandwich, apple, and a bottle of water. A simple plastic meal that folks a short mile away would do just about anything for. I sit down at one of the long tables, every one of them empty this time of morning. It dawns on me who Beth looks like.

Danica Patrick. That's who you look like. You know, in a few years.
Sent: 8:53AM

I still have a good thirty minutes before Ben should arrive. I pull the laptop from the satchels and find the last entry to Logan.

```
It's been three days.  Three short days and
seemingly everything's changed.  Again.  I gave
the bike to someone, along with most of the
riding gear and useful bits.  I'm back in Port-
au-Prince.  And I'm eating a chicken salad
sammich' on a runway.

I'm not really sure what to tell you about Beth
that you probably didn't predict right away.
Insta-heartbreak!  Just add me!  Yuk, yuk.  I
hate the situation, but something's suddenly
very different in my noggin now.       I'm
frustrated.  This wasn't in the script.    It
wasn't something I thought I was even capable
of anymore.  I dunno.  It hasn't had time to
really percolate yet.  I tried to see her last
night.  Let the record show that I did indeed
try.  But for now, I'm back in the capital city
and she's on the other side of the universe and
that's all there is to say about that.
```

There's a guy here in Port-au-Prince who's running what sounds like some sort of garage. He's going to give me a little tour in a few. Long story short, he and his merry band went out and bought up a bunch of old cars, trucks, 'sickles, and such. The point of this operation, as I understand it, is to repair and ration those machines to people who need them most. How they went about securing these machines is another story. I haven't yet decided how I feel about that. Stay tuned for a fair and balanced opinion there, old sport.

So, here I is. Back where I probably should have been all along. Beth said something a few days ago I can't stop thinking about. She told me not to head west after Jacmel. 'There's nothing out there,' she told me. 'You'll just be that douchebag American tourist you didn't come here to be.' Or something to that effect. But I couldn't help but wonder...was she asking me to stay? Closer to her?

See what I mean? Pitiful! I'm actually going to send this to you here and now considering I've been bitching and moaning for what amounts to a serious chunk of time. I'll write more tonight, provided I'm not dragged into indentured servitude by this mysterious Ben fella' and chained to some rusted-out Beezer. Keep your eyes skyward for my emergency smoke signal. If you see it, send help. And by help, I mean send a biggish case of hooch, toot sweet.

I copy the letter to an email and send it. Unsecured Wi-Fi here. Amazing to think any cheap motel back in the States is probably more secure.

The cell phone vibrates and skitters across the table.

**u need to have your
eyes checked!**
Received: 9:12AM

**About to get a tour with Ben.
Wish me way more than luck.
Miss you.**
Sent: 9:13AM

GL! it'll work out!!
Received: 9:13AM

**we're practically neighbors,
k? we go to cap-city all the
time. no pity party. miss u
too.**
Received: 9:15AM

Before I can even celebrate, my phone rings.

"You gotta' remember one thing here, kid. These folks are happy to see us." Ben's barking. He has to over the ruckus of the open-top Jeep.

"When people first get here, all anyone feels is sorry. Sorry for them. Sorry for the whole damn mess. But let me tell ya' what. They don't want no tears. They don't want no goshdamn hand outs. They don't mind some help, don't get me wrong, but what they don't want is a buncha' people making 'em feel less than shit. Like the bag you put it in."

He's a gruff guy, all belly and beard with a ballcap he must have stapled down tight the day he retired ten long years ago. He wears round rimmed glasses that he snaps temporary shades over and khaki shorts many years too small for him. Like many people here, he straps his calloused feet into sandals.

"Now, keep that in mind? It'll keep this shit from swallerin' ya' up. Trust me. I seen it happen. When'd ya' get in?"

"Last week!" I yell back. "Just been here since—"

"Shit, son! You only been here one week?"

"Yup!"

"I thought you'd been out there highfalutin since the quake!"

"Nope. I'm pretty green, I guess."

"Well, ya' need be where people's at to help, right? See much down south?"

"Not much. I made it a half-day west of Jacmel is all. Not very far."

"On foot?"

"No, I had a bike."

"Had?"

"Yeah. I kind of donated it to someone."

"You mean it kind of got stole?"

"No! Nothing like that. It's a long story."

"Well, I like long stories. Maybe tell me later. I'll even buy the beer."

"There's beer here?"

"Of course we got beer here!" He almost looks disgusted with me. "The town's crippled, kid. She ain't *dead.*"

He drives through town at a brisk pace that underscores his familiarity with everything. Where I'm exposed here in the Jeep, I feel an unexpected comfort I didn't tucked away in the big tap-tap.

"I'm gonna show ya' our stack first," he says. "We gotta' sort the wheat and focus on those worth fixin'. The rest we'll scrap or strip for parts and whatnot, but I want ya' to see some scope."

"Sounds good to me!"

He looks me over a few times.

"You're an agreeable type, ain'tcha'? I get that way sometimes. Where ya' staying?"

"Here?"

"Yeah. Got a place?"

"Not yet. That's next on the list. I was camping on the bike."

"Well, ya' ain't camping here. We got a few rooms at the hotel still. Mostly pens and brass come through, but I can square ya' there for a day or two if need be."

"Really?"

"You bet. We'll swing past after."

The route he's chosen leads us to the outskirts of the city, somewhat southeasterly from the looks of things. After a few turns down narrow little side streets, we angle onto a shallow alley where a tall barbed-wire fence skirts one side. He pulls the Jeep right up to a newer looking section of fence, hops out, and works a giant padlock. With it popped, he puts his shoulder to the beam and gives it a heave, sending the section screeching open on crooked wheels bound up in their tracks. He gives it a good kick for the last foot and it stops, opened just wide enough to squeeze through.

"Had to take my dang side mirrors off to fit!" he bellows as he plops back heavily into the seat, nodding at some paint transfer on the fence posts.

"What I mean is I had 'em taken off for me!"

It's a full lot alright. A real graveyard for cars. There's some order to the organization; smaller cars here, larger cars there, and trucks lined up in their own long column. But I don't see a single bike.

We hop out and he walks over with his hands in his pockets to stand next to me.

"Most this shit don't run. 'Course everyone said they run when they saw cash. But if it did? It mighta' run two more minutes. We got took on a lot of 'em, but I 'spose everyone got what was needed."

"You're wondering 'bout them bikes, ain't ya'?"

"A little, yeah," I admit. "I can help with cars, too. But I'm better with bikes."

"No, that works out. I only got the one guy for bikes."

He pauses and scratches the back of his neck.

"If you're still interested, I'll take ya' there."

"You're not working on them here?"

"The cars? You bet. But bikes we got cross town."

"Wouldn't make much difference to me where it is."

"Well," he frowns, "it might. I just wanna be straight with ya'. It ain't the best spot."

"Can't be that bad, can it?"

"Look. Ya' just need to know what the deal is. We'll head that way in a minute."

"Sounds good."

"But do me a favor? Gimme' a quick sec?" he asks and rushes into a little metal garage that looks to be made entirely from steel siding. He slams the single door behind him with a loud rattle.

I walk between rows of cars and trucks, looking for familiar metal. There's a lot of stuff here I don't recognize. Manufacturers I've never even heard of. Some are a few years old and still perfectly workable. Others are skeletons and hint at nothing they might have been.

I pull out my phone to snap a few pictures. I haven't taken a single picture in Haiti and I smirk at these first chosen subjects. The most recent shots in the gallery are from my last night in Portland. I know I shouldn't, but I scroll back, back, back and before long I'm staring at the girls.

I lied to Beth about calling her. It wasn't on purpose. It was a selfish deflection in the spur of the moment. Maybe she's right. Maybe I should call her.

You should call her.

I sigh. It sounds like her.

Hush.

I dial and close my eyes.

"...hello?"

"Janet?"

"Jesus," she covers the mouthpiece for a second. *"Greg?"*

"Yeah, it's me."

"Are you okay?"

"What?"

"Are you okay? Are you hurt?"

"I haven— no, I'm fine."

"Jesus! Is this really you?"

"I doubt very much anyone would pretend to be me right now."

"Where the hell are you? Are you coming home?"

"Well, I'm not, I don't know. I'm in Haiti."

"You're...*where?*"

"Haiti. Port-au-Prince. Well, just outside of town right now, but yeah."

"Whe—" I know she's shaking her head. "What on Earth are you doing there?"

"I came to help. After the quake."

"Have you been there this whole time?"

"What? Since the quake?"

"No, I mea— how long have you been there?"

"A week? Not even. Not very long."

"Jesus, Greg! Can I ask you something?"

"Of course."

"Are you out of your fucking mind?! Really? What the hell is wrong with you? Are you high? Did you finally drink yourself stupid?"

She tries to sigh, but it comes out as one big hitching gasp. "Are you safe at least? They say it's getting worse!"

"Oh I'm sure it is. It's not the happiest place on the planet right now."

"I imagine not," she snorts. "So? Is it as bad as it looks?"

"Yeah. It is. It's worse in spots, not as bad in others. It doesn't make much sense. I mean, you see it and your eyes relay it all, but it doesn't really square upstairs."

I take a deep breath.

"Is Maggie there?"

"No. It's Monday."

"Ah. Right."

She taps her fingers on something.

What color are her nails?

"She needs to see you. I've done what I can, but she's losing faith."

"I know."

"You're on a really long bike trip. That's all she knows."

"Is that what you think?"

"What, that she needs to see you?"

"No. That I'm just out on some really long bike trip?"

"I don't know! What do you want me to say? I thought you'd be back after a week or two!"

Where was I back then?

"That wasn't the plan. I didn't have a plan."

She's doesn't speak.

"I left, Janet. I'd never survive divorce. I told you that."

"Yeah, I *know*. You mentioned it once or twice. I wasn't real happy about it either. Do you think this is my fault? People get divorced! They move on! It doesn't have to be this big, drawn-out production."

"I never wanted a production! It just seemed easier for everyone this way. No boat rocking. No big display. I wasn't done, Janet. You were."

She sighs. She's always detested melodrama.

"So, again, it's my fault? You weren't the same person! And what do you mean no big display? Vanishing like that? Please tell me what you call that if not one great big fucking display?"

"I didn't know what else to do! Every option sucked. There wasn't one that just worked. You know? Part of me wondered if you were fucking around! And the more I thought about it, the less I cared to know. And then I began to wonder if I even cared at all. How's that okay? What good comes of that? You know? Let's say for a moment that I knew the truth. What would I do

with that? Where do I keep it? And if I shoved it in your face?
Game over, right? But if I ignored it? Then it's game over in a
very *different* way. There was no preferable outcome. It doesn't
matter now. I left. I went with the least painful option."

"No. You went with the least painful option for you."

"That's not what I mea—"

"Well, guess what? That's exactly what happened. You hurt
her, Greg."

"That's not fair, Janet."

"She rings that goddamn bell every night!" her voice cracks.
She clears her throat and waits a moment. No reason for her to
concede anything now.

"Taking off like that hurt her. Seeing her hurt? That hurts
me. So, good job. Bravo. Fair enough?"

"It was a fight or flight response and I flew. It's not like I'm
proud if it."

"Well, it *hurt*."

"I was trying to minimize that! I didn't want her to see us
beating each other up anymore."

She's quiet.

"Look, all we can do now is react to what did happen. I had
my reasons. Sure, they're not great. Maybe they're not even
defensible. But I didn't run away just so I'd hurt less. Leaving
you two killed me. Over and over. Every single night. Some
days I couldn't even ride. I had to hide out in some shit motel
room or wherever I was. I didn't want any of us to hurt."

She sighs.

"She rings the bell?"

"Every night. It's heart breaking, *Greg*. Can you understand
that? Am I supposed to tell her that it doesn't work anymore?
She keeps telling me you still might hear it. How can I tell her
she's wrong?"

I lean against the rear fender of some rusting derelict. She's unable to say my name without sarcasm. She's never said it like this before.

"What does she say?"

"She says, 'Maybe he has the sound on his ears turned off.' It's always the last thing she does before bed. After stories. After scratches. I figured it was just some routine for her, like circling the grass or whatever. She thinks you're coming home."

I close my eyes.

"So? Are you?"

"Janet—"

"Don't say you are for my sake."

"I know. It's just, well, I think I can really do something here. I think I can do something that matters to people. I think it matters to me."

She's quiet.

"Would you guys come here?"

"Excuse me?"

"Would you guys ever consider coming here?"

"You're kidding."

"Not at all."

"To stay?"

"No..."

I don't think that's what I'm asking. Am I?

"To visit. Stay a while. You guys can see things first hand."

"I don't know if it's the safest place to be taking a five-year-old."

"How do you think mothers of five-year-olds here feel?"

"That's not what I meant, Greg."

"Look, it's not like everything you've seen on TV. Yeah, it's terrible. There's a big hurt here and a lot of it's broken. But the people? They don't get them right in the news at all."

"I don't even know what that means."

"I mean they inspire me. I wish I was more like them. They're sincere and caring in ways I'm not sure I'm even *capable* of. They make me hate things a little less. Things in me."

She's sighs.

"Just say you'll consider it."

"But why would I do that, Greg? Even if I did, I'd have to come there by myself first which means I'd have to take time off from work."

"I took work off to be here," I interrupt.

"Very funny. You took work off *permanently.*"

"Sure, but it allowed me to be here. Janet, I'm not wrong about this. You should see it. She should see it. It's tough, but she'll be fine. There are days I feel ten times safer here than back there."

I still don't know where 'back there' even is.

"Where are you?" I ask.

"Work."

"No, I mean where's work?"

"Uh, Dallas?"

"You didn't move?"

"No, I didn't move. I wasn't going to take our daughter away to some other state."

"So you didn't sell the house?"

"Why would I do that?"

"Or the bikes?"

"I should have. Greg, I wasn't going to take her anywhere. We were going to be wherever you were." She sighs. "Look, I've got to go. I have someone waiting here."

"Wait," I stop her. "Wait."

"What."

"Do me a favor."

"What."

"Box up that bell. Send it to me. I'll get an address and email it to you."

"Greg—"

"Please. You don't have to agree with me on this. Just say you'll consider it. Hell, let her decide. Tell her why."

"*I* don't understand why. That's the problem."

"So I can ring it. For her."

"...I'll think about it."

"That's all I ask."

"Okay."

"She misses you," she sighs. "We miss you."

"We?"

"Yes, moron. I miss you."

"You shouldn't. You didn't lose a very good husband."

"You might think that. And maybe you're right. Who knows. But I know I lost my best friend."

Don't drop it. Don't drop it.

"Greg? Hello?"

"What?"

"I really gotta' go."

"I know."

"Be careful."

"Never."

"Cute."

"Tell Maggie I love her."

"She knows. I tell her every night. I'll ask her about that stupid bell."

"Okay."

"Alright."

I tuck the phone into my pocket and exhale.

"Heya!" Ben calls out from the Jeep.

I wave and pace back through the abandoned machines.

"What's it gonna' take to get you in one of these little beauties today?" he cracks.

"How about eighteen-year-old Scotch and a soft bed?"

"How 'bout cheap rye and an inflatable mattress?"

"Deal."

The phone buzzes in my pocket. I pull it out. It's a text from Logan.

Got your email. Holy shit! More later. Crazy here. Shelly and I just found out we're expecting! Celebrate or bender???
Received: 10:37AM

That's fantastic news! Trust me, you will never feel love again like that first day. I'm happy for you!
Sent: 10:38AM

"Any good with that stuff?" Ben asks, nodding at my phone from the drivers seat.

"Nah, not really. I actually kind of despise it. I've wanted to throw it away about a million times."

"I don't like 'em either, but it's evil we gotta' live with I 'spose."

"I guess so. I just miss what it replaces."

"I just hate them itty buttons!" he bellows.

We weave through the city, taking roads he knows will shave time. He's a cautious driver and reads everything well. His shifts are precise and his uptake on the clutch is smooth, with a gentle and linear throttle tip-in that nearly masks the engagement altogether. This, no less, in a forty-year-old Jeep.

"This place we're headed? It's a rough patch. It ain't real dangerous. No more than most. But it's far away from everything else here. If ya' do decide to work on them bikes, you're gonna see shit ya' can't unsee."

"So, why this location?"

"It was this here or sharing some shack way outta' town with this real cocksucker from North Carolina." He looks at me with a stern frown. "You'd know what I mean if ya' met him."

"I don't doubt it," I smile back.

He looks at the road, then back to me with a big grin growing somewhere in that bushy beard.

"I can't quite figure ya'."

"You'd fall asleep."

"Bah!"

He wasn't exaggerating. He zigzags through a series of side roads and alleys that lead us to a city block no shorter or longer than the others here. But it's utterly ruined, like it was shelled just this morning. It's a mess. It's the middle spot under the rug where everyone else has swept their remains.

Most of the buildings in this block have collapsed. Some, Ben tells me, have been razed in botched rescue attempts. But there's a little green building in the middle of everything, all by itself. It's the only color here.

"Guess which one!" he laughs as we squeal to a stop.

There's no sign out front, but there's glass in the window frames and the paint looks fresh, the door a darker shade of green. I peer through the windows, but nothing's visible beyond the dark glare.

"Privacy glass. *Bulletproof*," he boasts. "Installed it myself."

"I'm impressed!"

"C'mon. Let me show ya' what we got."

He springs the lock with a small brass key, one of hundreds swinging from a ridiculously huge ring. We step inside and the darkness draws in complete when he shuts the door behind us. I hear his rough hand slide along the wall for the light switch.

It's a small space. There's clean sheetrock all around, still unfinished with the fine snow of installation salted everywhere on what appears to be a fresh concrete floor. We leave crisp, white footsteps as he leads me through.

"This whole damn place was broke. But it was mostly upright. I gutted it, tossed in some sheetrock, and poured a half inch floor. Took a few days. No big deal. But it made a worlda' difference. I'm thinking this here's where the finished bikes go. Like a showroom?" he asks, like he's selling me. "I just liked the idear' of seeing 'em all shined up."

We walk through an open doorway and into the back room. There, a sea of motorcycles packed a little too close together fills the space. There must be a hundred bikes.

"There's some thirty odd out back, besides. Mostly junk."

Most of them look to be twenty or thirty years old, worn honest with years of service.

"All of these run?"

"Some do. These here I think we can use."

A slow realization forms as I scan the maze of plastic, metal, and chrome. There's a lot of scrap, sure. But there're a few vintage bikes hiding here as well. Properly important bikes. From where I'm standing, I can already see three old Triumph Bonnies in the back, triplets from '66 I believe. Several BSA models and a few beefy Honda CB750s. A pair of Beemers missing their badges, but unmistakably RS60s. Maybe a dozen or more faded red Cushmans. To Ben, this is all just one heap of stuff that may or may not ever run again. But it's something else entirely to me.

"Do you have all the keys?"

"Most. We asked for keys, paperwork. Whatever they had. If they had other shit to toss in? Why we took that, too."

"Some of these are good bikes."

"Well, I don't know 'bout none of that. I just know we got 'em now and folks need 'em."

I start to argue a point I quickly abandon. People of means would pay serious premiums to get their hands on some of these bikes in *any* condition. But something clicks before I admit this to him. We could rebuild them to workable levels, to support normal people in functional and everyday ways. They won't be gracing some climate-controlled garage or museum where they'd

just sit, useless perfection rotting away in stasis. They have a
chance to live on as honest machines.

"So?" he drawls.

"I think this is really cool."

"You like this kinda' stuff, don'tcha?"

"I do."

"Well, shoot. This might work out. But," he grabs his hips.
"We got one or two things need ironin' out. Things you need to
know."

"Okay."

"Well, like I said, there ain't no pay. Not now, anyhow.
Maybe some day we might swing a few bucks, but this here's a
strictly volunteer gig for the time being. The other guy?
Makandal? He's my local and him I gotta' pay. He's got kids,
and he's helped me out these past few weeks, so I gotta' do right
by him. Good guy. Quiet. I like him so you'll like him. But
there just ain't no pay."

"That's not a problem."

"I don't know how on Earth that ain't no problem, but I
reckon that's not my business. Now, the second problem has to
do with *you*."

"Oh."

"Yup. Sounds like ya' ain't got a place to call home yet. And
that's fine. We'll set ya' up at the hotel for bit until ya' find
something. But I gotta' know you're staying somewhere so I
ain't worrying. Follow?"

"I do."

"Which brings up another issue, come to think of it. Sounds
like ya' ain't got no way of getting down here each day. We
ain't real close to the hotel here, so ya' can't walk it. And I just
ain't got time to be your personal taxi. So that needs figurin'
out. Sounds like ya' gone and gave away a perfectly good bike
once already and I ain't gonna judge ya'. That's some big deal. I

bet you made someone's day. But ya' can't be giving none of these bikes away."

"They're not mine to give away."

"Damn straight. Not even mine. People gonna' get on this list and they gonna' get a ticket. We'll process all that in the order that best suits everyone. Sometimes we're gonna' hold a lottery and a few folks more each month'll get a shot at something. Some car. One of these bikes. Whatever suits 'em best. But that's how it's gonna work. I gotta' be firm on that. We can't have bikes just vanishing. Which brings me to my last point."

"Which is?"

"Which is this here shot-to-shit spot. This ain't a friendly place. People need stuff. And when they get away from prying eyes, well, they get brave. I bought this hole before we collected all this junk. It was cheap and standing up and I didn't exactly know it was that bad 'round here. So that's all on me. I'll own that. But I hate that cocksucker from North Carolina and there wasn't no *way* I was gonna share Jack nor shit with him."

I laugh. "I understand. It's a little Old West out here right now."

"That's right. So you're gonna' keep one eye on everything here, and one eye on that road. Think ya' can handle that?"

"I can."

"Well, alright. Alright." He nods slow with a distant look in his eyes. "You know? I'm getting a decent feeling 'bout this."

"Me too," I say. "I think this makes a lot of sense."

We walk back to the front room.

"Now, it's gonna be rough. Need parts? You're gonna' have to figure that out your damn self. There ain't no corner parts store, so when ya' need stuff you're gonna' have to make some calls. And let me tell you something else. Deliveries here *will* take a long ass time. It's a tad better'n before, but it's a far cry from what it need be. Tools..." he drifts off for a second. "Kid, I really don't know what to tell ya' there. Makandal has some, but he'll be working here, too. No differn't you. If you two are sharing thisn'that, or if ya' don't have the right one—"

"Not a problem. I can order tools for the both of us. And the car guys, too. If you'd like."

"Greg, now listen. I think you're missing a real important point. I ain't got no cash for that."

"And you don't need any."

"I don't follow."

"I'll pay. I can order a few other things that will really help. Equipment we can use for anyone who comes in. A tire mounting machine, for instance." I point at the far corner. "There's enough room in here for a pair of those. And a balancer. One of the good ones. A few bike lifts would be nice. Helps the back and keeps you from ruining every other pair of jeans. A sandblast cabinet and an eighty-gallon compressor would help a ton. We could clean up a lot of these bikes without having to repaint a single thing."

"See, I know for a fact those goshdamn wheel balancer deals ain't cheap. You mean to tell me you're gonna' just up and *buy* one?"

"I mean exactly that."

I smile, but he seems unconvinced.

"I made a lot of money in a former life. More than I deserved."

He watches me a moment. Like he's waiting for the punch line. I look around the room again and imagine the potential. I'm seeing a way to help. And it's good.

"Kid, I gotta' tell ya'. You're alright."

I smile. It's not much. It can't be, given what's happened. But it's something. It's enough on a day like today.

"Not yet. But I'm working on it."

It's been three months now, or as close to it as I can figure. Makandal, whom I've nicknamed Vale, and I have turned the little green building into a functional and well equipped shop. We have the tools and equipment to completely dismantle a bike, replace or repair whatever's needed, and reassemble with just enough bloom to make it shine.

I keep an eye open for one of our 'babies' out there on my ride to the shop every morning. I know they're out there, shuttling someone to their job or getting their kids off to school. People still work here. Kids still learn. What we do isn't much, but it's enough for me. Even better, word's getting out and people from all over are starting to find us. Sometimes they need something looked at on their own bikes. Sometimes they need a part we can source for them. I was even able to order new carburetors and air filters for Remy and their Honda powered water pump.

One of the first things I needed to deal with was basic transportation. As luck would have it, that issue worked itself out while Ben was showing me around that very first day. I went back through the storeroom again to start a quick mental inventory, just to have a better idea of what we had to work with. As I poked around and took pictures of this and that, I found her in the far corner, lost among myriad Hondas and Kawis - a 1951 Vincent Black Shadow.

I knew she was rare. I told Ben as much right there on the spot. But it was only later, when I had a chance to look it up online, that I learned how truly rare she was.

"Ben, that bike doesn't belong here."

"What's that 'sposed to mean?" Ben grumbled through foamy sips of local brew.

"That's a special bike. I don't even know what it's doing here. They didn't make very many of those. I'm not saying we can't build it out for someone, but—"

"Take it."

"No, wait. That's not what I'm sugg—"

"Hogwash and horsefuckery! Take the goshdamn thing. We can't sell 'em for profit anyhow, so if it really is rare and special like you seem to think then it's probably fuckin' delicate to boot. Right? And you ain't gonna' have time for a repeat customer, if you catch my drift."

"Well, I *do* need wheels."

"I *know*, kid! I can't be driving ya' around. Call me selfish."

"What about Makandal?"

"You kidding me? He hates motorcycles!"

Over those first few weeks, Vale and I used the Vincent to break in the new shop equipment and rubber in our methods. It gave us a chance to work together on something we wouldn't have to worry about. It was perfect practice.

It took a little over two weeks to get the Vincent up to snuff. I was steadfast from the start that I didn't want to restore her. I just wanted to freshen it up and replace the things that really needed attention. She's good. She's a real sparkwheel. I've named her Asticot.

We've cranked out a total of thirteen bikes since then. We compliment each other well, Vale and I. He doesn't say much while I tend to carry on.

Right now I'm working on a real bastard of a bike. Every bolt on the damn thing's seized up, likely frozen in place years before I was born. Solvent, heat, time, cursing, rubber mallets – all the best tricks are failing today and I'm breaking far more fasteners during teardown than I should. Some of the bikes are in surprisingly good shape and often nearly complete in their assembly. But some, like this '57 Beezer, must have been left outside, uncovered and forgotten, for decades. There are days when we feel more like archeologists than mechanics, unearthing strange things from their rusted out bowels. Sometimes the findings are interesting. Sometimes disturbing. We find lots of little bones.

To my delight, Maggie convinced Janet to mail me her bell.

"He heard it, mommy! I told you!" she'd said. "Now he can ring it and I can turn the sound off on *my* ears!"

Janet and I are able to speak like adults again when we talk on the phone. It isn't much, but it's better than it's been in some time. Maggie and I talk every weekend for as long as I can keep her on the line. She tells me about her week and what she's doing in school, and I tell her what filthy, miserable bike I'm saying very bad words at. She seems to like it. I know I do.

I hear Maggie's bell jingle out in the front room. I nailed it over the front door there as our welcome chime. My little girl used to ring it when she needed me. People here in Haiti ring it now for the same reason.

It tinkles again. Twice. *Ting, Ting.* Like someone's pawing at it.

"Greg? You back?" Vale peeks his head into the back room. He's been working on his English, and he's getting much better.

"Oui, je, umm, sauvegarder ici...?" I reply. I've been working on my French, and I'm still quite terrible.

"Someone here. She say you know her."

Born in 1974, LW Montgomery spent his youth lost in the library. He would spend years sacking groceries, building hard drives, and co-founding the game studio *Gearbox Software* before eventually returning to his first love.

Promise of Departure is his first novel.

18012430R00155

Made in the USA
Charleston, SC
11 March 2013